Mara closed her eyes as the familiar feeling swept over her.

Night had fallen. She went to the window, though she knew there was nothing to see except darkness and more of the same.

The impressions grew stronger, and she stopped fighting them. The picture of a man formed in her mind. He was tall and muscular. His hair was the brown of forest shadows, and his eyes were the clear, iridescent gray found at the borders of thunderclouds.

His name eluded her.

She asked herself why she was envisioning this man, a stranger. Unease filled her. Then, as suddenly as he had appeared in her mind, he vanished.

Mara wanted to forget the last few minutes. She wanted her life to be exactly as it had been before.

She knew better than to hope for such a thing.

Dear Reader,

Many of you love the miniseries that we do in Intimate Moments, and this month we've got three of them for you. First up is *Duncan's Lady,* by Emilie Richards. Duncan is the first of "The Men of Midnight," and his story will leave you hungering to meet the other two. Another first is *A Man Without Love,* one of the "Wounded Warriors" created by Beverly Bird. Beverly was one of the line's debut authors, and we're thrilled to have her back. Then there's a goodbye, because in *A Man Like Smith,* bestselling author Marilyn Pappano has come to the end of her "Southern Knights" trilogy. But what a fantastic farewell—and, of course, Marilyn herself will be back soon!

You won't want to miss the month's other offerings, either. In *His Best Friend's Wife,* Catherine Palmer has created a level of emotion and tension that will have you turning pages as fast as you can. In *Dillon's Reckoning,* award-winner Dee Holmes sends her hero and heroine on the trail of a missing baby, while Cathryn Clare's *Gunslinger's Child* features one of romance's most popular storylines, the "secret baby" plot.

Enjoy them all—and come back next month for more top-notch romantic reading…only from Silhouette Intimate Moments.

Yours,
Leslie Wainger
Senior Editor and Editorial Coordinator

Please address questions and book requests to:
Silhouette Reader Service
U.S.: 3010 Walden Ave., P.O. Box 1325, Buffalo, NY 14269
Canadian: P.O. Box 609, Fort Erie, Ont. L2A 5X3

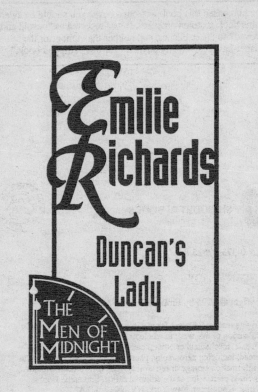

Emilie Richards

Duncan's Lady

THE MEN OF MIDNIGHT

Silhouette

INTIMATE™MOMENTS®

Published by Silhouette Books

America's Publisher of Contemporary Romance

SILHOUETTE BOOKS

ISBN 0-373-07625-8

DUNCAN'S LADY

This edition published by arrangement with Harlequin Enterprises B.V.

® and TM are trademarks of Harlequin Enterprises B.V., used under
license. Trademarks indicated with ® are registered in the United States
Patent and Trademark Office, the Canadian Trade Marks Office and in
other countries.

Printed in U.S.A.

Books by Emilie Richards

EMILIE RICHARDS

believes that opposites attract, and her marriage is vivid proof. "When we met," the author says, "the only thing my husband and I could agree on was that we were very much in love. Fortunately, we haven't changed our minds about that in all the years we've been together."

The couple live in Ohio with their four children. Emilie has put her master's degree in family development to good use—raising her own brood, working for HeadStart, counseling in a mental health clinic and serving in VISTA. Though her first book was written in snatches with an infant on her lap, Emilie now writes five hours a day and "rejoices in the opportunity to create, to grow and to have such a good time."

For the Jarvis family,
who willingly shared their home and country
with strangers

Prologue

1965

Bairns, wee bairns everywhere. And no one else to bring them into the world.

Dr. Angus Sutherland wished he hadn't sucked quite so hard on the bottle of Glenmorangie that a grateful patient had given him. But it was a cold night, with hardly a star visible; Hallowe'en night, in fact. A night for a bottle of good malt whiskey and a strong lock on the door. Unfortunately, he'd had one, and not the other.

"Three of them. I can no' believe it. Three at one time. So far this year we've had only four babies born in the hospital." Jeanne Maxwell put her hands on her wide hips and pursed what little lip God had blessed her with. "I've a pot of tea brewing, and you'll drink it strong," she continued. "But you will no' have time to savor it. You'll need to pour it down. Every last drop."

"And you think they'll all be delivered tonight?" Angus unwrapped his scarf and shrugged out of his overcoat. He supposed it was the whiskey pleading for reassurance. Jeanne had already given her opinion, and loudly.

Jeanne hung the coat on a peg. "Aye. I think they'll all deliver immediately. With or without you. And better with."

"It's a cold night, Jeanne. A wet, cold night. We should both be snug at home in front of a good fire."

"Well, we can send the ladies home and ask them to come back tomorrow."

Even if everything else was as foggy as a Highlands autumn morning, Jeanne's expression was absolutely clear. She was a sturdy, capable woman, never pretty even in her prime, but eternally fresh-faced and steady-eyed. And, tonight, disapproving.

Angus sighed. "Fetch the tea while I wash up." He went to the sink in the corner and turned on the water so that he could scrub. "Who is it you're thinking I should examine first?"

"I'd see Lady Ross. She's the laird's wife, after all. But she will no' deliver first. Nae, that'll be Mrs. Sinclair." She paused. "The good Lord willing."

"And Mrs. MacDougall?"

Jeanne shrugged.

He read the truth in that lift of her shoulders. Jeanne really had no idea in what order the three women making assorted noises in the next two rooms were going to have their babies.

Angus had been a physician since the war's end, and eighteen of those years had been spent here in the gray stone cottage hospital of the tiny village of Druidheachd in the remotest part of the Highlands. He was still considered a stranger, the Edinburgh doctor who had come on holiday from one of Auld Reekie's finest hospitals, never to return to the city again. Some thought he had stayed for the clear mountain air; others said a witch had cast a spell on him to keep him nearby. Only a few understood that the war had taught Angus the value of simple things and people. He knew the names and stories of every person for twenty miles. And now he supposed he was about to deliver three more stories within hours, possibly minutes, of each other.

"To my dying day, I'll never understand why the ladies all waited so long to come in," he said as he quickly lathered, rinsed and lathered again.

"Mrs. MacDougall planned to give birth at home with her auld granny helping, but she changed her mind when Granny kept nodding off. The laird and lady started toward Glasgow at the first sign of labor but realized they were no' going to make it in time and turned around. And Mrs. Sinclair just refused to believe the baby was coming so fast. Then there was the wee matter of you falling asleep and neglecting to answer your telephone, and me having to send a passing lad to wake ye."

He ignored the last. "I'll see Mrs. Sinclair first. That'll be her yelling the loudest, I ken."

"It's nearly midnight." Jeanne checked her watch. "And her husband's no' back. He brought her in, then left again."

"Donald Sinclair's no' a man to offer comfort. He's probably at the pub counting the night's profits. She'll need a bit of reassurance."

"Terence MacDougall's no' here, either," Jeanne said. "It's his pounds that Donald Sinclair's counting, I'm thinking."

Angus's head began to ache. "And the laird?"

"Standing beside the lady's bed. Waiting for you."

Angus quickly discovered that fact for himself. The noise from the rooms beyond grew louder. He skipped the tea and the last few moments of scrubbing. As he donned rubber gloves, he saw Jeanne washing and donning gloves, too.

The first room held two beds. A regal man with silvering hair stood beside one. He was Malcolm Ross, the tenth laird of Druidheachd. Mary, his wife, was to have set up housekeeping in Glasgow next week to be near a modern hospital with the most up-to-date medical care. Either the baby was early or a highly acclaimed specialist had never learned how to count.

Thrashing from side to side in the bed beside Mrs. Ross was Melissa Sinclair, the wife of the innkeeper. Angus knew Mrs. Sinclair hadn't wanted to give birth here. She was an

American, and she hated everything about Druidheachd, including—he feared—the Scotsman she'd married.

In the next room, out of sight but not out of earshot, was Jane MacDougall, wife of the town's colorful ne'er-do-well. When he wasn't drinking or recovering, Terence Mac-Dougall fished or else fleeced the occasional tourist who ventured this far into the Highlands for a glimpse of Loch Ceo's resident monster.

"My wife first," the laird announced calmly.

Angus had little choice. He felt a stab of pity for the two other women whose men had left them to fend for themselves. He started toward the Rosses.

"It's coming! The baby's coming!" Melissa Sinclair wailed.

From the room next door, the same wail sounded.

With an unsteady hand Angus drew back Mary Ross's covers and saw that although she was grimly silent, her situation was identical. There was little left to do except catch the laird's son as Mary gave a mighty push. Jeanne reached Melissa Sinclair at almost the same moment and with the same result. And as they delivered the babies side by side to the chiming of the town clock, they heard a lusty new cry from the other room. Angus plopped the laird's new son into the outstretched arms of his astonished father and dived for the door.

One glance told him that Jane MacDougall had managed quite well without anyone's help.

The next morning, the three births were the talk of Druidheachd. Three healthy male infants, born at the same moment. Born at midnight, to be exact. No one, not the doctor, not Jeanne Maxwell, and certainly not the proud new mothers, could say which of the wee laddies had come first.

"Margaret Henley says it's a sign, the three weans being born at the same moment," Jeanne confided to Angus that afternoon over a well-deserved dram of the Glenmorangie he'd opened the previous night. "She says they've started this life together and can no' be separated now. She's calling them the wee laddies of midnight."

Angus knew that whatever Margaret—not a day over ninety—said was widely accepted in the village, since she was known by one and all to have the sight. The poor wee laddies of midnight would bear that title until they were men. "They'll go to school together when they've grown a bit," he said. "But do you think that lads of such different backgrounds will be raised like brothers? I can no' believe it."

But Margaret's pronouncement spread through the village. It wound through the front door of the moss-etched stone hotel, up the wide spiral staircase of the laird's manor home, and in between the planks of a humble cottage beside Loch Ceo. Duncan Sinclair, Iain Ross and Andrew MacDougall were bound together by the peculiar circumstances of their birth. They were destined to live their lives in each other's shadows.

And they did. Even as men.

Chapter 1

One moment the hills below the peak where Mara stood were dappled with bright patches of sunlight. The next, shadows stole across them, shadows and writhing, flailing wisps of fog. With a shiver she pulled her long cloak around her and turned toward home.

As a child, Mara had visited the south of England, and she had been surprised to find that night fell there with calm, ordered regularity, even in summer. Here in the Highlands, even more than the rest of Scotland, there was either an abundance of night or not nearly enough of it. Now that winter was almost over, the black velvet curtain that extinguished the afternoon fell later and later, but the days still weren't long enough to suit her.

Guiser, the border collie Mara had gotten in trade for a dozen hanks of hand-spun wool the previous year, fell into place beside her. Her small flock of sheep were all safely in the stone pen behind her, and the cows were in the byre. Guiser would assume his watchdog role after tea, but until then, he deserved a rest.

"Aye, it's time we were getting home," she agreed. "I've a full pail of scraps for you and soup simmering on the hearth." Guiser trotted up the hill at her side and along the winding path that led to the thatched cottage that Mara called home. Inside, he stretched out in front of the fireplace, but his eyes followed her as she went to the cupboard.

"You'll like what I'm serving tonight. There's nowt in Glasgow or Edinburgh that compares. You'll be dining like a king." She took the pail of scraps she had assembled that morning and started toward his bowl. She reached over to fill it, but her hand froze in midair. She closed her eyes as a familiar feeling swept over her.

She tried to focus on something, the smell of soup simmering or the acrid tang of the peat fire, but she knew how futile it was to resist the impressions forming in her mind.

Guiser growled; then he leaped to his feet and started toward the door she hadn't closed tightly behind her. He wedged his nose in the crack and nudged it open. In a moment he was gone.

Night had fallen. Mara went to the window, but there was nothing to see except darkness and more of the same. She followed Guiser's trail in her mind. The dog would be a black and white blur streaking down the mountainside toward the road that was the only route off Bein Domhain. In her mind she watched as he patrolled silently back and forth, waiting for something he couldn't possibly understand.

It wasn't the first time that the dog had discerned his mistress's feelings. She had no idea why he always seemed to know when she sensed something was about to happen. She imagined that without meaning to, she communicated her own apprehensions to him. He was an extremely intelligent animal. She called him Guiser, the Scottish word for a person in disguise, because she had never been convinced he was just a dog. That was foolish, of course, since no male human she had ever encountered had Guiser's sensitivity.

The impressions grew stronger, and she stopped fighting them. The picture of a man formed in her mind. He was tall, but not a giant. Muscular, but not a weight lifter. She was a spinner and a dyer, and she thought of colors by their connection to the land and sky. The man's hair was the brown of forest shadows and his eyes the clear, iridescent gray found at the borders of thunderclouds.

His name eluded her.

Mara asked herself why she was envisioning the man, a stranger, now. Unease filled her. Then, as suddenly as he had appeared in her mind, he vanished, and his face was replaced by another. This face she knew. It belonged to Geordie Smith, who lived alone in a farmhouse on the road to Druidheachd. Geordie Smith, who believed he was a poet when he had half the contents of a bottle of whiskey warming his insides, and the bens and braes of his beloved Highlands stretched out at his feet. Geordie Smith who was known far and wide as a man with more heart than brains.

With her eyes still closed, Mara saw Guiser give up watching the road. He turned and started up the mountainside, ready to be fed.

Mara wanted to forget the last few minutes. She wanted her life to be exactly as it had been before them.

She knew better than to hope for such a thing.

Duncan Sinclair had forgotten that night fell so swiftly in a Highland winter. These days there was little but frost in his heart; he was almost surprised to discover that winter existed outside of him, too.

Duncan hadn't lived in Scotland since the age of eight. He had finished his childhood in New York, where he had lost his accent, his roots and his innocence. As a boy he had returned for a month every summer to visit Donald Sinclair, the father he had buried today in the cemetery at the village kirk. But it had been more than twenty years since Duncan had seen the Highlands in March.

As the sky darkened, his breath formed clouds in front of him, and his glove-encased fingertips grew numb. He thrust his hands deeper in his pockets as he hiked on. He wasn't sure when he had realized that he'd better start back to the minibus. One moment he'd been trudging down a narrow path toward the small mountain loch where he and his best friends Andrew MacDougall and Iain Ross had camped as boys, the next he'd turned back, his goal unrealized.

He wasn't a man who gave up easily. There were few battles he hadn't fought to conclusion, few ambitions he hadn't satisfied. He had left home at eighteen, worked his way through college, and, fresh out of it, he had started an advertising agency, which at its peak had captured some of the most lucrative accounts in southern California. Along the way he had wooed and won the woman he had been certain he couldn't live without.

Then, last year, at twenty-nine, he had forfeited everything he owned in order to attain the most important goals of his life: a divorce and sole custody of his six-year-old daughter, April.

So why had he turned back today? He supposed thoughts of April had influenced him, even though she was thousands of miles away in New York with his mother and sister, Fiona. He no longer had the luxury of taking risks, even small ones like walking along a mountain path at twilight. Duncan was the only stable force in April's life.

He paused to take a breath. The darkness settled around him, chill and damp. It seeped through his ski jacket and wool slacks. Even his feet, encased in heavy socks and waterproof leather, were quickly growing cold.

How far had he come? He wasn't sure. His friends Iain and Andrew had cautioned him to be careful. They had pointed out that distances in the mountains could be deceptive and that he had probably forgotten more than he remembered about their boyhood jaunts. He had shrugged off their warnings the same way he had shrugged off the condolences of the villagers after the funeral. He didn't like advice any more than he liked sentiment. And today he hadn't liked the way he had responded deep inside to the warmth of both.

He started back up the path and stepped up his pace, searching the thickening gloom for reassuring landmarks. He rounded a bend and halfway expected to see the hotel's old minibus sitting beside the single-lane road, but there was only mountainside beyond him and the faint tracing of the path.

At the next turn a boulder rose high in a clearing. The shape was unusual, wider at the top than the bottom and nearly level. As he stared, memories surfaced of scrambling over it as a boy. He, Andrew and Iain had played king of the mountain here, scratching their way up the lichen-crusted surface, then shoving each other over the side. He hadn't noticed the boulder earlier, but now he was reassured. At least he wasn't lost.

He paused for a moment to watch fog waltz through the clearing. Broad and long, the clearing was as lush as a meadow in the summer, a surprising splash of tall grass and wildflowers. Now the vegetation was brown and shrouded with snow. There were springs hidden in the rocks beyond him and caves in the mountainside. He had explored the caves as a teenager. At sixteen he had considered moving into one when his father, stern under the best circumstances, had discovered that all the tomato plants in the hotel glasshouse had withered and died because Duncan had neglected to water them.

As he stared into the distance, remembering the man he had buried today, something moved at the edge of his field of vision. He narrowed his eyes and searched for the source. Not far away rowan trees twisted in the rising wind, and just beyond them thick clumps of hazel and beech swayed restlessly. He peered into the darkness behind the dancing silhouettes, but little else was visible.

He had already started back down the path when a piercing whistle stopped him. He faced the trees again, but the whistle was nothing more than the wind, at most a warning that night was falling fast and he should hurry back to the bus. He started forward again, when something brought him up short. He turned for one last look. There was a noticeable change in the elements surrounding him. The whistle expanded into a shriek, almost a howl, and the remaining light seemed to fade away. The wind, which he had blamed for the whistling, died completely. Even the trees were still.

But something moved behind them.

He stepped forward, squinting into the darkness. "Hello? Is anyone there?" he shouted. There was no answer.

"Hello?" he shouted louder.

There were animals in these mountains, sheep and the occasional fox or wild dog. But Duncan didn't expect to see any four-legged beasts. Whatever he had glimpsed was taller and two-legged. Either he was imagining things, or another human being was out there.

He hesitated. If someone was there, that person wanted to be left alone or he would have answered. Perhaps a farmer from one of the surrounding properties was looking for a stray sheep. Duncan wasn't sure that he had the legal right to be on this path, which probably cut across privately owned lands. His knowledge of Scottish property laws was as foggy as the meadow. But whether he had the right to be here or not, he didn't have the right to disturb the property owner.

He had convinced himself to leave, but he still didn't move. Like his father, he had never been a man who acted on feelings, but something kept him rooted to the spot. Annoyed with himself, he shouted once more. "Hello?"

No one answered, at least not in the way he had expected. There wasn't any movement now, but a shaft of light illuminated the spot where he thought he'd seen someone. It was too early in the evening for the moon, too late for the sun. He stepped forward, intrigued. The light was finely focused and intense. He'd never seen anything quite like it, but he wasn't frightened. The day was dying, and the fog was thickening. There were a billion possible combinations of twilight and mist and mountain air currents. He was witnessing one.

He balanced his need to get back to the road with his need to explore a little further. Shrugging, he picked his way across the clearing. The trees were farther than he'd thought, and the light glowed brighter. As he drew closer he noticed that it had a peculiar greenish tint. The color was odd enough, but odder still was the shape. It was a narrow beam, the width of a small tree or a person. Channeled through a leafless canopy of branches, it was as concentrated as a laser.

No one was nearby. Duncan wondered if he had mistaken the light for a person. Perhaps it had played a trick on his eyes. His hands and feet were growing colder, and he began to lose his enthusiasm. His goal was just ahead, but there seemed to be little point in walking the final fifty yards. Then he heard the shriek again.

He began to run. There were no more thoughts of farmers searching for lost sheep or interesting shafts of light. As he charged through the trees, he could see the ground where the light was centered. A man lay on his back, his eyes closed.

Duncan fell to his knees and patted the man's cheeks. "Hey, you there. Can you hear me?"

The man was short and dark, well-padded with fat but not dressed for the elements. An empty whiskey bottle lay on the ground beside him. Duncan shook his shoulders. "Can you understand me?"

"I doubt he'll be understanding anything for a good while."

Duncan's head snapped up. At the edge of the light, just in the shadows, stood a figure wrapped in a long, hooded cloak. "Where in God's name did you come from?" he demanded. "And just how long have you been standing there?"

"Long enough to be glad you came along."

The voice was a woman's, soft and as delicate as sea foam. Duncan squinted into the darkness, and as if to give him a better view, she glided forward. Her cloak billowed around her, yards and yards of wool that looked as soft as her voice.

"Do you know this man?" Duncan asked. "And do you know what in the hell he's doing here?"

"By the look of him, I'd say he's freezing to death."

"I had that part figured out."

"His name's Geordie Smith. And I think he's in this state fair often."

It was too dark to get a good look at her. Her hood was drawn around her face, hiding everything but a glimpse of nose, an impression of eyes. He could just make out even white teeth gnawing her bottom lip in concern. He looked back down at the man on the ground. "Well, right now it doesn't matter how often he gets this way, just whether he's going to survive this particular binge or not."

"He'll survive. Now that you're here, he'll be all right."

As if to prove her words, the man's eyelids fluttered open, and he began to moan. Duncan bent closer. The man she'd called Geordie smelled like a distillery.

The moan changed to barely audible words. "Who's there?"

"My name's Duncan Sinclair. What in the hell are you doing out here by yourself?"

Geordie struggled to sit up. Duncan helped him into position. It took a great heave, then an arm around Geordie's shoulders for a moment to steady him. Geordie grew paler.

"Are you all right?" Duncan asked.

"Of course I'm no' all right. I'm dead."

"Do I look like an angel?"

"There's no use in ye sparing me feelings. I'm dead."

Duncan sat back on his heels. "Not yet. But you might have been if you'd stayed on the ground all night. What are you doing here? Or are you too drunk to remember?"

Geordie looked insulted at the question. "Och, I'll have ye know I'm no' a drunk. I'm . . . a poet, a bard."

"Well, that explains it."

"I'm here for ins . . . ins . . ."

Duncan waved away Geordie's twin attempts at explanation and dignity. "Can you walk?"

Geordie considered.

Duncan was afraid Geordie might ponder the question all night. "Let's get you to your feet and see."

"I'm still thinking . . . I'm dead."

"You'll just wish you were tomorrow."

"Then if I'm no' dead . . ." He narrowed his eyes. "Just who was the lady in green?"

Duncan looked up. He wanted to find out the answer himself. He hadn't thought to ask the woman's name or what she was doing on the mountainside. But now the place where she'd been standing was unoccupied. He leaned forward and peered into the darkness, but there was no sign that anyone had ever been there.

Duncan wanted to be back at the hotel in front of a good fire. His patience and sympathy with Highlanders were abating. The woman hadn't even stayed to be sure that Geordie was going to be all right, and the evidence that Geordie had brought this state on himself was lying on the ground at his feet. "Look, man, you're still drunk, and your body temperature's probably dropped a few degrees. Don't waste my time talking. Just see if you can get to your feet. We've got to get you someplace where you can warm up."

"It was a lady I saw. In green. All in green." Geordie put his face in his hands. "If she was no' an angel..."

"She wasn't," Duncan assured him.

"Och, then she was a ghost."

"What?"

Geordie began to cry, big sloppy tears that threatened to freeze on his cheeks. His shoulders shook. "She saved me. I've been saved by a ferlie."

"I saved you."

"No. She brought ye here."

"Look, there was a woman here, but she left as soon as she saw I could take care of things. She was just an ordinary human. That's all. There's no such thing as a ghost. And if you don't get moving, Geordie whoever-you-are, there won't be any such thing as *you*, either."

With Duncan's help, Geordie managed to get to his feet. He staggered a few yards, his elbow firmly in Duncan's grasp. "She told me to lie down, the ferlie did. She said I'd be safe."

"The only thing worse than a ghost is a ghost who gives bad advice."

"Yer no' from the Highlands," Geordie said. He lifted his head and held it high, even though his chin wobbled badly. "Ye...can no' understand."

"Oh, I'm from here, all right. And I'm afraid I understand all too well."

Geordie shivered and fell silent. Duncan wanted nothing more than to leave the little man in the clearing, but he knew that by the time a search party from Druidheachd came back for him, Geordie would be a ghost or an angel himself. He stripped off his jacket and placed it around Geordie's shoulders. The wind cut through his wool sweater, but unlike Geordie, he was in no danger of dying of exposure. They trudged on. To Geordie's credit, he struggled to keep pace.

"Can you make it back out to the road?" Duncan asked, when they had crossed the clearing and were near the path again.

"Oh, aye. With yer help, I'll make it just fine. She promised I'd be safe."

It had been a day unlike any other in his life. Duncan's patience snapped. "You're drunk, man. And you were passed out on the ground because you were too drunk to stand! I don't want to hear anything more about ghosts."

Geordie stopped moving. He pulled his elbow from Duncan's grasp and turned in the direction they'd come. "Dressed in green, she was, with a face like an angel."

"Come on." Duncan took Geordie's arm. At this rate it would be very late when they got to the bus—if they got there at all. "Don't worry about anything now except walking."

"She's there still."

"Sure she is."

"She's there." Geordie pointed.

Duncan looked up. The pale green light was no longer focused. It had diffused into soft, gentle curves. His breath caught. For a moment, just the fraction of a moment, the light appeared to take on the shape of a woman. Then it dissolved into the darkness. Somewhere out of sight a dog began to howl.

"Farewell, lady," Geordie said softly. "And thanks to ye."

At that moment, all the reasons why Duncan could never be happy in Druidheachd were absolutely clear to him.

"What is it ye say they call ye?" Geordie asked.

Duncan jerked the little man back onto the path, and Geordie came willingly. "Duncan Sinclair."

"Yer not Donald Sinclair's son? One of the wee laddies born at midnight?"

"That's right."

"And will ye be staying in Druidheachd now that yer father's passed on?"

Duncan could feel his jaw clamp tight, but there was only one answer he could give. "I will. God help me, but I don't seem to have been given a choice."

Chapter 2

A month later Duncan looked out on the sheets of rain sweeping Druidheachd's High Street. Spring had arrived officially, but the days were still chill and gray.

A woman's voice sounded behind him. "There's a lovely fire in the sitting room, dearie, and a pot of tea to warm you. Come away from the window now, and forget your troubles."

Duncan unwillingly faced Frances Gunn, the hotel's cook. She was apple-cheeked and white-haired, a storybook-perfect granny with a lap wide enough for half a dozen children and a smile wide enough to let them all know they were welcome. "I'd forgotten how gray it can be on a spring evening, and how cold," he said.

"Aye, gray it can be. But in Druidheachd, spring's the time of year when good friends become better ones."

Duncan turned back toward the street and didn't respond. He had friends here, the only two people in the world besides April and his sister, Fiona, who really mattered to him. Iain Ross and Andrew MacDougall had drawn him to the Highlands as much as a need to put thousands of miles between his daughter and Los Angeles. But there was little

else of value for him in Druidheachd, a village so backward
that the eighteenth century seemed to beckon from the future.

"You will no' be having that tea?" Frances asked.

"No. Thank you, Frances, but I've got to tuck April in
bed. I promised I'd read her a story."

"She does look forward to your time together."

"So do I."

"She likes it here, you know. She feels like she belongs.
And you belong, Duncan. You always have."

He wasn't cruel enough to contradict warm-hearted Frances Gunn. He managed a smile and was rewarded with one
of Frances's own. He waited until the click of sensible shoes
against the granite floor died away before he gave up his
view of the street for that of the interior of the building that
was the only thing of value—however dubious—that he
owned in the world.

The Sinclair Hotel was gray like the street in front of it,
and nearly as cold, despite a fuel bill that threatened daily
to put him out of business. One room faded into another,
austere, colorless rooms with threadbare furniture and tattered carpets. Little had changed since his childhood. He
imagined that in the eighteenth century the hotel had sprung
to life in exactly this form. One moment there had been a
narrow parcel of barren land facing what passed for a street;
the next moment the Sinclair Hotel, shabby and weather-
beaten, had risen intact from the stone buried deep inside
the earth.

Duncan had taken his first steps here, read his first halt-
ing sentence. He had played hide-and-seek in these narrow
halls, but those moments of laughter and friendship seemed
to have left no mark. Now he couldn't imagine anyone
laughing within the confines of these three-feet-thick walls.

"Daddy?"

Duncan looked up to the top of the stairwell rising to the
second floor. A small, thin figure was perched on the top
step, her chin resting in her hands. He felt a familiar mixture of love and regret.

He pointed a finger at her. "I thought you were in bed. I was just coming up."

"I *was* in bed, but I got so lonely."

"I know what you're doing. You're just looking for an excuse to stay up a little longer."

"It's not a very big excuse."

"Just big enough to keep you out of bed." He started toward her. "And look at you. You're not even wearing a robe, as cold as it is."

"I'm not cold. I only get cold when I'm all alone in my room."

Duncan had painted his daughter's room a sunny yellow and added flowered curtains, comforter and pillows. There was a small heater in the corner to steal the ever-present chill from the air, and shelves of toys to steal the chill from her small heart. But nothing he'd done for her could possibly be enough.

At the top of the stairs he presented her with his back, and she obligingly climbed on board for a ride to the apartment at the hall's end. She was lighter than a thick Highland fog. When he deposited her on the rumpled comforter in the middle of her bed, he hardly noticed the absence of her weight.

Duncan sat on the edge as she slid under the covers. "Now listen, Springtime. You know I'm never far away. I'm always somewhere in the hotel when you're sleeping, and I come up to check on you often. You've got the intercom right beside your bed if you need me, and if I have to go out, I always have someone come up here to stay with you."

She gave him a tremulous smile. "I just get scared sometimes."

"I know you do. But you'll see. I'll never leave you alone."

Solemn gray eyes exactly like his own stared back at him. He knew what she was thinking. He took her hand and kissed it, then stuck it back under the covers. As he did, his fingers brushed something cool and solid. "Did you pick out a book already?" he asked.

Her eyes grew larger. "No."

He felt resistance when he tried to tug the book from under the covers. She was obviously doing her best to prevent it. He lifted a brow in question.

"I want the one about the beaver pond," she said.

He almost gave in, but something about her expression warned him that there was more here than she was acknowledging. "Let me see what you have there first."

"It's just a book."

"April..."

She looked away and relaxed her grip. He pulled the book from under the covers and read the title. *"Duncan and the Fairies?"* He flipped through the pages. The book was small and beautifully illustrated. Golden haired fairies garbed in gauzy green nearly danced off the pages. Even without reading the text, he could see that his poor namesake Duncan, a clumsy-looking lout, was no match for them. "Where did you get this? Did someone in the hotel give it to you?"

"No."

He waited.

"Will you read me the book about the beavers now?"

"I'd like to know who gave you this."

She still didn't look at him. "Mara."

"Mara? Who's Mara?"

"Just a lady."

Had the mysterious Mara been just any lady, Duncan knew that April would have chatted on and on about her. But obviously Mara was already someone special, and therefore not to be discussed. April had learned early to keep the things that really mattered close to her heart. "Where did you meet her?" he probed.

"She lives by Mrs. Gunn, at the end of her road. Jessie took me there to get milk. Don't be mad, please?"

"Mad?" He finished flipping through the book. There was nothing like it in April's sizable library. She had books that carefully explained the world around her, books about nature and science, and several about divorce and children with feelings just like hers. But there were no fairy stories.

That was no accident.

He rose and set the book on her shelf. "April, there aren't any fairies. And there aren't any ghosts or leprechauns or witches. It's all make believe."

"But Mara says she's heard the fairies singing!" She sat up. "They live under the ground near her house, and she's heard their music late at night. Mara looks like a fairy, like the prettiest one in the book, except she's prettier and—"

"This Mara, whoever she is, is just making that up. Fairies, elves and gnomes are all pretend." He found the book he was looking for. "And people who pretend they're real, shouldn't."

"Mommy read me fairy tales."

He didn't know what to say. There were plenty of other things Mommy had done that couldn't be talked about.

"I think Mommy believes in fairies, too. Like Mara," April said.

"She might believe in fairies, but that doesn't make them real." He took his place at her bedside again. "Have you ever seen a fairy yourself?" He waited for the reluctant shake of her head. "A witch? An elf? Don't believe in anything, Springtime, not unless you can see it with your own eyes. And then question what you see, because even your eyes can lie."

"I like that book." Her bottom lip sank an inch. "Mara gave it to me, and I like Mara."

"How often have you been to see this Mara?"

April shrugged.

More than once. That was obvious. Duncan wondered why Frances Gunn hadn't told him about the visits, and why April had never mentioned them before this. Displeasure curled inside him. April didn't need another unstable, fanciful woman in her life. As it was, the damage inflicted by her mother might never be repaired.

He smiled at his daughter, making sure that no sign of his feelings showed on his face. This was something he could take care of. His hands had been tied before, but this time no court would stand in his way. April was his now; he could protect her. And that was exactly what he planned to do.

He opened the book about life in a beaver pond and began to read out loud. When she was sound asleep, he tucked
the covers around her and checked to be sure the intercom
was on. The clerk at the front desk would hear any noise in
the room and alert him if April awoke.

Then he headed downstairs to find Frances.

An hour later Duncan watched Iain Ross sip a dram of the
hotel's finest whiskey. His back was to the hotel bar, and his
white hand-knit sweater gleamed like a beacon in the smoky
haze.

"What is it you're wanting to know about Mara, Dunc?"

"What do *you* know?" Duncan signaled Brian, the bar-
man, and Brian obligingly brought him a pint of the pub's
bitterest ale.

"You don't have that much time." Iain sipped, watching
his friend as he did. He was perfectly capable of downing
half a dozen shots without flinching, but Duncan knew he
preferred to take his time and savor his liquor.

"You're jerking me around, Iain."

Iain lifted one dark elegant brow. He looked every inch
the laird of Druidheachd.

"She gave April a book," Duncan said. "And Frances
Gunn says that no one knows much about her background
or why she's chosen to live in Druidheachd."

"And those are punishable offenses in America?"

"I just want to know who she is."

"She came here from Perthshire. About two years ago.
Actually, I sold her a parcel of land. I take it you haven't
met our Mara yet?"

"How do you know that?"

"I think the look in your eye might be a wee bit different." Iain stared at him as he finished his drink. Then he set
his glass on the counter. "Mara's a good woman, bonny and
courageous and far too lovely a person for me to get involved with."

Duncan knew that said quite a bit. Iain navigated through
romances like a sailor on a round-the-world cruise. He en-

joyed his times in port, but he never looked back when the ship put out to sea again.

"What else do you know?" Duncan asked.

"That you're worrying about nothing. Mara would never do a thing to hurt April."

"Do you know, that's exactly what Lisa said to me the first time I confronted her?" He then mimicked his ex-wife, "Duncan, how can you say those things? You know I'd never do a thing to hurt my baby."

"Mara's not Lisa, Dunc. And this isn't California. You've been so far away and for such a long time, you've forgotten how we take care of each other in Druidheachd."

"I haven't forgotten. That's one of the reasons I stayed away so long."

"Ask Andrew what he thinks about Mara." Iain nodded toward the door. Andrew MacDougall was just striding in. Rain clung to his dark macintosh and shaggy red hair. It took him a while to cross the room, because the other pub guests all had to have a word with him first. But when the three men stood together at the bar, the other patrons kept a respectful distance. Duncan remembered that it had always been that way. Ordinary men when they were alone, the three friends were considered extraordinary together.

Duncan experienced the irritation that was the sum total of his feelings about the village of his birth. He nodded to Andrew. "Watch. No one will come near us now. What do you suppose they're afraid will happen? That as a body we'll put a curse on them? Turn them into frogs or seals?"

"Nowt quite so dramatic," Andrew said. He pointed to Duncan's glass, and Brian brought Andrew the same, sliding it toward him from six feet away.

"Look at that. Even Brian doesn't want to disturb us," Duncan said.

"Be glad," Iain said. "If we'd been ordinary weans, born where and when we were supposed to be, we never would have been raised on top of each other."

"We would no' have taken our first steps right here in this hotel together," Andrew said. "Or said our first words at the laird's fine table."

"Or had our first ride on the loch in MacDougall's boat," Iain said.

Duncan shook his head, and Andrew grinned. He slung his arm around Duncan's shoulder. "There's nowt to be gained by fighting your feelings for Druidheachd quite so hard, Dunc. Or your feelings for us, for that matter. There's nowt womanly about loving your friends."

Duncan shook Andrew off, but a reluctant smile formed. "What do you know about a woman named Mara Mac-Tavish?"

Andrew winked and whistled.

"If you want to meet her for yourself, you've only to cross the road." Iain gestured lazily toward the window. "She's over at Cameron's now. I saw her go inside."

Duncan set his glass on the bar. If he wanted to know more about the MacTavish woman, he was going to have to get his facts straight from her. His friends weren't going to be any help. "That's what I'll do, then. Just tell me how to recognize her."

The other men exchanged a look that told Duncan what he needed to know. He left without another word.

Outside he pulled his jacket tightly around him and crossed his arms to hold it in place. Cameron's was the grocery store, the liquor store, the post office and the unofficial center of gossip. No Cameron had owned it in a hundred years, and for a hundred years a series of new owners had hung new signs. But Cameron's it was to the people of Druidheachd, and Cameron's it would always be. The building was one story, with stone painted white and woodwork black. Boxes adorned the windows and pale sprouts promised that someday, if the sun ever shone, there might be flowers in them.

Inside it wasn't any warmer than outside, but at least it was dry. He stamped his feet, and water droplets flew. He used the time to survey the neatly arranged aisles.

"Is it help you're needing, Duncan?" the proprietor, a man in his fifties, asked.

"Thanks, but no."

"We've a new shipment of videos."

Duncan shook his head. His gaze traveled from aisle to aisle, past an old woman holding tightly to the hand of a rosy-cheeked cherub, past a thin young man choosing a bunch of carrots. As he was about to admit his friends had played a trick on him, a length of green unfolded from the farthest aisle, and a woman appeared in the midst of it.

She was tall and slender, or at least that was his guess, because most of her body was shrouded in a forest green cloak. Straight, pale blond hair hung over the hood, which was pushed back over her shoulders. As if she knew he was watching her, she turned, and her eyes met his. She didn't smile, and neither did he.

Now Duncan understood April's description and Iain's comments. Even a heart as jaded as his could still respond to beauty. And Mara MacTavish was more than beautiful.

It was one more strike against her.

He started toward her, and she waited, as if she knew that she was the reason he was here.

"And fresh young kail," the proprietor called after him. "Frances Gunn told me to let her know if we got good kail."

"I'll tell her."

The proprietor muttered something behind him, but Duncan didn't take his eyes off Mara. He stopped just a few yards from her and crossed his arms. "I'm Duncan Sinclair. You've met my daughter, April?"

She held out her hand. "Mara MacTavish. Your daughter's a bonny wee girlie."

He didn't want to touch her, but he knew the whole village would hear about it if he didn't take Mara's hand. He stretched out his own. Hers wasn't soft, as he'd expected, but callused. He looked down and saw short nails and sun-blotched skin. He dropped it quickly.

"She was fair taken with my dog," Mara said in a soft, musical voice. "He's no' used to children, but he was taken with her, too. I was afraid he might try to herd her and Jessie's Lolly into one of my pens, but he worshiped at their feet."

Mara's voice seemed familiar, but Duncan couldn't place it. Nothing else was familiar, though. Despite April's description, he had visualized a rosy-cheeked, sturdy-boned crofter. Instead, Mara was as delicate, as ethereal, as the fairy in April's new book. "Mrs. Gunn tells me you have a farm near her house."

"Nothing so grand. It's a wee croft. No one would call it a farm."

"But you raise cattle? April says Jessie buys her milk from you."

"Jessie does, and a few others, but I only have two cows. I raise sheep."

He really had no interest in what Mara MacTavish did or had, except when it concerned his daughter. He went straight to the point. "Would you mind telling me how many times April's been to see you?"

She seemed puzzled. "I'm sorry, but I have no' been counting."

"I didn't know anything about her visits until tonight."

"I suppose there was no' much to tell. She enjoys my animals."

"You gave her a book."

"Oh, I see." Her face had been lovely in repose. Adorned with a smile, it was breathtaking. "You're worried that she took a gift from a stranger. I'm sorry. I never thought. She was just so interested in my stories about the fairies. The book was mine as a child, and I thought she'd enjoy it. You dinna have to worry. She said a proper thank you."

He was growing more irritated. He thought he was making himself clear, but she seemed purposely to misunderstand. "It's not that you gave her a gift. It's the gift you gave her."

The smile faded. "Oh?"

There were things he couldn't tell her, not without a lengthy explanation, which he wasn't inclined to offer. He couldn't tell her that despite a hundred differences she reminded him of his ex-wife, with her delicate bones, translucent skin and sweet feminine smile. He couldn't tell her that he was desperately afraid that she would remind April of Lisa, too, and make it harder for April to forget her mother.

But he could tell her part of the truth. "April doesn't need stories about fairies in her life. Not fairies or witches, ghosts or leprechauns. She's a little girl, and little girls can't always tell the difference between the truth and a lie."

"A lie?"

"I've met a few adults who can't tell the difference, either."

"Mr. Sinclair, I have no' told your daughter any lies."

He shrugged. "April's still young. She doesn't understand that not everything a grown-up tells her is a fact. I want her to understand that the world's a certain way. No ghosts and goblins, just good people and bad. No magic, just a world that works on certain fixed principles."

"And you understand everything about the way the world works?"

"I don't make up stories to explain the things I don't understand."

"I see."

She seemed to see quite a lot. Her eyes were a pale green and perfectly steady. They didn't flicker from his. "I'm not trying to be harsh or ungrateful," he said. "It's just that April is my responsibility, and I take that responsibility seriously."

"I can see that."

"I've asked Frances not to let her visit you again. April's still getting used to living here, and I want to be sure she's...adjusted before she starts meeting people. I'd appreciate it if you'd send her back to the Gunn's if she and Lolly slip over to visit without permission."

"No."

Duncan knew exactly how he'd sounded. Autocratic, unyielding, an undisguised bastard. But he didn't really care. April *was* his responsibility, and the fact that Mara Mac-Tavish couldn't possibly understand his fears didn't change a thing. "Would you mind telling me why not?"

"Mr. Sinclair, I've no wish to hurt your daughter. If I thought I might, I'd send her home in a minute. But despite everything you've heard about me, I would no' hurt a child, *could no'* hurt a child, if my very life depended on it."

Something had changed. Duncan didn't know what or why, but the balance between them had shifted. Now she was angry, and he was the one who was mystified. "Heard about you?"

"Oh, I can guess what you've been told. I know what's said about me in the village. Dinna pretend you dinna understand."

"I *don't* understand."

"Well, try to understand this. I'm no' in the habit of rejecting children, no' for any reason in the world. Your daughter seems to want my friendship, and she'll have it if she finds her way to my house. If you're determined that she can no' visit me, then you'll have to supervise her more carefully. I will no' discipline her for you, and I will no' send her away."

Her voice hadn't changed. It was still light and lyrically accented with the country of her birth, but the words were flawlessly aimed. Duncan felt their barb. *He* was the one at fault. He didn't supervise his daughter closely enough. He was trying to protect April from an important friendship. He was asking a total stranger to reject her.

Except that Mara wasn't a total stranger. Duncan stared at her. Her voice had been familiar from the beginning. Now he understood why. "Wait a minute. I don't know why I didn't realize it before. You're the woman I met on the mountain last month."

"Am I?"

"Look, I don't want to play games. You helped me rescue Geordie Smith. There's not much chance I'd be allowed to forget you. Since I came back to live in Druidheachd, I've seen Geordie every day at the hotel, and he reminds me of that night every time I see him."

She started past him, but he took her arm, catching folds of forest green wool. "Where did you go that night? You just disappeared."

"What does Geordie say?" She pulled her arm from his grip and faced him.

"He babbles."

"And what does he babble?"

"That he was saved by a ghost. That the ghost of a lady dressed in green saved his life. I don't get much of the credit."

"I'm sure that's upsetting, feeling about ghosts as you do."

"Well, at least now I can tell him exactly who his ghost was."

"But I would no', Mr. Sinclair. It will just worry him more."

"What do you mean?"

"Dinna you see? Half the people in Druidheachd already believe I'm a ghost or a witch or a fairy." She smiled, but it didn't warm her eyes. "If you tell Geordie it was Mara MacTavish he saw on the mountain that night, he'll be absolutely certain his life has been touched by magic. And we both know you would never want to be responsible for that."

Chapter 3

Daffodils blanketed the slopes leading away from Mara's cottage, and new spring lambs frolicked in the afternoon sun. Mara sat on a stone bench under a tall copper beech and listened to the humming of the bees as they waltzed from flower to flower. From time to time she hummed, too, a ballad her auntie had taught her as a child about Highland glens and lost love. On the ground before her, spread out to take advantage of the sun, were a dozen fleeces of newly shorn sheep.

She was so absorbed with the lock of wool in her hands that she wasn't aware she had company until Guiser sprang to his feet beside her. She looked up and saw April Sinclair standing in the distance, on the knoll opposite the cottage. Mara couldn't see the little girl's face clearly, but she could tell that April was terrified to come closer. And she knew what was frightening her.

"Stay, Guiser," she warned. He whined, but he sat obediently. She stood and started toward the knoll, skirting the fleeces. As she passed the last one, she lifted and rolled it into a neat bundle, then started toward April again, holding it up for the little girl to see.

"It's just a sheep's wool," she called when she was close enough to be heard. "No' a real sheep. Look." She pointed in the distance, where the newly shorn sheep grazed contentedly. "They've given me their coats so I can spin them into wool."

She stopped a short distance from April and waited. Once she had been a fanciful child herself. She knew that April needed a moment to absorb this new and better explanation for what had appeared to be a dozen slaughtered—and flattened—sheep.

"They're not dead?" April asked at last.

"Och no, no' dead at all. The sheep are busy growing more wool right over there."

"Why are their coats on the grass?"

"I'm letting the sun soften them. Come here and feel one."

April moved slowly toward her. Several feet away she stopped; then she stretched out her hand. She rubbed her fingertips over the fleece, and her eyes grew wider. "It feels funny."

"When I'm done with it, it will feel wonderful, all soft and cuddly, like a wee bittie lamb."

"What do you do with it?"

"Well, right now, I'm teasing the wool."

"Like my daddy teases me?"

Mara couldn't imagine Duncan Sinclair teasing anyone. It had been weeks since he had confronted her at Cameron's, weeks during which she had relived those short minutes in her mind and gotten angrier in the process.

She had known men like Duncan before. Her former husband, Robert Fitzwilliams, was one of them. Robbie had known what was best for everyone, too. Like Duncan, he was a physically appealing man, a man who would catch a woman's eye, then imprison her in a web of his own conceit and self-righteousness. She had learned more from Robbie than he would ever know. Most of all, she had learned to see him in others.

She put her arm around April's shoulders and guided her toward the house. "You can help me with the wool, if you'd like," she said. "But first you have to tell me if anyone knows you're here."

April was silent. It was answer enough.

"Will they no' worry?" Mara asked.

"No. Jessie thinks I went home after school."

"Then how did you get here?"

"I came on the bus to the end of the road with Lolly. And I made her promise not to tell anybody."

"Your father will be worried, will he no'?"

"He thinks I'm at Jessie's. He wrote me a note for the bus." April looked troubled. The complex strategy had obviously taken its toll. Mara guessed that April seldom disobeyed her father.

"You must have wanted to come here very badly." Mara stroked a lock of April's hair.

"Daddy..."

Mara knew what April wanted to say. "I know. He'd rather you did no' visit me. But surely you can understand why. I'm a stranger to him, am I no'?"

"Daddy says there's no such thing as fairies."

"Well, perhaps he's right."

"But you heard them singing!"

"I'm very fond of fairy tales. Perhaps I only want to hear them." They reached the bench where Mara had been sitting.

"I want to hear them, too."

"Perhaps you will one day." Mara sat, and April joined her. Mara snapped her fingers, and Guiser, all wags and lolling tongue, lavished canine affection on April.

She hugged him like a favored teddy bear. "May I tease some wool?"

Mara gazed into April's pleading gray eyes and knew she couldn't refuse her. "Aye, you may. But then we're going to have to take you back to Mrs. Gunn's house, are we no'? We can no' have anyone worrying about you."

"I'll just stay a little while."

For the first time in two years Mara wished she had a telephone. But her cottage lacked everything that most people considered conveniences. There were neighbors closer than the Gunns, but their houses were still a good distance away. There was no easy way to let anyone know where April was.

She picked up a lock of wool. "A sheep's fleece can get matted and creeshie when it's covering the sheep."

"What's creeshie?"

"Greasy, like your hair or mine if we did no' wash it. So after it's sheared, I set the fleece in the sun. The grease warms and makes the wool soft. Then I can take the longest fibers, like these, and tease them apart with my fingers. If they're no' too tangled, I can spin them without carding them."

"What's carding?"

Mara picked up two wire brushes on the ground beside the bench and turned them over. "You put the wool on these and rub them back and forth. Like this." She demonstrated. "The brushes straighten the wool and blend it. But I like to tease the best part without carding it, because after I've spun it, it takes dye in a bonny way."

"What will this be?" April took the wool from Mara's hands.

"That's the best part. I dinna know. Someone will buy it when I've spun it into yarn, and use it for weaving or knitting, whatever their imagination tells them it should be."

She demonstrated how to tease the wool, taking another lock in her left hand and separating the fibers. Then she helped April do the same with hers. The sun was warm, and the little girl was fascinated by the new task. Minutes slipped by. "You have perfect fingers for this, nimble and strong," Mara said at last. "Look how even your fibers are."

April glowed at the compliment. Mara knew that expression. For this brief moment, the child believed in herself. It made the moments that had come before and those that would come after seem more poignant.

"Would you like to try more?" Mara asked.

"Can I?"

They worked in silence for a while. April showed no signs of tiring, although Mara watched her carefully to be sure. Skylarks wheeled and sang overhead in accompaniment to

the hum of the occasional car on the road below. Dragon-
flies flitted from shadow to shadow.

Even though she knew it was time to take April back,
Mara bent over to get more wool. The little girl's company
made the afternoon perfect, and she was reluctant to see it
end. She was searching for one last easy clump to guarantee April's success when Guiser began to bark. She knew
whom she would see if she straightened. She supposed his
arrival had been inevitable, despite all April's scheming.

"Quiet, Guiser." Mara sat up. She noticed for the first
time that dark shadows had cut across the sunlit expanse of
daffodils. Even the baby lambs seemed chastened as they
huddled closer to their mothers.

"April." Duncan stood at the end of the path that led
down to the road.

Duncan's arms, encased in a dark blue jacket, were
crossed over his chest. The sunlight glinted against his
brown hair but ignited no sparks of gold or red. If there were
hidden depths, sensitivities or emotions inside Duncan Sinclair, there were no signs of them now. His striking face,
with its dark brows and shadowed eyes, was expressionless.

April moved closer to Mara, as if for support. But Mara
knew better than to come between father and daughter. "I
think it's time you were on your way, April," she said. "I'm
sorry."

April stood. Mara watched Duncan closely. She couldn't
keep him from taking April home, but neither would she
allow him to mistreat his daughter. April lacked the natural
confidence and spontaneity of most children her age, and
Mara was afraid she was about to witness the reason for it.

But Duncan surprised her as April approached him. He
squatted so his eyes were level with the little girl's, and he
didn't raise his voice. "Just what do you think you're doing, Springtime?"

She hung her head. "I wanted to see Mara."

"There are people who worry about you, me at the very
top of the list. Didn't you realize I'd be worried if you
weren't where you were supposed to be?"

"But I fixed it so nobody would worry!"

He lifted her chin with a gentle hand. "I'm afraid you didn't."

April looked down at the ground again. Duncan gently cradled her chin in his hand and lifted it again. "I called Jessie to see if you'd gotten there yet, and she told me you hadn't come home with Lolly. You never thought I might call her, did you?"

April shook her head.

"Haven't I told you that I always check to be sure you're safe?"

"Yes."

"And I mean it. That's my job, and I'm very good at it. I'm going to be sure that nothing ever happens to you."

"I just wanted to see Mara."

"Next time, you have to tell me."

"But you'll say no!"

Duncan looked up, and Mara met his eyes. She lifted a brow in question. He lowered his gaze to April again. "Whatever I say, you still have to tell me. I have to know where you are."

April began to cry. Duncan pulled her closer and held her in his arms. "Now look, I parked the car on the road. I want you to go down there and wait while I talk to Mara."

Mara rose. "Guiser will go with you to keep you company," she said. "He needs a good walk, anyway. Will you take him for me?"

April, tears still running down her cheeks, nodded. She broke away from Duncan and started down the path. Mara signaled, and Guiser followed in pursuit.

The shadows seemed to lengthen as Duncan and Mara stared at each other.

"Well, I'll give you this," he said finally, when the sound of April's footsteps had died away. "You meant what you said at Cameron's."

"And what was that?"

"That if April ever found her way here again, you wouldn't do a thing to be sure she got back home."

She knew it was useless to defend herself. He wouldn't believe she had intended to take April back to the Gunns. "Aye, I suppose I did say that."

"That's pretty irresponsible, don't you think? Did it occur to you that I might be worried sick?"

"No. But it did occur to me that if you found out she'd been here, your ego would take a terrible beating."

"My ego?"

"It can be very threatening, can it no', when a child takes it into her head to do what she wants? April defied you, and I'm guessing you're no' a man who likes defiance."

"You think that's what this is about?"

She watched him, and she saw what she had refused to see at first. She sighed. "No. That's no' all it's about, I suppose. You were worried. I'm sorry."

"You obviously don't have children."

"No. But I understand them, and I understand that your April finds something here that she's no' getting anywhere else."

"And what might that be?"

She knew better than to provoke an argument. She shook her head.

"I give April everything she needs. There's nothing I wouldn't do for her."

Mara wondered what Duncan's face would look like if he smiled. It would still be a strong face, a face defined by bold, uncompromising angles. But his mouth fascinated her. It was a grim slash that just hinted at the possibility of transformation.

"Then let her come to see me," Mara said. "If there's nowt you will no' do for her, let her come here sometimes. She needs it enough to defy you. Let her take what she needs. I will no' hurt her."

He looked beyond her to the cottage that was her pride. "I don't know you or anything about you, except the little I've heard in the village." His eyes flicked back and condemned her.

"And the way I live is hardly a recommendation, is it?" She lifted her chin. "I gather you're no' a man with simple tastes, Duncan Sinclair."

"Your name provokes a strange reaction whenever I hear it mentioned. Why is that?"

"What kind of reaction?"

"Something close to fear. You told me yourself that half the people in Druidheachd think you're a witch."

"Among other things."

"Yet you think I should turn my daughter over to you."

"You told me yourself, you're no' a man who believes in the supernatural."

There was a commotion on the road below. Duncan whirled, as if he expected to find April in trouble. But it wasn't April who was approaching. A white-haired woman was coming toward them. Mara recognized her closest neighbor, Marjory Grant, at once, just as she recognized the feelings that assailed her. She felt for the bench behind her and sat. Her hands began to tremble. Somewhere in the distance, Guiser began to howl.

"Mara MacTavish, I'm wanting to speak to ye," the woman said when she was close enough to be heard. "And I will no' be put off. Do ye ken?" She stopped several yards from Duncan and stared at him.

Duncan stared back.

"Ye look like yer father," the woman said.

Duncan nodded and remained silent.

The woman faced Mara. "I've come for the truth. I'll have nowt but. I want to know about my Fergus."

"Please go home, Mrs. Grant. There's nowt I can tell you."

"Last week he was peely wally, so I put him to bed thinking that would take care of it."

"Mrs. Grant, there's nowt I can do for you."

"Then last night he took a turn for the waur. The doctor says he's fair ill, and they want to remove him to Glasgow."

"I'm sorry, I truly am, but I can no' do a thing to help you except look after your sheep till you get back."

"Ye can tell me what I'm facing! And some in this glen say ye can even cure Fergus—if ye've a mind to!"

"Those who say that have no idea what I can or can no' do." Mara stood, although her legs felt as weak as a newborn lamb's. "I can no' cure your Fergus, Marjory. I'm no' a doctor."

Marjory's hand, spotted and gnarled by age, swept the air, gesturing to the land behind Mara's cottage. "I've seen yer garden. What grows in that patch of earth? No tatties, no kail. Yet, for a' that, ye tend it like a mother tends her weans. What is it ye do with the plants ye grow if ye dinna use them to heal?"

"Come back later in the spring and I'll show you potatoes and cabbages. But I also make dyes from what I grow. You've seen me dying yarn yourself, out here under the trees. And I grow herbs and flowers for sachets to sell in the stores in Inverness and Fort William. I grow none for healing."

"My Fergus is dying!"

Mara swallowed tears. Marjory Grant and Fergus, her son, had not welcomed her to Bein Domhain. Jessie and Roger Gunn and Roger's mother Frances had extended friendship immediately, and some of the other residents along the mountain road had been gracious, if cautious, but Marjory had been suspicious and antagonistic from the beginning. Still, that hardly mattered now. She was suffering, and Mara knew what it meant to suffer.

"I'm so sorry," she said. "You've no idea how sorry I am."

"Then he is dying." Marjory moved closer. "And yer sorry because ye can see it. It's just as everyone says. Ye can see the future, and ye can see that my Fergus will no' survive this." She moved closer again, her eyes narrowing. "Tell me what ye see. I have to know! Tell me or I do no' know what I'll do!"

Mara felt the woman's approach as clearly as she saw it. There was almost a malevolence about Marjory's determination to know the future. She had moved beyond grief to some place more frightening. She would sell her soul to save Fergus. She would challenge the devil.

"Mrs. Grant!" Duncan stepped in front of the old woman. "No one can see the future, no matter how much they might want to. Any stories you've heard about Mara are just that—stories."

Marjory Grant swayed, as if she were balanced on the edge of a chasm no one else could see. Duncan steadied her with a hand on her shoulder. "I have to know," she said. But the threat had gone from her voice.

"I wish I could help." Duncan dropped his hand. "I know Fergus from the pub. He's a fine man. I'm sorry he's ill."

"No one will tell me anything."

Duncan shook his head sympathetically. Mara witnessed the transformation she had only imagined before. His face softened, and his eyes warmed. For a moment he seemed capable of a full range of human emotion. "Maybe I can help you there," he said. "I know Dr. Sutherland well. He delivered me."

"Aye. Yer one of the wee laddies of midnight."

"Shall we talk to him together? I'll go in with you, and I'll be sure he answers all your questions. I'll drive you in now, if you'd like. We'll go to his house if we have to."

Mrs. Grant seemed to crumble. "Ye'd do that?"

"Of course."

"I can no' go now. But they told me I could see Fergus after tea this evening. Ye'd go with me then?"

"I'll meet you at the cottage hospital at half past six."

"The doctor will listen to you."

Duncan smiled warmly. "I'll make sure he does."

She didn't smile back, but she looked as if a burden had been lifted from her shoulders. She turned to Mara. Her eyes narrowed. "I'll remember that ye would no' help me when I needed it. And I've rowan growing beside my fence. Remember that if ye come to call."

"I'll pray for Fergus," Mara said. "And for you."

The old woman sniffed. "Does God listen to the prayers of the likes of ye, Mara MacTavish?" She turned without waiting for an answer and started down the path to the road.

Mara felt the bench against her legs and sat. She put her head in her hands. She didn't know how much time passed before she felt a warm presence beside her. In the wake of Marjory Grant's words she had almost forgotten that Duncan was still there.

"Rowan?" he asked.

"Dinna you know? Rowan keeps away witches. I'm surprised she does no' wear a cross of it when she visits me."

"She's an old woman, and she's very upset," he said quietly. "Don't let her get to you."

She opened her eyes and found him sitting beside her. His leg was stretched along the length of hers. She could feel his warmth through her wool skirt, sense the complex essence of the man in the air that surrounded them. His presence seemed both an invasion and a peace treaty.

"I guess I hadn't given much thought to what it must feel like to be branded a witch in a place like Druidheachd. In California, where I'm from, it would be pretty ho-hum. There's probably a coven on every block."

She didn't know what to say.

"I was always one of the different ones here," he continued. "I was born..." He shrugged. "I guess that doesn't matter now. Let's just say that right from the start, I was considered different. So I guess I should have been more sensitive to your situation. It doesn't take much to set off the locals. A dog howling late at night, chimney smoke that curls in the wrong direction, the size of a rising sun. They read signs here like people in other places read the newspaper. Druidheachd may look like a hundred other Highlands clachans, but underneath, it's pure seventeenth century. Brigadoon risen from the mists."

He faced her, and for the first time since she'd met him, his eyes were unveiled. She glimpsed the whole man, both the man he tried to be and the one who lived deep inside of him. There was understanding in his eyes, and even a reluctant compassion. She was stirred in a way she hadn't been in years. And frightened.

Frightened. She looked away. Her hands began to tremble again. "Marjory has reason to be worried."

"I guess I'll find out tonight how much reason."

Her voice trembled now. Her voice, her hands, even her heart seemed to tremble. "I tell you, she does."

"What do you mean? Do you know something she doesn't? Have you heard something?"

She raised her eyes to his. It was easier than imagining the worst. "Heard something? No. But Fergus Grant is dying. He'll be dead in a fortnight, at the full of the moon. And there's nowt any doctor in Glasgow or anywhere in the world will be able to do to prevent it."

Chapter 4

"**D**id you know Fergus Grant died last night?"

Duncan looked up from his desk to find Andrew lounging in his office doorway. His mind was filled with figures confirming that the Sinclair Hotel had always been a losing proposition. "I'm sorry, what did you say?"

"Fergus Grant died last night. In hospital in Glasgow."

Duncan stared at his friend. "He was doing better. They said he might even be able to come home after the weekend."

"Aye, Fergus will be coming home, all right. In a kist." Andrew's expression was solemn, a rare event and a powerful thing to see.

"What happened?"

"A clot of some sort. Took him like that." Andrew snapped his fingers.

Duncan felt more than sadness. It had been two weeks since Mara had predicted Fergus's death. And last night the moon had been full. He knew because he had lain awake and stared at it through the sheer curtains of his bedroom.

"It's a coincidence." He stood and came around his desk.

"A coincidence?" Andrew shook his head. "It's no' a coincidence when any of us die, Dunc. We're meant to. It's inevitable. No' even the Americans have figured out how to avoid it. It was Fergus's time. That's all."

Duncan didn't explain himself. He hadn't told anyone about Mara's prediction. It had been too bizarre to discuss, and he had been angry with himself for reaching out to her and provoking it. "Don't tell me you believe in fate, Andrew. You think there's somebody up in the clouds with a clock and a gong waiting for some prearranged moment to end our lives?"

"Well, put like that, it sounds a bit gyte." Andrew clapped his hand on Duncan's shoulder. "You're taking it harder than I thought. You hardly knew old Fergus."

"It's a surprise, that's all."

"I'm just home for a few days. Do you have time for some snooker?" Andrew was an engineer on an oil rig in the North Sea. For most of the year he came and went according to his work schedule, but in the summer he remained in Druidheachd and took the few tourists who wandered into the little village out on Loch Ceo to look for the resident monster.

"Did you just get paid, by chance?" Duncan asked.

Andrew grinned. "What would make you think such a thing?"

Duncan smiled, too. Andrew had always been able to make him smile. "Sorry, but I don't have an extra pound that doesn't have to go into this slag heap. If I don't have the plumbing fixed soon, I'll have to build outhouses back behind the carriage house and advertise the hotel as an authentic bit of old Druidheachd."

"I'll play you for a wee dram and the sheer joy of beating you."

Duncan looked at his watch. "I can't. I promised April we'd have supper together up in our flat so we can discuss her birthday. She's going to be seven this weekend."

"Ah, if she were only about twenty years older, I'd be knocking at her door."

"And I'd be on the other side of it with a shotgun."

The room seemed empty when Andrew left. He filled any space he wandered into with good humor and exuberance. From the moment of his birth he had drawn others to him. He had been a hearty, laughing baby and a child who could make anyone see the best side of life. Even Donald Sinclair, Duncan's father, had been a different, warmer person when Andrew was around.

Duncan couldn't remember a time when Andrew had brought him bad news. But he had today.

He found himself at the window, staring through the ancient, wavy glass at the street that ran beside the hotel. Fergus Grant was dead, and Mara MacTavish had foretold the hour of his death. Duncan knew it was a fluke; he wasted no time on wondering how it had happened. But the odd timing of Fergus's death brought back the afternoon two weeks before at Mara's.

He had been stunned at her prediction, so stunned that at first he had only stared at her. Then anger had gripped him.

"What in the hell are you trying to do?" he had demanded. "Are you trying to make me believe you're as strange as they say you are?"

Her eyes had been fixed on some point in the distance. "I dinna care what you believe. I dinna care what anyone believes."

"Well, if you don't care what anyone believes, maybe you ought to give some thought to keeping quiet. Then maybe no one would pass judgment on you. But you're inviting them with crazy talk like this."

"Crazy?" She rose and faced him. "You think I'm no' sane?"

"What else can I think? It's not all that normal, is it, to announce the hour of somebody else's death." He stood, too. "At least you had the sense not to tell Mrs. Grant her son was going to die. We can be thankful for that."

"There was nowt to be served by telling her."

"And nothing to be served by telling me, except to convince me that my daughter really isn't safe here. She's had one unstable woman in her life. She sure as hell doesn't need another."

"Unstable?"

Duncan had a moment of regret, but just a moment. There was no point in beating around the bush. "April's vulnerable right now. The last thing she needs is a role model who thinks she can see into the future. Just what do you get out of a stunt like this, Mara? It must have been clear to you that I wouldn't be impressed."

She didn't look away. He saw pain in her eyes as deep as any he'd ever witnessed. "Aye. I knew better than to tell you. I dinna know why I did." Then she slid past him. He watched as she disappeared into the trees beside the absurdly primitive thatched cottage that she called home.

And that had been the last time he'd seen her.

What was she thinking now? Did she know that Fergus Grant had died at the full moon, exactly as she'd predicted? Did she see the irony, or did she believe it was not a coincidence at all, but proof that she had that dubious gift the Highlanders called the sight?

He told himself he didn't care, but he couldn't get Mara out of his mind. He remembered the pain he'd seen in her eyes. And when he moved away from the window, he knew in his heart that she would feel nothing but sorrow that her words had come true.

"I can have anything I want for my birthday?"

Duncan smiled across the dinner table at his daughter. "Well, anything within reason. I don't think I could afford a pair of dancing elephants or a tiger who nibbles on the hotel guests."

April giggled. "What if it was something that didn't cost much?"

"Then I would be especially pleased to give it to you."

"I want to go on a picnic."

He cocked his head in question.

"A picnic with you . . . and Mara."

She'd caught him by surprise. He didn't know what to say.

"A picnic that lasts all day. In the mountains. And Guiser has to come, too."

"I'm not sure we can do that."

"You said anything."

Just six months ago Duncan had prayed for the day when April would feel secure enough to assert herself. Six months ago, she wouldn't have asked for a piece of bread. Now he knew he couldn't say no. He had waited too long for this flash of independence. Going to Mara's against his wishes had been a sign that April felt secure enough to reach for what she wanted. And now she was brave enough to ask for more.

"Mara may not want to go. She might be busy," he warned.

"But you'll ask her?"

He had said some hard, cruel things to Mara, and he was ashamed. Fergus's death didn't change his feelings about her prediction, but it did remind him that he was fast becoming a man more comfortable with condemning others than trying to understand them. And he suspected that Mara needed understanding now, more than she had two weeks ago.

He poured himself a cup of coffee. "I'll ask her." Mara would refuse, he was sure. She would have no reason to want to spend time with him. But if she agreed to come, it would give him a chance to observe her up close with April. He could discount most of what she'd said to him, but one thing she'd said was true. April obviously did need something that Mara offered her. And he needed to find out what it was.

By the time April was sleeping, he had decided that nothing would be gained by waiting to ask Mara if she would picnic with them on Saturday. April had talked about nothing else as she'd gotten ready for bed, and Duncan was afraid that if he waited too long, April would be profoundly disappointed when Mara refused.

He asked one of the chambermaids if she would stay with April while he went out for a while, and she settled in with a thick murder mystery and a plate of Mrs. Gunn's shortbread. Before he left he played a fast game of snooker with Andrew, lost immediately and grudgingly told Brian to give Andrew free drinks that night.

Outside, a soft, chill mist filtered through his raincoat and made him nostalgic for California sunshine. But the air had never smelled this way in Pasadena. There was a sweetness here that defied his attempts to name any particular plant that produced it. It was the smell of a Highland spring, green and fertile and tinged with the promise of new life. A snatch of music, the piercing laughter of a child, the tinkle of a shop door. All the sounds of Druidheachd drifted around him like the mist.

The mist thickened as he drove, and as the road beside Loch Ceo wove back and forth through neat stands of Forestry Commission pines, he slowed his pace. There was an eerie beauty here. He could almost understand the Highlanders' preoccupation with the unknown. The landscape promoted it. It was easy to imagine ghosts rising from these mists, witches in stone cottages set between desolate, craggy mountains, fairies in tiny underground villages roofed with purple heather. Druidheachd was a Gaelic word meaning magic, and at moments like this, he could understand why the name had been chosen.

His car climbed steadily until it was time to turn off the main road to the single lane track that zigzagged up Bein Domhain to Mara's cottage. He couldn't fathom why a young woman had chosen to live so far from civilization. After their last encounter, he'd made a few inquiries. Mara's nearest neighbor, Marjory Grant, was more than a quarter of a mile as the crow flew, and a human would need wings to travel that route, since a wide creek, or what the Scots called a burn, flowed between their properties.

If Mara wanted to reach a neighbor by foot, she would have to walk nearly half a mile around the mouth of the burn and over a rocky, inhospitable landscape, or along the single lane track for more than half a mile. The journey would be relatively short by car, of course, but he had seen the ancient Morris Minor parked behind her cottage, and he doubted it was reliable. In the worst weather she was probably trapped at home for weeks.

She obviously didn't mind. Iain said that Mara had bought her land from him. Duncan couldn't imagine it had cost her much, since it had little to offer. The house was worth nothing, and the land was steep and unproductive. But if she could afford a large plot in the mountains, surely she could have afforded something smaller and closer to town. Instead, she had chosen isolation.

He felt that isolation as his car climbed along the track. The mist had deepened into fog now, and it grew denser as he climbed. The sky was dark, and his headlights illuminated only a short stretch of road.

He slowed even more. If he crept along he would be safe, he knew, at least as far as his own driving was concerned. He could see enough of the road not to miss a twist or turn. The real danger lay in cars coming down the mountain. Even with good visibility, the road was treacherous. One car could be on top of another with no warning. There were frequent passing places, small clearings beside the road so that one car could get out of the way to let another pass. But with the fog, there were even fewer signals than usual that it was time to find one.

Another five minutes went by, and he began to curse himself for choosing tonight to talk to Mara. He wasn't a complete stranger to these mountains. He should have known thick fog was inevitable. Now he had ignored it until it was too late to turn back. He had no choice but to continue, and the wind was steadily growing stronger. His car windows rattled in protest.

He estimated he was only a few minutes from the turnoff to Mara's cottage when he saw the light. He was approaching a particularly wicked curve, and he had taken his eyes off the road for the briefest moment to gaze down. Something glinted just beyond the next passing place. It was little more than a twinkle, an earthborn star winking along the fog-enshrouded mountainside. He caught just a glance, but it was enough to intrigue him. By the time he had reached the passing place, he had made up his mind. He pulled over and got out of his car. Then, with a flashlight in his hand, he walked as close to the edge as he dared.

At first he could see little. There was a sharp but short drop-off that culminated in a wide ledge. Beyond that ledge was infinity, a sheer drop of hundreds of yards to the glen below that spelled instant extinction for anyone unlucky enough to step over the side. He turned off his flashlight and peered into the darkness. He could see next to nothing now, just fog, shifting and whirling with each gust of wind.

He was almost ready to turn back to the car when he saw the light again. It was just below him, a tremulous fountain of green that blinked for an instant and then disappeared.

"What the hell?"

He wasn't anxious to get too close to the edge. If he fell, he might miss the ledge altogether and end his life in some Druidheachd garden, planted head first among an old lady's poppies and bluebells. But he was more than curious now. He was determined to find out where the light was coming from. He'd only seen light this color once before. And Geordie Smith was alive because of it.

He lowered himself to his hands and knees and felt his way to the drop off. He was afraid his flashlight would ruin his view, so he kept it off. The ground fell away just in front of him, and he dropped to his belly, sliding close enough that his chin hung over the side.

For a minute or more nothing appeared. Then, just as he was beginning to wonder if he had imagined it, a light formed, a pale green light the color of Mara MacTavish's eyes. As he watched, transfixed, the light seemed to coalesce into human form.

He told himself it was the moonlit residue of some mysterious gas seeping through the rocks and the age-old deposits of carbonized plants. But even as he told himself that the light was completely natural, it formed into the shape of a woman in a long, flowing gown. She lifted her arms in entreaty.

He could no more have moved at that moment than if he had been chained to the ground.

He had no idea how long he stared at the light; time seemed suspended. He was only aware of its passing when a roar sounded on the road behind him. He pushed himself away from the ledge, cold and surprisingly stiff from his sojourn on the wet ground, and sat up. He turned just in time to see a truck with its headlights blinking crazily swoop by at a tremendous speed, barely negotiate the next curve, then, with tires squealing in protest, careen down the mountain track.

If he had been on the road, as he should have been, he would have been directly in the truck's path. And his small sedan would have been no match for the forces of gravity and several tons of solid steel.

If he had been on the road.

He was chilled inside and out. His hands began to shake. He rarely played the game of "what if." But he played it now, and the answer was simple. If he had been on the road, he would be a dead man.

He peered over the side of the cliff again. There was no light now, not even moonlight tracing the ledge below. He got to his feet and realized his knees were weak. He stared over the cliff, but nothing appeared, not light, not a woman, not a sign of anything out of the ordinary.

He stared at nothing for a long, long time.

Mara was fond of her sheep, particularly the lambs. But even she had to admit that more foolish creatures didn't exist anywhere on the food chain. As she and Guiser were penning the sheep for the night, she had realized that one of her ewes and the ewe's two lambs were missing. She was exhausted, and she hadn't liked the idea of going out to look for them. She had been up early to work with the shearer who had come to finish her sheep. She had paid close attention to everything he'd taught her and attempted to shear the last sheep with his help.

There were some things, she'd discovered, that not even the most self-sufficient crofter should do herself.

Ordinarily she wouldn't have worried about the missing sheep. But the ewe was a first-time mother and not suited for the role. She was completely capable of leading her lambs into danger. Several days before, Mara had found one wedged between two rocks while the mother grazed contentedly some distance away and ignored the lamb's pitiful bleating.

So Mara had been out since nightfall searching. For once Guiser had been little help. All day he had done the work of two dogs, and now he was determined to take his well-deserved rest. He had skulked beside her as she tramped her fields, lantern in hand, but he had shown no enthusiasm or initiative. Just as she'd been about to give up, she'd found the ewe with both lambs, encamped under a chestnut tree. Now they were safely penned with the rest of the flock, and she was ready for a warm, fragrant bath and a three-course supper prepared by a gourmet chef.

Except that warm, fragrant baths and gourmet meals were only memories from her past.

She was unfastening her cape to hang it on a peg beside the door when a knock sounded from the other side. She was startled. Guiser was asleep beside the fire, and he didn't even thump his tail in response.

"Who's there?" she called.

"It's Duncan Sinclair."

She was sorry she'd asked and confused that she hadn't anticipated his arrival. She regretted the ancient Highland code that declared a welcome should be extended to strangers.

She opened the door and stepped back to let him in. There was light from the fire and the lantern she had hung on a hook in the rafter. She could see his face clearly enough to watch his expression change as he gazed around the room.

"Whatever you paid Iain for this cottage was too much," he said bluntly.

"I did no' pay Iain anything for this."

He frowned. "Nothing was still too much."

"I did no' pay Iain anything for *this*." She gestured to include the room. "I built the cottage myself. Stone by stone. I paid Iain for the land, and it was a fair price."

"You built it?"

"Aye, and proud I am of it."

He was silent. She knew what he saw. The cottage was small, divided into two rooms, what the Highlanders called a "but and ben" cottage. There were fireplaces at both ends, the one farthest away crowded with pots and kettles suspended from chains. She was inordinately proud of her fireplaces. She had studied and planned and sketched them a dozen times before laying the first stone. Never had she expected them to draw properly. But somehow they had.

"This is incredible," he said at last.

"Why have you come, Duncan?"

He looked down at her. Her hair was plastered against her cheeks and lank against her neck. She was wearing the dark green cloak in which he had first encountered her. "You've been outside?" he asked.

"I have." She finished removing her cloak and hung it on the peg. Her back was to him. "You sound as if you're surprised by that. Crofters live outside, or at least once they did. A house was only for sleeping."

"What were you doing out there? Where exactly were you?"

She faced him. "Is something the matter?"

"Were you down by the road?"

"As well as a hundred other places."

"Were you down by the road just a little while ago?"

She saw what had been invisible to her at first. He was upset, as upset as a man like Duncan Sinclair ever got. Something had shaken his confidence.

She found that satisfying.

She turned away and crossed the room to pour water from a kettle into the wash basin on the hearth. She soaped and rinsed her hands, then took a cloth and soaked it in the water. She wiped the cloth across her forehead and cheeks and finished by wringing it out once more and wiping her neck. "I'm sorry, but I'm soaked to the skin and spattered with mud. I hope you dinna mind."

"You don't have running water, do you?"

"No. And I dinna have electricity or a telephone, which is why I could no' phone you about April's visit here. But I have a nice warm fire and two chairs beside it. You can join me over here for a cup of tea if you'd like."

She didn't watch to see what his decision would be. She shook tea leaves from a jar on her shelf into a brown ceramic teapot and poured the remaining hot water from the kettle into it. "I have some crumpets we can toast," she said. "I have no' eaten tonight, and I'm near starving."

"Why haven't you eaten?"

His voice sounded from right behind her. She never seemed to know exactly where he would be, and that was disconcerting. "I've been out looking for one of my ewes and her lambs. It's been a long day."

"And were you looking out by the road?"

"I told you, I've been all over."

Duncan wondered if he was losing his mind. He looked at her and saw light in the shape of a woman. The figure he had seen was Mara's size, with flowing hair and a long dress—or perhaps a cloak.

He lowered himself to one of the chairs; his legs were still surprisingly weak.

She took the other chair and drew it closer to the fire. Then she picked up a hairbrush from the fireplace ledge and held it up with a whimsical smile. "My hair dryer," she explained. She began to pull it through her hair, holding the long locks out toward the fire. With each stroke it fell to her shoulders in fine clouds, like the angel hair on Duncan's childhood Christmas trees. She brushed her hair for a long time in silence. "What happened on the road, Duncan?" she asked at last. "Did you have trouble getting up Bein Domhain in the fog?"

"I got up just fine. There was the small matter of a truck going down at the same time."

Mara paused for a moment. "You do understand about our passing places, do you no'?"

"I understand perfectly. I'm not sure that the driver of the truck understood. If he'd driven any faster, he would have been airborne."

"But you're all right? You were no' hurt?"

"No. I had pulled off the road to look at something."

She resumed brushing her hair. "I'm glad of that. The drivers on this road are usually cautious. Maybe his brakes failed. You were fortunate that something caught your attention. What was it?"

She had finished her hair, and she set down the brush before he answered.

"It was just a shrub caught in a stray moonbeam or the truck's lights. There's a full moon out tonight, even if the fog's nearly obscured it."

"I'll get the crumpets."

Duncan watched Mara busy herself beside the fire. She wore a long sweater of heathery green and violet, and a dark wool skirt that fell past the tops of her boots. She moved with an uncommon grace, and under different circumstances it might have been a pleasure to watch her. But the world wasn't the same place it had been before his brush with death. He was too wrought up to appreciate her feminine allure.

"Fergus Grant died last night," he said. "Did you know?"

There was just a slight pause in her movements, so slight he might not have noticed it if he hadn't been watching so carefully. "Aye." She reached for a tin and removed the cover. She put crumpets on two crockery plates before she turned. "The neighbors have organized to take food to Mrs. Grant."

"You don't seem surprised, Mara. The rest of us thought he was improving."

She didn't reply.

"The moon was full last night," he said.

"I'm well aware of the cycles of the moon."

"You said Fergus would die at the full moon. And you were right."

"Aye. And I'm wishing I'd been wrong." She turned to look at him. "And I'm wishing I had never spoken of it to you."

"But you did."

"I did." She sat down again, placing a tray with a crock of butter and the two plates of crumpets in front of him. She reached for two long-handled forks hanging from a hook embedded in the fireplace mortar. She handed one to him.

He took it without a word.

She speared her crumpet and held it in front of the flames, just close enough to heat it. "So what do you think, Duncan? Am I simply unstable, as you said the last time you were here? Or is there more at work than meets the eye?"

"How did you know Fergus would die? And how did you know when? Do you have medical training?"

"I have medical training. But do you know a university anywhere in the world that can teach a student to name the hour of a patient's death? Because, if you do, I would be properly grateful. Then I would know there's a scientific explanation for what I've been able to do since I was a child."

"And that is?"

She didn't answer.

He wanted to scoff. He wanted to leave. But the world was no longer exactly the place it had been. "Why don't you tell me about it?"

"Can you listen with an open mind?" She pulled the crumpet toward her to inspect it. Then she glanced at him before she thrust it back to the fire again.

He didn't know if his mind was open. He had witnessed the effects of New Age philosophy up close, had watched it destroy his marriage and nearly his daughter. He had always been a skeptical man. In the past three years he had moved far beyond skeptical.

But Mara was not Lisa.

He watched her at the fire. Mara had none of Lisa's nervous, almost manic energy. She didn't seek reassurance. There was a quiet self-possession in everything she did. And she had built this cottage, this extraordinary re-creation of an old Scottish croft. She lived in it by herself under conditions most people would find grueling, at best. And she was proud of everything she'd accomplished.

He didn't want to be intrigued by Mara MacTavish; he didn't want to be intrigued by any woman, particularly not one with roots here in the Highlands. He only planned to stay in Druidheachd until he could fix up the Sinclair Hotel and make a decent profit on it when he sold it. Then he was going to take April faraway and start a new life and a new business.

He did not want to be intrigued by Mara MacTavish, but he was.

"No, my mind's not open." He reached for a crumpet and speared it on his fork. "I'm not even sure anymore that an open mind is an asset. I've seen too many minds that were so open every rational thought drained right out of them."

"You've been hurt."

"Is mind reading one of your talents, too?"

"No more than anyone's. But hurt's audible in every word you speak. Was it April's mother who hurt you?"

"I don't want to talk about me."

"Do you ever?"

"What's that supposed to mean?"

"Do you ever share any part of yourself? I'm no' a mind reader, but I'd guess that almost everyone you've ever counted on has failed you. And that's part of the reason you've given up believing in the things you can no' see. I'm no' even sure you believe in the things that you can."

"How did you know that Fergus was going to die yesterday? Or was it simply a guess? Because that's what I think. A lucky—"

"Unlucky for Fergus." She faced him.

He shrugged. "Unlucky guess."

"Do you truly want to know?"

He started to say yes, then reconsidered. There was more to her question than what appeared on the surface. She was gently pointing out that he was asking for more than a simple explanation. He was asking for a part of her.

"Are you going to tell me the truth?" he asked.

"I've never learned to lie."

Did he want to know about her? Because he realized in that moment that he already knew something that he hadn't wanted to know. Mara MacTavish was sincere. She might be misguided, but she had none of Lisa's deceit. She wouldn't twist the truth to make her own life easier. And whether he liked her explanation or not would be of no importance to her. She could only tell him what she believed to be true.

He leaned forward. "You believe that you have second sight, don't you? That's what this is all about."

She reached over and pushed his fork away from the fire. "I dinna know what I have, Duncan. Labeling it only makes it easier for other people to accept or condemn. But I've never understood it, myself. I only know that far too often I can see the future." She smiled sadly. "And most of the time, the news is no' very good."

Chapter 5

"And you've been able to see the future since you were a child? You're telling me that you always walk around knowing what's going to happen next?"

Mara took the toasting fork from Duncan's hands and removed his crumpet. She buttered it and set it on a plate. "I'd be a rich and famous woman if everything in the future were that clear. Just think what I could do on your Wall Street."

He took the plate from her hands. His fingers brushed hers, and their eyes met. Hers were steady, the pale green of a fountain of light that had probably saved his life. Disturbed, he looked away. "Then what do you see?"

"Much more than I want to."

She rose to pour the tea, and she handed him a cup. She sat back down, clutching her own to her chest, as if for warmth. He realized she was shivering. "I was still a young child when I realized that what was simple for me was impossible for others. At first my parents excused the things I said as the ramblings of childhood. But when I was four, I told them a neighbor had been in an accident. My mum thought I'd overheard someone talking, and she went next door to see if she could be a help. Nowt had happened, of course, and she was terribly embarrassed that I'd lied. But the next day, the accident took place just as I'd seen it. I was too young to know the difference between what I saw in my head and what I saw with my eyes. And to a child, past, present and future are very much the same.''

Everything Mara said was an affront to Duncan, but he couldn't fault her sincerity. Clearly she believed her story was true. ''What did your parents do then?''

''I frightened them and still do. They're good people. My father is an elder in our kirk. But he and my mother are very sure they have all the right answers, and their answers dinna include a daughter who can see things before they happen. They told our minister what I'd said, and he told them such talk came from the devil. I was punished and told I must stop lying. It took me a while to understand. I became afraid to tell them anything, because I wasn't always sure if what I was relating was something that had happened or something that was going to. If I made a mistake, I was punished, and the punishments got harsher each time.''

She stopped to sip her tea. Duncan didn't know what to say. He didn't want to feel compassion for the child Mara had been, because compassion implied belief in her story. But he felt compassion anyway. And anger at the insensitive people who had raised her.

''By the time I was in school, I'd learned to keep everything to myself, but I'd lost all confidence. I barely spoke, and when I did, I stuttered. I was sent away to school because I was an embarassment. The school had a rigid curriculum and uncompromising rules of conduct. If anything, I grew quieter. By then I'd learned to ignore my visions of the future, even to doubt they were real.''

''But obviously something happened to make you change your mind,'' Duncan said.

She picked up her crumpet and buttered it. She finished every crumb, and still she didn't speak. He watched her stare into the smoky peat fire, and he thought that she was reliving those years, remembering how it had felt to be an outcast. He could almost feel her pain. He didn't know what was wrong with him. He didn't want to feel this connection to her.

Finally she wiped her hands and faced him again. "When I was old enough to think about a career, I decided to choose medicine. I wanted to be a nurse. I suppose the way I'd grown up made me want to reach out to other people who were suffering. I even thought that if I tried to help people, I might stop imagining that I knew their futures. I enrolled at a school in Edinburgh, and at first, when I was just taking classes, I thought I'd made the right decision. I discovered that I learned quickly in a relaxed environment, and that the world was a far more interesting place than I'd been led to believe. But then I began to work with the sick. Just a little at first, then more often as my studies lent themselves to it. And that's when I found out that after one encounter with a patient, no matter how brief, I could tell if that patient was going to live or die."

Duncan set his cup on the hearth. Mara had engaged his sympathy, but now sympathy disappeared. "One encounter?"

"Aye. I know how it sounds, Duncan. I can no' make it sound any different."

"You're saying that you only had to walk in a room and you knew if a patient was going to die?"

"No, it was worse than that. I'd never lived in a large city before. Suddenly I was surrounded by people. One day late in my second term it was as if a floodgate opened. I could no' walk down the street without being assaulted by impressions of the people around me. This man was going to die the next month. This man was going to lose a loved one. This woman had a son in a foreign country with a grave illness that had no' yet been diagnosed. I took to staying in my room whenever I could. I went out at night, when the streets were less likely to be crowded. I chose my friends carefully, only associating with people whose futures seemed out of my reach."

"This is increasingly difficult to believe."

She smiled sadly. "I know."

"What happened then?"

"One day I considered taking my own life." The words were matter-of-fact. "And on that day, I realized I had two choices. I could accept myself and my ability and try to use it for the benefit of others, or I could end my life. Because the third choice, trying to pretend I was someone I was no', was slowly driving me insane."

Duncan wondered what he could say. On the face of it, she'd made a good decision. But to tell her so was the same as admitting her story could be credible. And her story was preposterous. As he had so many other times in their short but emotionally charged relationship, he said nothing.

"I started to take stock of what I knew. There were some things I could do nowt about. If a patient had a fatal illness, I did no' have the skills to intervene, and often it was clear to me that no one had the necessary skills. That person was going to die whatever I said or did. Like poor Fergus. But sometimes I sensed a situation that I could affect."

"Such as?"

"Once I purposely lost the discharge papers on a patient who was to go home one morning, and that afternoon she suffered a heart attack. She survived because she was still in hospital. Another time I scribbled a note in a chart and forged a signature. It led a doctor to order more testing and saved another patient's life. A classmate complained of menstrual cramps, and I dragged her to casualty. Her appendix had nearly ruptured."

"Come on, Mara. Those were all things you might have noticed or known because of your training."

"There was a young doctor at the hospital, Robert Fitzwilliams. Robbie told me one morning that he was going to fly to Austria for a skiing holiday with his friends over the weekend. I saw an avalanche and certain death. I was terribly worried, but I did no' know what to do. He was no' a particularly sensitive man. I knew he would only laugh if I told him what I'd seen."

She stood and faced the fire, crossing her arms as if she were still chilled. "The night before he was to leave I saw Robbie making rounds. I went into the doctors' lounge and went through his jacket and found his airplane ticket. I took it and hid it under my cardigan. By the next morning, when Robbie discovered the ticket was gone, it was too late to replace it, and he missed his trip. He was furious enough to make inquiries. Someone remembered that they'd seen me leaving the doctors' lounge, a place I never should have been. Robbie confronted me, of course. I did no' know what to do except tell him the truth and return his ticket."

She turned. "Robbie said he was going to report me on Monday when the hospital administration returned. That night there was an avalanche on a trail at the resort where he'd been scheduled to stay. Several skiers died, among them Robbie's friends."

"Surely he saw it was a coincidence. Avalanches aren't uncommon."

"No' one of that dimension. Robbie believed he'd escaped death because of my intervention. He was grateful. I was lonely. Gratitude seemed to lead naturally to love. We married the next year. I was certain that at last someone understood my strange gift, and that he would help me deal with its burdens. And at first he did."

"At first?"

"Robbie was . . . is a fine doctor. But nowt in his training could compete with my predictions. After a few months he began to resent me. He wanted victory over death. He worked twelve hour days, and when he was no' working, he studied. But I had only to walk into a room and I could tell if a patient was going to live or die."

"I gather you're not married to him now?"

"No, I left him. Robbie did what my parents had done. He began to make me doubt myself. He questioned me constantly, but he never wanted to hear my answers. He belittled me to his friends and colleagues. At home he found fault with everything I did and was."

Duncan might not believe that Mara had the gift she claimed, but *she* believed it, and it had caused her nothing but sorrow. He wanted to reach out to her, but he was too cautious and too skeptical of all she'd said. He could only manage a gruff "I'm sorry."

"Thank you, but I'm no'. I stayed with Robbie for three years. I believed in marriage, but I did no' believe in myself. Now I believe in both, but they have to go hand in hand, do they no'?"

She had revealed so much, in the spaces between sentences as well as in the sentences themselves. She talked with reserve about her marriage and her childhood, but he suspected there was a great deal more to each than she'd related. What had her husband done to make her leave him? And what about her parents? She'd said that their punishments had gotten harsher as she'd aged, but what exactly did that mean? And the school where she'd been sent? What had the teachers done to continue the destruction of her spirit? How had she survived the continued onslaught on her self-respect?

Duncan didn't believe in Mara's abilities, but he believed in her. He realized it, and battled it the next instant. "I can't accept any of this," he said. He stood. She was only a few feet from him.

"You are no' the first, Duncan."

He saw resignation in her eyes and not a trace of anger. She didn't expect support or even understanding. She had come to the Highlands to learn to live without either. She lived alone because she believed that was her only salvation.

Perhaps if she had expected more from him, he would have turned away. He thought of that as he moved toward her. He reached out, and he saw her tense. But she didn't move away. She had schooled herself to face whatever was thrown at her.

He touched her shoulder. His hand rested lightly there. "I can't accept any of this," he repeated. "But I accept that you believe it, Mara. I don't believe that anyone can see the future. I don't know what you see, and I don't know why. But I know you're not lying to me."

She didn't relax under his touch, but she didn't move away. "You realize you'll have to reconcile that someday, do you no'? You'll have to find a way to explain to yourself that I'm no' lying but I'm no' telling the truth."

"Why don't we just leave it the way it is?"

"Why should we leave it any way? We're strangers. We can remain strangers."

She was right, but she didn't feel like a stranger. He was unwillingly entranced by the delicate curve of her shoulder under his palm, the sheen of her hair in the firelight, the candid, wounded green of her eyes.

"Can you see your own future?" he asked.

"No. And I can no' see the future of anyone I love."

"Can you see mine?"

She paused. "No."

"Then I'll be easy for you to know."

She shook her head. "There's nowt easy about you, Duncan Sinclair."

"And nothing so hard." He dropped his hand. "Right now I'm just a man with a favor to ask."

She took a deep breath, as if to cleanse herself of all she'd said. "What could I possibly do for you?"

"Would you join April and me for a picnic on Saturday? It's her birthday, and she wants you to help us celebrate."

"And all the things you said before? After tonight you must know I have no' changed, but I have no new way to explain the things I see."

"I'm sorry." The words tasted strange against his tongue. He had said them so rarely, but never with more sincerity. "I shouldn't have said the things I did. I know you won't hurt April. And you were right. She seems to need something you can give her. She wants you in her life."

"And you?"

He wasn't sure what she was asking. "I would be grateful if you'd be our friend."

She hesitated before she spoke. He could see her sifting through answers, and he couldn't rate his chances of success. "Shall I pack a picnic tea, or shall you?" she asked at last.

He was surprised at his own pleasure. "I'll have Frances put a basket together for all of us. Will you choose a place? Is there somewhere near enough to walk to?"

Her lips turned up slowly into a smile. "Aye, I know a place. I can almost guarantee you'll feel at home there."

"Good."

"You'll be careful going back to the hotel tonight? No more clashes with lorries on my road?"

He had already turned to go, but he turned back. "You don't know something I should know, do you?"

She shook her head.

"Mara, have you considered that you didn't predict I would have a brush with death tonight?"

"I've considered it, aye."

"And?"

"You did no' die, did you, Duncan?"

He wasn't dead; that much was true. He had gone in search of lights where no lights should have been, and that bit of whimsy had saved his life. He had been spellbound by stray moonbeams and swirling mists, by an illusion that for moments had seemed like a woman beckoning.

Scotland was getting to him.

Duncan had planned to go back to the hotel after leaving Mara's, but instead he found himself heading toward the Ross estate, several miles in the other direction. He turned onto the road that girdled Loch Ceo.

As a boy he had taken this trip often. Had the circumstances been different, he might never have shared more than a word or two with Iain Ross. But the good people of Druidheachd had proclaimed that the wee laddies of midnight would be raised together. And the Rosses, like the Sinclairs and MacDougalls, hadn't been courageous enough to refuse.

The Ross home, Fearnshader, had been a second home to Duncan. And Iain's parents had welcomed him and treated him with the same mixture of reserve and warmth with which they treated their son. Only Andrew had been treated differently, Andrew who had never thought twice about crawling up on the lap of Lady Mary Ross and throwing his chubby arms around her neck. There had always been an extra smile for Andrew, a glance the other way when he misbehaved, an extra scone or spoonful of jam when no one was looking.

The elder Rosses were gone now, Malcolm Ross of a sudden illness when Iain was only ten, and Mary Ross of heartbreak—diagnosed as pneumonia—less than a year later. Iain had been sent away to school in England. On holidays he had grown from youth into adulthood under the care of servants and an aged great-uncle who rarely left his bed.

There was a legend repeated in Druidheachd, one as old as the village itself, that the Rosses of Iain's line would never know happiness. There had been a curse on one of Iain's ancestors, a chieftain of his clan, and the modern-day Rosses still labored under its spell. No one knew the particulars of the curse—at least, no one who was willing to talk about it—but almost anyone in the village could count back generations and relate stories about Rosses who had died under mysterious circumstances or lived desperately unhappy lives.

Legends and curses, the stuff of the Middle Ages, but still a vital part of the lore of Druidheachd. As he drove, Duncan wondered about his own decision to return. He had come here to give April a stable place to recover from her mother's neglect, and he had wanted to make a success of the hotel so that he could make a greater profit when he sold it. But what exactly had he done? Apparently even he wasn't immune to the effects of Druidheachd's magic. Witness his sympathy tonight for one green-eyed fairy-witch who believed she could see into the future.

The fog had lessened as the night wore on. The road ahead of him was clear. It widened perceptibly as he approached Iain's house. He had been on Ross land for miles. There was little of the surrounding area that Iain didn't have title to, although most of it was leased to others.

He rounded a bend and saw the skeletal outline of Ceo Castle beside the loch. It was daunting in moonlight, daunting in sunlight. He knew every stone, every step, every grisly reminder of ancient tortures deep in the castle dungeons. He had romped through the halls with Andrew and

Iain, camped in chambers where princes had slept, shot handmade arrows through slits in the north tower. Ceo Castle was as much a part of the mystery and reality of Druidheachd as the glistening midnight waters of Loch Ceo.

He turned away from the castle and started up a drive that led to an inlet of the loch. He drove until the castle had disappeared behind a grove of alders at his left, which gave Fearnshader—alder house—its name. He parked beside a small, vacant gatehouse and started toward the house. Rhododendrons as tall as small trees lined the path. Duncan knew that in a month or two peonies, roses and sweet william would perfume the journey to the front door. In Mary Ross's day the gardens of Fearnshader had been renowned throughout the Highlands.

He paused at the doorway and reconsidered his visit, but only for a moment. He let the knocker, a ferocious bronze gargoyle, fall against the carved mahogany door. Then he waited.

Iain answered on the third knock. His household staff was small. He was seldom at home, and when he was, he liked solitude. More than once Duncan had been ushered into the cavernous kitchen to find Iain at the stove alone, frying his own sausages for supper.

Duncan stared at Iain, lounging in the doorway. He was casually dressed in dark trousers and a shirt of finely woven cotton. His hair was rumpled, as if he had finger-combed the curls he despised on the way to the door.

"Are you alone?" Duncan asked.

"Unfortunately." He stepped aside, and Duncan entered.

Fearnshader was large by the standards of anyone except other landed gentry. The hallway was wide enough for a bevy of servants to pass without touching; the rooms were many and varied, all with elaborately ornamented plaster cornices and skillfully carved woodwork.

"I've got a fire in the sitting room."

"Am I interrupting something?"

"Contemplation. You're welcome to interrupt."

Duncan followed Iain through the hallway. On those rare Highland days when the sun shone, the sitting room was awash in light, but tonight the heavy formal draperies were drawn against the chill, and the massive dark furniture that cluttered every square foot seemed on guard against pleasant thoughts.

"You need to have a garage sale, Macbeth," Duncan said. "Scrap everything in here and start all over."

"Better men than you have sat on these chairs, Sinclair."

"And after spending a few evenings in here, they probably didn't even flinch when their heads were lopped off or their kingdoms snatched out from under their noses."

"You have no respect for tradition." Iain flopped into a particularly aged chair with fraying upholstery. He gestured to the one beside him.

The fire was warm, and despite the gloom, Duncan could feel himself beginning to relax.

"Just out for a drive?" Iain asked.

"Have I ever, in all my years, just gone out for a drive?"

"That's one of the things that's wrong with you."

"Do you want to tell me the others? Or don't we have that much time?"

"You're overly cocky and underly appreciative of the value of my friendship."

"I'm here, aren't I? And I came solely for a chunk of your remarkable insight."

"Then you don't have enough time. It would take me years to set you on the proper course."

Duncan put his feet out and his arms behind his head. He stared at the flames, and they reminded him of the fireplace at Mara's cottage. "I was just up at Mara MacTavish's."

"At this hour?"

"April wanted me to invite her for a birthday picnic. You and Andrew are invited to the hotel Saturday night, by the way, for cake and ice cream."

"I wouldn't miss it."

Duncan knew Iain was sincere. Iain adored April. He lavished her with affection, brought her dolls and dresses from faraway places and, this year, the first primroses and violets from Fearnshader's gardens. He was her beloved uncle, and she worshipped him and Andrew equally. "Seven o'clock," he said. "And be on time, even if Andrew isn't."

"You weren't just up at Mara's to invite her on a picnic, were you?"

"No. We'd had a run in."

"And you went to apologize? The guilt must have been overwhelming."

Duncan smiled. Iain understood him so well. "She's not your everyday run-of-the-mill beautiful woman."

"You've been listening to the good folk of Druidheachd?"

"I haven't needed to. She gave me a small sampling of her so-called abilities a few weeks ago. You know, don't you, that she claims to be able to see the future?"

"I know quite a lot about Mara. Is that why you're here?"

"Yes."

"What is it you plan to do with whatever I tell you?"

Duncan considered. The bantering was over. "I don't know what I'll do. I don't even know why I'm interested."

"You said it yourself. She's a beautiful woman."

"But I'm not in the market for another beautiful woman with her head screwed on backwards."

"Mara is not Lisa."

"Why don't you tell me who she is, then? Start with why you sold her such a godforsaken piece of property. Or better yet, tell me how you met her."

The fire had burned down a little more before Iain answered. "I met her through her husband...her ex-husband. He was my physician."

"He practiced a little too faraway to treat colds and stomach aches, didn't he?"

"I had a problem I had to consult him about." Iain didn't elaborate. "He's very capable and, on the surface, quite a pleasant chap. He invited me out to dinner after an appointment. Mara met us at the restaurant. It became a tradition of sorts. Whenever I was in Edinburgh, or later, after they moved to Pitlochry in Perthshire, we would dine together. It was a harmless habit, one I saw no reason to break. But eventually I couldn't close my eyes to the way Fitzwilliams treated Mara. He seemed to pride himself on humiliating her."

Duncan recognized the edge in Iain's voice. He knew from childhood skirmishes how deceptive Iain's patrician manner could be. He was perfectly capable of going from bored lord of the manor to avenging angel in the blink of an eye. "She said that he belittled her."

"That's gently put. The last time the three of us were together, she was a bit late getting to the restaurant. Fitzwilliams entertained himself and me with two extra rounds of drinks. By the time she arrived he was in fine form. He told me that Mara fancied herself able to tell the future, but she couldn't tell when her own car would get stuck in traffic. She tried to quiet him down, but he got more loathsome as the night went on. He told one tale after another about Mara's strange abilities, twisting them to make her look like a fool. I tried to leave once, but he wouldn't let me, and I didn't want to make a scene, because I knew it would upset Mara more."

Iain turned so that he and Duncan were eye to eye. "Finally, Mara tried to leave. But Fitzwilliams wouldn't allow that, either. He'd had far too much to drink by then. He leaned over the table, and he said that Mara was just upset because he'd told her that morning that he never wanted children. He was afraid a child of hers might have the sight, too. He said he didn't want another freak in his family. One was more than enough."

"The bastard!"

"Aye, but he's like too many of us, Dunc. He's frightened of anything he doesn't understand."

Duncan felt the sting of Iain's rebuke. "And you understand Mara? You really believe she can see the future like that old Margaret Henley, who decreed that you and Andrew and I had been born together for some great purpose and we shouldn't be separated?"

"There's magic in this place, Duncan. We both know it. There will always be things that happen here—and everywhere, for that matter—that we can't understand. I don't know what Mara sees, and I don't know why. But I know her. I stood by her during her divorce, and I offered her that godforsaken bit of land because she needed isolation. She needed a place to build her confidence. I could give her that, and I did."

"Did Fitzwilliams leave her destitute?"

"Oh, not at all. She has money. She lives the way she chooses to live. She's building her self-respect with every stone of that cottage, with every hank of yarn she spins, with every plant in her garden and sheep in her steading."

Iain didn't let himself care about people easily. But he cared about Mara; that was obvious. Duncan knew he had to let the things Iain had said to him settle. There was just one more thing he had to know.

"What did you do to Fitzwilliams when he called Mara a freak?"

Iain smiled for the first time that night. "I threw him halfway across the room. It was a very nice restaurant. I'm afraid I quite spoiled a platter of roast duckling and a six-layer torte."

Chapter 6

With his heart in his throat, Duncan watched April fling herself at Guiser, but before he could intervene, the dog methodically covered the little girl's face with canine kisses.

"I suppose this proves she needs a pet," he told Mara, who had come down the path in front of her cottage just after the dog.

"A wee kitty, perhaps. Imagine the havoc a dog with Guiser's energy would wreak at your hotel."

Duncan almost protested that the hotel didn't belong to him. It belonged to his father, and he was only managing it until it could belong to someone else. But he supposed Mara was right. The Sinclair Hotel was his, as well as his sister's, at least temporarily, even if that thought made him feel a thousand years old.

"One of my neighbors has a cat with kittens just old enough to give away. We could stop there on the way home this afternoon." Mara was careful to be sure that April, still occupied with Guiser, didn't overhear her.

"It would make a good birthday gift," Duncan admitted.

"Then might I give one to her?"

He pretended to consider, but he used the seconds to study her. She was dressed in a green sweater and skirt as pale as the newest leaves of spring. Her hair was pulled back in a long braid that fell past her shoulder blades, and she wore a straw hat with a wide brim that shaded her face from the day's rare and glorious sunshine. Perhaps he had known more beautiful women, women who understood fashion and artifice and made the most of both. But he had never known anyone whose beauty appealed to him more.

He shook his head. "I used to be in advertising. I had an account a couple of years ago that depended on finding the perfect model. I lost it because nobody I found could even come close to the image we were trying to promote. And here you are."

She smiled. "You're saying that it was someone like me you were looking for?"

"Exactly."

"What was the product?"

"Fabric softener."

Her smile widened. "Should I be flattered?"

He thought of the ad campaign that had come to nothing. Of acres of billowing clouds and a woman dancing just above them, as feather light and delicate as a fairy. "Flattered? I don't know. I've never really understood the way women think. But you'd have made money."

"I've never wanted to be rich."

"Just happy?"

"Perhaps not even as grand a thing as that."

"Can I have a kitten, Daddy? Please?" April jumped to her feet, pushing the fawning Guiser away. "Can Mara give me a kitten?"

Duncan raised a brow, and Mara shrugged. "I can no' be blamed. Her hearing's exceptional," she said.

"If Mara is willing, I'm willing," Duncan said.

"We'll have to check with my neighbor first," Mara warned. "No promises."

"But you think she'll let me have one?"

"Aye. I think it's possible."

Duncan watched April run toward the cottage with Guiser close at her heels. "Thank you for coming with us today," he said. "I don't know that I'd have been as charitable as you are, under the same circumstances."

"What circumstances are those?"

He saw humor in her eyes. "I haven't exactly been fair to you."

"I think you must have your reasons."

"And I'm still not sure how I feel about all this."

"You're sure, Duncan. You think I'm a wee bit daft. But you're willing to overlook it. I take what I can get."

He realized that had become his philosophy, too, at least as far as Mara MacTavish was concerned. He couldn't dwell on her supposed gifts, because he found the idea so impossible. But he was beginning to think he might be able to wall away his doubts.

She was worth a little effort.

"I've packed a few extra treats. Let's get them, then we can start our walk."

He fell into step beside her. "We're walking from here?"

"Along a sheep path. You might be surprised where sheep will go."

There was a lilt to her voice that intrigued him. "You sound like you're enjoying this already."

"I've been looking forward to it."

He read between the lines. She'd been looking forward to today because she had so little contact with people. And she loved children—he could see that in the way she treated April—but she seldom had a chance to be with them.

She surprised him when she continued. "I've been looking forward to knowing you better."

"Have you?"

"Aye. I dinna think you're the dour, humorless, judgmental and arrogant skellum that you pretend to be."

She'd said it with such charm, he couldn't feel insulted. "I'm relieved. I think."

"Dinna fash yourself, Duncan. I think you're a sensitive man who feels things so deeply he does no' know what to do about them. So he tries no' to feel them."

"What if you're wrong?"

"Well, I suppose I will have had a wheen happy hours just pretending you're a better man than you are."

He laughed, and she laughed, too. He couldn't remember suffering such ferocious criticism so gladly. He felt rebuked and forgiven, and he realized, for the first time, that he had needed her forgiveness. He didn't examine it too closely; he was just glad to get it.

The door to the cottage stood open, and April had already gone inside. Duncan followed Mara through the doorway. He crossed the threshold and stopped, examining her handiwork as she and April gathered containers from the kitchen and put them in a canvas backpack like the one firmly in place on his own back.

With sunlight streaming through the doorway and windows, he could see the details that he had ignored on his last visit. The cottage was simple, almost primitive in its construction, but everything had been put together with craftsmanship and an eye for detail and beauty. The rafters were hand-hewn hardwood. He imagined they had once graced a barn or stable. Bunches of dried herbs and flowers hung from them in colorful, lacy disarray. Without peat smoldering in the fireplace, he could smell their subtle perfume.

The walls were a patchwork quilt of shapes. The stones had been assembled so expertly that they seemed to form pictures. He imagined that on a cold winter night, they provided hours of entertainment and fantasy.

Almost everything in the cottage had been handcrafted, and possibly a great deal of it had been crafted by Mara herself. The furniture was simple, certainly not as crude as might have been found in the but and ben houses of old crofting settlements, but chosen with utility and modest elegance in mind. The walnut table in the kitchen shone from a century of careful polishing. Hand-thrown pottery of subtle hues adorned it, along with a bouquet of golden daffodils and grape hyacinth. The bed loomed large not more than three yards from him. It was high off the stone floor, a wide wooden rectangle with what looked to be a comfortable mattress. He found himself staring at it, imagining

Mara asleep there at night, surrounded by the fragrance of smoldering peat and drying herbs, her long blond hair flowing over the pastel pillowcases.

"Do you approve, Duncan?"

She had asked the question humorously, a woman who'd caught a man with more on his mind than decor, but he sensed she really wanted to know. Did he approve of everything she'd accomplished? And did he approve of her?

"It's extraordinary. You're extraordinary for living here."

"There's still much to be done. It has no' been easy, nor will it be. But it's mine."

"And you've done it all by yourself?"

"Could you see me lifting those timbers for the roof alone?"

"No. I can't see you hauling stones, either."

"Well, the stones I did. There was a settlement here once, and stones aplenty for the taking when I began to build. Sometimes late at night I like to imagine the lives of the people who lived among them."

"You hauled the stones and set them in place?"

"The stones are not as large as you might think. These walls are a double thickness. Did you know?"

"Double?"

April was busy with Guiser again. Mara beckoned Duncan to the doorway. "If this frame were gone you could see how it's done. There are two rows of stones, filled in with earth and whatever was handy. It was a natural way to insulate against wind and cold. My house is snug in the coldest winter."

"Is that how the old houses were built?"

"It was. I tried, as best I could, to do everything the same way."

"Why?"

"I've always been interested in history. My ancestors lived not more than fifty miles from Druidheachd before the Clearances, and probably had a croft much like this one. I had an auntie who knew our family history, and she used to tell me stories." She paused.

He could almost see her editing what she would say next. "What did she tell you?"

She looked away. "This and that. But I always found the stories of life in the Highlands fascinating."

"I find stories of the Romans fascinating, but I've never built my own amphitheatre or hired gladiators to entertain at my parties."

"Will you promise no' to laugh?"

"Scout's honor."

She didn't look convinced. "When I've finished what I've set out to do, I'd like to bring schoolchildren here to teach them the old ways. No' because all the old ways are better, mind you, but because we are sometimes in danger of forgetting where we came from and what we once knew."

"What would you teach?"

"A bit of everything. Caring for animals, the spinning and dying of yarn, construction methods, gardening and preserving food, the old customs and beliefs."

"It sounds ambitious."

"It is ambitious. I won't be ready for a year or two, and then only just the smallest number of children could come for a week in the summer. But it would be a beginning, would it no'?"

"I think it's a fine idea."

"But would you send April?"

He started to say that this was not April's heritage and therefore there was little need for this in her life, but even as the words formed, he realized how false they were. He was descended from crofters himself. And not just from his Druidheachd-born father. His mother had been a fifth generation American, but a branch of her ancestors, like a multitude of Scots, had been transported to the United States against their will in the early 1800s. The Clearances had rid the mountains of the troublesome, clannish Highlanders and made them safe for the sheep of wealthy Englishmen. And when that tragic time had finally ended, there had been more Scots living outside their own country than within its borders.

"I would send April," he said. "It might be her only chance to know something about her history."

"Why? She'll be taught it in school."

"We won't be here long. Just long enough to put the hotel on its feet and sell it. Then we'll be moving on."

"I did no' know."

"I think I owe it to April to raise her somewhere more cosmopolitan," he said dryly.

"Do you now?"

"You don't sound convinced."

"There are things to learn everywhere. She'll learn things in Druidheachd she'd never learn in New York or London and vice versa. Who's to say which is more valuable?"

"*I* say."

She smiled. "And so you should, like a good father."

He wanted to protest. He wasn't a good father. He had been an abysmal failure when April most needed him. But Duncan never talked about his failures—or his successes.

"Can we go?" April asked, coming to join them. Guiser wagged his tail as if to repeat the question.

"Aye, I think it's time," Mara said. "Do we have everything?"

"I hope so. I feel like I'm carrying half of Scotland on my back."

She laughed. April and Guiser scampered through the doorway, and Mara followed. Duncan was the last out. "Shouldn't I lock the door?" he called after them.

Mara turned, and the sunlight wasn't nearly as bright as the expression on her face. "Silly mannie. We trust each other here. We dinna have to lock our doors. I suppose that's just one of those things you will no' be learning in New York."

The spot Mara had chosen for their picnic was the meadow where Duncan had first encountered her at winter's end. Duncan hadn't been aware that it was so close to her house, because by the road, it would have been a twisting and treacherous drive. But by foot, along a trail blazed over the centuries by flocks of cloven hooves, the meadow and the small loch that he had been headed toward that day were only a pleasant hike.

They stopped for everything. April wanted to examine every rock, every sprouting wildflower, every clump of fern or heather. She threw fallen twigs for Guiser and collected shining pieces of agate to set on the windowsill of her room.

It was after noon when they reached the meadow. A profusion of violets and cowslips greeted them. The tall grass seemed to turn a deeper green as Duncan watched, stretching toward the cloudless sky and rippling in gratitude.

"It's a rare and perfect day," Mara said. "The sun is out for your birthday, April. It's God's own present."

"The sun doesn't shine here much, does it?"

"I'm afraid no'."

"So when it does, you notice it. Like now. I never noticed it at home, because it was always there."

"Then you like this better?"

April considered. "No. But it makes a good present."

Duncan and Mara laughed together. "Just tell me one thing," Mara said, after April scampered off. "With a bonny name like April, why is her birthday in May?"

"She made a late arrival, a whole month late. She was supposed to be born in April," he said.

"And you liked the name so you could no' bear to change it?"

"My ex-wife never let anything as unimportant as reality stop her from doing whatever she wanted," Duncan said.

They chose a spot not far from where Duncan had seen the light show that had led him to Geordie Smith. Duncan cleared away the largest stones and spread a thin blanket on the ground. In a companionable silence he and Mara unpacked their backpacks, while April and Guiser searched unsuccessfully for the season's first forget-me-nots.

Frances Gunn had outdone herself in honor of April's birthday. There were tiny sandwiches of smoked salmon and cucumber, and more of a tangy local cheese garnished with the tart watercress that grew along a small burn near the hotel. There were apples saved over the winter in Frances's fruit cellar and freshly baked oatcake studded with plump raisins.

Mara had added raspberry jam made with berries from her own garden and scones she had baked that morning, along with thick cream from Bluebell, her best milk cow. Mara and Duncan drank fragrant tea from one thermos, and April finished two glasses of fresh, sweet milk from another.

Duncan stretched out with a backpack as a pillow after a determined April and Guiser went off to search for forget-me-nots again. "Bluebell is a health hazard."

Mara stretched out beside him. "I'll have you know she's been examined and vaccinated, and she's a very proper cow, as cows go."

Duncan didn't think about his next move. He reached for her, repositioning her so that her head was pillowed on his well-satiated belly. "So you can watch April, too," he explained. "It takes two to keep a good eye on her."

"Guiser will watch over her."

Duncan felt an urge to stroke Mara's hair. Her braid lay across his chest, and he wondered if it was as silky as it appeared. He wondered what she would do if he touched her in such an intimate way. He wondered what *he* would do.

He kept his hands by his side and chose a safe subject. "Bluebell's a health hazard because her milk is so rich. I can feel my arteries clogging."

"When you lived in Los Angeles, did you nibble on lettuce leaves and have your own personal trainer?"

"I was always too busy. The only way I got to the gym was if a client was there and wanted my company."

"You said you were in advertising."

"I had my own agency."

"And did you give it up because you had so little time for anything else?"

The obvious answer was no. Duncan had thrived on hard work. His adrenaline had soared higher and higher with each success. There had been nothing else in his life that had come close to the exhilaration of winning a new account.

But there was a less obvious answer. "In a way I gave it up because I didn't have time for April," he said.

"In a way?"

"When I divorced April's mother, she told me I could have all the time with April that I wanted if I was willing to pay a small price."

"A price?"

"Lisa traded sole custody of April for all my financial assets, including the agency. She took our net worth. I took our daughter."

"You made the better bargain."

Mara hadn't even hesitated, although he knew she must have been shocked by his revelation. "I did," he agreed. "And now April's mine, and Lisa can never hurt her again."

"Hurt her, Duncan?"

He debated whether to tell her a little about Lisa. If Mara was going to spend time with April, she needed to understand. "Lisa was worse than a failure as a mother. She foisted April off on anyone who would take her. I was working too hard, and for too long I didn't know what was happening."

Mara shifted so that her cheek was against his shirt and she could see his face. The intimacy of the position wasn't lost on him. He wondered how it would feel to have her against him this way, cheek to bare skin. She too easily inspired those kinds of thoughts.

"But dinna a lot of people find that adjusting to a child takes time?" she asked. "Was your wife so unusual?"

"I wish it had been that simple. But Lisa never wanted to face the real world. When I met her, she was a struggling actress, a good one, but without the self-discipline or drive to succeed, so she married me. And after April's birth, she found that the real world still wasn't much fun, so she retreated into the New Age. I don't think I'll ever know everything she did. Some of it was harmless, even healthy, like meditation and yoga. But she quickly moved on to other things. For a while she was an astrologer and self-proclaimed psychic. She surrounded herself with crystals.

She claimed to see auras. She talked endlessly about her past lives. At one point she believed she could teach herself to travel anywhere in the universe while she was lying on our bed, which she did for days at a time.''

"But dinna a lot of people search for answers? Perhaps her choices were no' traditional ones, but do we all have to follow the same paths?''

"I told myself the same thing. And I shut my eyes to how obsessed she'd become with all of it, and how completely oblivious she was to April. After more than two years of floundering and searching, Lisa found her answer. She became the disciple of a man who preached brotherly love and psychic healing, along with total and complete obedience to his teachings. His church—if it could be called a church—was named the Temple of Knowledge and Joy, and I suppose those were the things Lisa was searching for. She began to spend all her time at indoctrination sessions. She sold all her jewelry and gave him the profits. She took huge chunks out of our savings and signed over a number of our investments. She'd always handled our personal finances, so I didn't find out until it was too late.''

"So you divorced her and took April?''

He wished with all his heart that it had been that straightforward. "No. I left Lisa, but I let her keep April. I could see that Lisa's behavior was unhealthy, but I couldn't see what it was doing to our daughter. When it came time to decide custody, Lisa promised me she wasn't involved with the Temple anymore, and I believed her. I really thought she loved April, and I didn't believe she would do anything to hurt her. I worked so many hours each day that I just couldn't see how I could care for April by myself.''

"Then you did what you thought was best.''

He was surprised that she sounded so certain. "Did I? When I visited April, she clung to me like she was drowning. I thought she just missed me, but that she would get used to our divorce the way I had gotten used to my own parents' divorce when I was a child.''

"Those would be natural explanations.''

Or the explanations of a man too obsessed with his own importance to care enough about his own daughter. But Duncan didn't add that part.

"After I left, Lisa went from leaving April with unsuitable people to leaving her alone. I went to visit April late one evening, and before I could even get the front door unlocked I heard screaming. Lisa hadn't known I was coming, so she'd locked April in her bedroom and gone out. I finally quieted April and got her to sleep, then I waited for Lisa. She didn't come back until early the next morning. When I confronted her, she claimed that someone from the Temple was supposed to have come over to stay with April, but she couldn't give me a name. When April woke up, I took her into the office for the day. At four o'clock Lisa arrived with her attorney, demanded that I give April back, and the negotiations began. I've told you how they ended."

"But could you no' have gotten custody without giving up everything? Would your American courts no' have preferred a healthy father to a mother with psychological problems?"

"Unfortunately, I couldn't prove what I knew. When I found April alone that night I didn't call anyone to come and help me verify Lisa's neglect. I was too upset to think that far ahead. And none of Lisa's neighbors would testify against her, because they were afraid some of her more dubious friends might retaliate. April was too young to be a reliable source of testimony. So I was told that either I could share custody of April with Lisa, or I could give Lisa whatever she demanded."

"And that's what you did."

"I'd have paid a thousand times more to get her out of April's life. I didn't want my daughter alone with her for a minute. Now April never has to see Lisa again."

Mara sat up. She stared down at Duncan. "You can no' mean you deny April the chance to see her mother?"

"That's exactly what I mean. That's why we're here. Lisa has a short attention span and very little desire to exert herself. She won't follow us to Druidheachd. April's safe here. And in a year, when the hotel's sold, we'll move somewhere else. By then Lisa will have forgotten she has a daughter.''

"Never."

He sat up, too. "You don't know her."

"Lisa sounds incapable of caring for a child, that's certain. But I can no' believe it's best for April never to see her own mother again. Does she no' miss her, Duncan? Does she no' ask about her?''

April *didn't* ask about her mother. Not anymore. She was more sensitive to nuance than any child should have to be. And Duncan knew that his clipped, evasive answers to the questions she *had* asked had been a warning that Lisa wasn't to be discussed.

Mara was still waiting for an answer. He could feel anger rising inside him. "Lisa will never put her hands on my daughter again. She doesn't deserve to be April's mother. She abandoned her and neglected her. My little girl still has nightmares about being left alone. I can't believe you think a woman like that should have any part in April's life."

Mara stared at him. Then she shook her head. "Duncan, when will you forgive yourself for no' being a better father?"

"How dare you pretend you can read my mind!"

She shook her head slowly, sadly. "It's no' your mind I'm reading but your heart. And I have no special powers to help me. Your guilt is visible to anyone who cares enough to look behind your anger."

"You don't know what you're talking about."

Her voice grew softer. "Am I wrong? Or are you no' distressed that you did no' protect April from so much sadness? Are you no' consumed with guilt that you worked so hard you had little time for her and ignored the signals that she was suffering? I think you're afraid that you and Lisa are more alike than anyone knows. And you can no' forgive her, because you can no' forgive yourself."

"Maybe you're not pretending to have psychic powers. But what gives you the right to psychoanalyze me?''

"I have no right, but I have no secrets, either. I've lived too many years pretending I have no thoughts or feelings about anything. I'll live that way no longer."

He wanted to stay angry. He didn't want this woman to understand him so well, better, perhaps, than he understood himself. But he was a fair man. At his very core he was fair—if nothing else.

She rose, as if to leave.

He rose, too, and took her arm. She looked down at his hand, then up at his face. He dropped his hand. "Don't go," he said. "I'm sorry I spoiled the afternoon. I shouldn't have dumped all my problems on you."

"You'll have to decide now if we're going to be friends or just acquaintances. Friends sometimes have to dump their problems—and sometimes have to endure suggestions on how to solve them."

He heard April's laughter from the grove of trees just beyond them. The same grove of trees where this woman had somehow—and improbably—entered his life. He wondered how he could have ignored what was now so obvious. He hadn't asked Mara to come today because of April. That had been a part of it, but there had been more behind his invitation. He had wanted to get to know her better, not to protect his daughter but to risk a part of himself.

By asking Mara to come today he had opened a door. She was giving him a chance to close it again, or open it wider. But there could be no compromise.

He took a step toward her. "I don't endure suggestions well. I'm sorry. I didn't want to hear what you said."

"And I'm sorry I was so blunt. But I've wasted too much of my life saying what other people wanted to hear."

"I appreciate honesty. Just not when it's applied to my life."

She smiled and put her hand on his. "Shall we walk down to the loch?"

The door was neither open nor closed. But it was still ajar. He felt her fingers brushing his skin. Her hand was soft, despite its calluses. He could almost feel reassurance flow through her fingertips, reassurance and a curious kind of strength. He didn't want to feel anything. And he didn't want to smile at her.

But he did, and he covered her hand.

"You're a far different man when you smile," she said. "I can almost understand why I'm wasting this beautiful day with you when I could be cutting peats or mucking out the byre."

She whistled for Guiser; he shouted for April to join them. And somehow, as they started down the path to the loch, their hands continued to touch.

Chapter 7

Mara watched April blow out the candles on an absurdly large birthday cake. Frances had designed the two layers to look like a spring bonnet covered with pink frosting roses and lemon peel daisies. Happy Birthday April was spelled out on the wide ribbon of frosting that circled the crown.

At first April had refused to let her father cut the cake. Frances herself had been forced to step in to convince the little girl that it was for eating as well as for looking at. Now, in the spirit of the occasion, April was smiling happily and basking in the attention of her guests, but particularly the three men surrounding her.

They were an odd mix, the three men of midnight. Mara had heard the story of their unusual births and the evolving legend that went with it. But she thought that more un-usual—and interesting—than their births was their unique friendship.

Three more diverse men didn't exist, yet they were united in their devotion to each other and, now, to Duncan's daughter.

Andrew seemed the easiest to know, although Mara knew him the least. He was open and forthright, consistently good-humored and warmhearted. He was a tall, brawny man, with a strong man's knowledge of his own power, so he conscientiously schooled himself to be gentle. There was a temper there that he kept under tight control, and possibly a vulnerable heart that only a few people had ever taken note of. She had liked Andrew MacDougall on sight because she had known instinctively that she would never have anything to fear from him.

On the surface, at least, she knew Iain the best. He was unfailingly well mannered and solicitous, a man of considerable charm and personal appeal. But under Iain's cultured exterior was a darker specter. He was haunted by his past and his future, a man who lived only for the moment because he had no faith in anything else. He never talked about his past, and she had never been able to glimpse his destiny. Her gift—or her curse—could not be manipulated. There was far more she couldn't see than she could. The real Iain was almost as much a mystery to her as Duncan was.

Duncan. Mara covertly watched Duncan with his daughter. He was helping April gently guide a knife through the bonnet's brim. When he was with his daughter his patience was infinite. He talked her through the destruction of the bonnet in low, supportive tones. Father and daughter were so much alike. April had her father's gray eyes, and although her hair was lighter now, someday it would probably be the rich brown of Duncan's. Like her father, she seldom smiled, but when she did, her solemn little face showed the promise of beauty.

When Duncan smiled . . . He was smiling now. Mara felt that smile blossom somewhere deep inside her. She had chosen a nun's life, but she hadn't a nun's inclinations. She felt no shame at the immediate, almost visceral reaction she had experienced after her first meeting with Duncan. She had stood in a mist-shrouded meadow and looked down at the man kneeling beside Geordie Smith, and as Duncan felt Geordie for signs of life, she had imagined those same hands gliding over her body.

It hadn't been a vision of the future. It had been lust, pure and simple.

Since then, her attraction to Duncan had grown. She didn't understand it. She had never felt anything like it, not with her husband, not with other men she had known. It frightened her, not because she was afraid of her own sexuality, but because the sheer power of her response to Duncan could change her life. And she was only just beginning to believe that she had a life worth protecting.

"Mara gets the first piece." April held out a plate with a huge slab of bonnet brim across it.

"I'm honored." Mara reached for the plate. Her eyes caught Duncan's. He wasn't smiling now. Not exactly. Something else glimmered in the thunder-curtain gray.

"She's thanking you for the puppies," he said.

"The puppies were no' my doing."

As if in protest, one of the three tiny hounds in the basket under the table began to howl.

"I said a wee kitty," Mara reminded him. "Never did I say a word about puppies."

"But there were no kitties left, were there, Mara? Just a basketful of puppies."

A basketful of puppies about to see their final hours on earth. A basketful of puppies with dubious lineage and no genetic guarantee that they would ever hunt or herd. A basketful of unredeemably ugly puppies with soulful eyes and lolling pink tongues and a master whose patience had run out.

"I understand the puppies were all born at midnight," she said, "and that their destinies are intertwined."

Andrew's laugh roared over the puppy's howls. "Then we should each have one, should we no', Iain and Duncan and me? It's only fitting."

"I get to choose first," April said. "And I don't know which one I want."

"Iain?" Duncan asked. His gaze never left Mara's. "Would you leave a poor puppy without a home?"

"Gladly." Iain glanced down at April and saw her distress. He lifted his eyes in resignation. "Gladly will I take one."

"Then it's settled," Mara said. "And easily at that."

"But I don't know which one I want!" April said again.

Duncan patted her shoulder. "You have until tomorrow afternoon to choose, then we'll take the others to Uncle Iain and Uncle Andrew."

April seemed satisfied. "Can they sleep in my room?"

Frances made a noise deep in her throat.

"It's all right," Duncan told her. "I'll clean up after them."

"And it's well you plan to, because *I'm* the one the maids will complain to tomorrow if the wee hellhounds make a mess!"

Andrew lifted the howling puppy from the basket and soothed him, while a mollified April passed out cake to the rest of her guests. Jessie, Frances's daughter-in-law, and her husband Roger had come for the celebration, along with her daughter Lolly and another of April's classmates. Members of the hotel staff came and went over the next half hour to have their slice of cake and pass along small gifts to April.

By the time everyone had gone home, there was no cake left, but there were a pile of presents, three snoozing puppies and one exhausted little girl in a pink nightgown.

"It's time for bed, Springtime," Duncan said, lifting April into his arms.

Mara gathered the last of the plates to take into the kitchen. "I should be going, too," she said. "Guiser will think I've left him forever." She was glad she'd insisted on bringing her own car so that Duncan wouldn't have to leave April.

"Will you read me a story first?" April stretched out her arms to Mara.

Mara looked to Duncan to provide her with an excuse. "She'd really like it," he said.

She was surprised he had encouraged April. "Well, if you're certain."

"I'll trade you." He strolled toward her with April. She set down the dishes and held out her arms. April wound her arms around her neck. For a moment Mara stood quietly and held her. She'd seldom been so physically close to a child, because she had always been afraid that such intimate contact would trigger a vision of the future.

April's small form nestled against her only triggered a yearning for the things Mara had never had. She rested her cheek against April's hair. "Shall you choose a story, or shall I?"

"Will you read me *Duncan and the Fairies*?"

Mara turned to Duncan for permission. He shrugged. "Aye, I'll read it to you," she said.

In April's room Mara set the little girl at the foot of the bed. Duncan had followed them as far as the doorway with the basket of sleeping puppies. He set the basket down and returned with newspaper to spread around it, although he didn't look optimistic about the chances of puppy success. "I've got to run downstairs to take care of a few things," he said. "Do you mind?"

"I'll stay until you come back."

"Maybe you should stay a little longer. It started to rain a while ago. I'll check when I go downstairs, but it sounds like a real downpour now. I don't like the thought of you going back up the mountain until it slows."

She tried to ignore the comfort his words gave her. Seldom in her life had anyone worried about her. The people who were supposed to have loved her had more often worried about what she might do or see.

"We were lucky the weather was so bonny today. It could have rained earlier," Mara told April when Duncan had gone.

"It wasn't luck. It was 'posed to be."

Mara smiled. "Was it, now? And how do you know?"

"My mommy says things always happen for a reason. Do you think so?"

"I can no' say." Mara turned back the covers on April's bed and fluffed her pillows. She couldn't imagine that Duncan would appreciate her talking to April about her mother. She tried to change the subject. "Do you like the rain?"

"Sometimes Mommy and me would go for walks in it."

Mara tried once more. "Guiser loves the rain because he loves to splash in puddles."

"I've got a picture of my mommy."

Mara understood defeat. "Do you?"

"Daddy doesn't know."

Mara sat on the bed beside her. "Perhaps you should no' be telling me, either."

"Can I show you?"

Minutes later Mara had seen more than a photograph. She had seen a shrine to the absent Lisa, a shrine in a carved wooden box hidden at the very bottom of April's toy chest.

Inside the box there resided an enameled earring in the shape of a unicorn and a silver rhinestone button. There was a tattered recipe for broccoli and brown rice that looked as if it had been tacked too long on a refrigerator and a postcard to Duncan signed "Lisa" in a bold, romantic script. There was half a tube of bright red lipstick and a tiny vial of perfume with most of the label rubbed off.

And there was a photograph of a lovely, ethereal brunette gazing down at an infant in her arms.

"How did you gather all this?" Mara asked. She didn't know what else to say. She certainly didn't have to ask who the baby was.

"I looked. When we were moving. I found things."

"And you put them in here."

April took the box from Mara's lap and, after one more quick peek, closed it and put it back in the toy box. "Lisa's pretty, isn't she?" She not only called her mother by her first name, she sounded more detached, as if by looking at the sad mementos, she had gathered enough objectivity to face her loss again.

"She's very pretty. You'll look a bit like her when you're grown, I think."

"Do you?" April turned. Her smile was huge. "Do I look like her now?"

Mara nodded, even though the resemblance was slight. "Aye."

"Daddy doesn't like her."

Mara saw no point in offering false hope. "Does he no'?"

"Sometimes I don't like her, either."

"And sometimes you do?"

"I haven't seen her in a long, long time."

And the longer April went without seeing her mother, the more importance Lisa would gain in her life. Mara could see the truth as if it were printed on a page in front of her. She wondered how Duncan could fail to see it.

"Don't tell Daddy about the box. Please?"

"It's your secret to tell." Mara brushed April's hair off her forehead. "But sometimes secrets are very heavy things."

"It would make him sad."

Sad. Not angry. Mara wondered how a child could see beneath an adult's surface with such perception. "Shall I read you that story now?"

"Will you make your voice like a fairy's voice?"

Mara leaned over and kissed her cheek. "You'll think it's a fairy reading to you."

Mara was standing at the window of Duncan's sitting room when he returned. April had fallen asleep before the fairies had taken poor, bewildered storybook Duncan down to their home below the hill.

"It was a very big day for a wee bittie girl," she said, turning to greet him.

"She'll need her sleep. I imagine the puppies will wake her sometime during the night."

"One of them is sleeping with her. He's a sleekit laddie, that one. He came to the bedside and yapped until I tucked him in beside her."

"I imagine he'll be the favored beast in the morning. I hope he was the most presentable."

She smiled and shook her head. "He'll take no prizes."

"It's still raining hard. I'd feel better if you'd stay a while until it slacks off."

She had taken care of the necessary chores before joining Duncan and April at the hotel. There were always things to do in the evening, yarn to spin, sachets to stitch, the cleaning she didn't get to during the day. But the appeal of wait-

ing out the storm where the roof and walls were watertight
and the fire warm was undeniable.

The thought of spending more time with Duncan was appealing, too. "I'll stay, but not long. I've an early day
planned for tomorrow, if the weather permits."

"And what will you be doing?"

She turned back to the window. "I've enough yarn spun
to begin my dyeing. If there's no rain, that's what I'll do. If
there is, there's still the byre to shovel and plenty of fleeces
left to spin. I'll be busy."

"Can you really make a living doing what you do?"

"No. If I had to depend on what I make from my crafts,
I'd be looking for work in the village, like most crofters. But
I meet a portion of my needs, enough to keep me from
draining all the profits from my investments."

"I'd like to see you spin."

She hadn't realized he had come to stand beside her. His
words skated along her flesh. He was so close, yet she hadn't
guessed he would join her. Duncan was a continual surprise.

She was a surprise when she was with him.

"What is it you'd like to see?" She stole a glance at him.
His face was turned toward hers.

"I imagine you're a study in grace. Everything about you
flows when you move. I can see you in front of the fire at
your wheel, swaying with the rhythm. What do you think
about when you're spinning? You spend so many hours
alone."

"I suppose I think about how glad I am to be alone."

"I watched you with April tonight. You're not always
glad."

She faced him. "No. But I'm always glad when the alter-
native is to be with people who are afraid of me."

"I'm not afraid."

"Perhaps no' of me. But you're still afraid of what I say
I can do."

"Aren't you?"

She considered. "There was a time when I would have
given anything to have the sight taken from me. Now I un-

derstand that it's a part of me, and if it were gone, I would be a different person. And I like myself, Duncan. I'm beginning to like myself very much.''

"I like you, too."

"But you would like me better if I had no peeks at the future, or if there was a rational scientific explanation for what happens to me. A disease with a Latin name and a cure."

He touched her cheek. "I couldn't like you better."

She couldn't pull her gaze from his. "I'm no' strong enough yet for this."

"Neither am I."

"I should go."

"Yes, you should." His fingers slid to her chin, then into her hair; his palm was warm against her cheek.

She smiled a little, just a little. "I dinna seem to be leaving."

"I don't seem to be letting you."

"I can no' change, and I can no' deny who I am and what I see. Dinna kiss me, Duncan, unless you're willing to accept that."

He kissed her anyway. She watched his face descend, and as her eyes closed, she felt the warmth of his lips against hers. She inhaled the masculine fragrance of his skin, tasted the dark wine flavor of his lips. His arms came around her, and she could feel her breasts sink against his chest. Her hips pressed against his, and she could feel desire stirring in Duncan as well as herself.

Her arms crept around him, even though she knew she should push him away. He kissed a sensuous trail to her ear. "Don't kiss me, Mara, if you can't accept a few doubts. I'm no different from you. I can't be anyone except who I am."

"I dinna want this unless we're going to be good for each other."

"I'm beginning to think we can be very, very good for each other."

She settled more fully into his arms. This time her lips parted beneath his. Her doubts drifted away; thought drifted away with them. She could feel his fingertips against her back, the rise and fall of his chest, the subtle shifting of his hips. Somewhere in the distance, thunder roared as their kiss deepened.

She had always thought that desire was a subtle thing; now it was as brilliant, as illuminating, as the lightning that split the night sky. Kissing Duncan was more than a need for comfort and human contact. Her blood surged, and her pulse sped wildly. Heat poured through her and settled in places that had never before known its power.

She held him closer. His knee slid between her legs as if he understood her need to be touched there. A moan formed deep in her throat. She wanted him to touch her everywhere. She wanted to run away.

Finally he was the one who stepped back. She opened her eyes and stared into his. She had been afraid she would see doubt or self-mockery. Instead she saw desire and a reluctant self-control. "You feel the way I thought you would. You taste the way I thought you would," he said.

She heard more than just words. She heard the unsteadiness of his voice and weeks of unconscious yearning. "You've thought about this?" Her voice was unsteady, too.

"More than once." He pushed her hair off her face. His hands rested in it. "In my dreams, most of all."

Duncan had been in Mara's dreams, too, although she hadn't known it until that moment. She had repressed all yearning for him, she who valued honesty above all. "I'd best be going," she said.

"The rain hasn't stopped."

"But I think that I have, at least for tonight."

"If we continue to see each other, a kiss won't be enough."

She knew he was right. Even now, it wasn't enough. Her body cried out for the solace of his. "Will you tell April that I'll finish the book the next time I see her?"

"Then you'll be back?"

"After awee."

"May we come to see you again?"

She leaned forward and kissed him again. Then she slipped past.

"Be careful on the road," he called.

She didn't turn. "Aye. It's canny I'll be. There'll be flooding tonight."

"Flooding? I doubt it. There's been just enough rain to soak the ground."

"There'll be flooding, Duncan. Tonight when they come to ask for your help with it, remember that I told you so."

Jamie Gordon hadn't drunk as much as his older brother Peter, but he'd had enough to propel him the first mile toward home without much minding the rain soaking his shirt and trousers. He wasn't sure where he'd left his mac. He wasn't even sure if he'd brought a mac to the pub.

He wasn't even sure which pub he'd been to.

"We could lie a bit under that tree," Peter said, waving a hand in the air in a dozen different directions. "Any tree. Just until the rain stops."

"A fat lot of good it'd do ye to lie down in this. We'd be washed away. Have ye nae sense left at all, Peter?"

Peter began to whistle. He coughed sharply when he inhaled water with his next gulp of air. "I will nae be having any more of this! It's the back way for me. Ye can come if ye want."

"It's no' safe in this rain. We'd have to cross the burn, and it'll be rising fast."

"Yer a poor excuse for a brother and a wee gyte at that. It'll nae be rising. It'll come to our knees. Nae higher. And we're wet all over, are we no'?"

Jamie continued to stumble down the road. He wasn't even sure he could find the back way home. He'd gone about twenty steps when he realized Peter was no longer beside him. He stopped and turned. Through the rain he could just see Peter's outline disappearing into the field at their left. He debated whether to follow; the rain seemed much more daunting without his brother beside him.

"Wait!" Jamie stumbled after him. "Peter, wait!" He caught up to him easily. "Ye know where yer going?"

"I know. Do you no'?"

"Haud yer wheesht! O' course I do!"

The ground under Jamie's feet sank lower with every step. He went quickly from uncomfortable to miserable. Brambles tore at his legs, and once he tripped over a stone, sprawling facedown in the mud. "We should no' have come this way," he said after Peter helped him to his feet.

"Ye can always go back."

Jamie thought of all the times that Peter had beaten him soundly at their childhood games. At eighteen, Jamie was still the thinker and twenty-year-old Peter the doer. But tonight they hadn't an intelligent thought between them, and nothing they were *doing* made any sense at all. He plodded on, lifting his feet higher, setting them down carefully. The rain seemed to be falling faster. He wondered about the burn.

"I've a rock in my boot." Peter hobbled to a boulder large enough to sit on and began to unlace his boot. Jamie crossed and recrossed his arms for warmth. He had never been this cold, not even in the midst of winter. Peter cursed repeatedly. His fingers were numb, not nearly as clever as usual, and the laces were soaked and knotted.

"I'm going on," Jamie said, when it was obvious Peter would be a while. "I'll go on just a wee bit." He wanted to see the burn and make his own decision about whether it should be crossed tonight. "I'll wait up ahead for ye, Peter. I'll stay in shouting distance."

"Och, go on. Yer setting my nerves on edge."

Jamie started in what he thought was the right direction. He moved slowly and carefully, never intending to get very far ahead of his brother, but as the ground sloped down, his speed increased. He entered a stand of trees and for the first time thought he knew where he was. If he was right, the ground would continue to slope and then level off. The burn would be just ahead.

When the ground began to level off, he felt a surge of pride.

He tried to decide whether to wait there for Peter or whether to forge ahead on his own. Peter wouldn't wait for him. That he was sure of. If Peter missed him in the dark, he would go on without him.

He took a few tentative steps forward, torn by the desire to be home in bed and guilt at leaving his brother behind. He had told Peter he would wait, and he was usually a man of his word.

He took a few more steps, and then he halted in his tracks and stared at the light coalescing just in front of him.

At first he couldn't believe what he saw. He couldn't remember how much he'd had to drink that night. He couldn't even remember where he'd had it. So why should he believe his eyes when they told him that eerie green light was forming into the shape of a woman in the midst of the trees ahead of him?

He put his hands over his eyes, then peeked through his fingers. The light—the woman—was still there.

"Who are ye?" he shouted.

The light seemed to move toward him. He took two jerky steps backward and fell. He could feel the earth under his backside and the rain on his face. He was still awake, and before him was a ghost.

He covered his face with his hands, and this time he didn't peek. He hadn't been inside the village kirk in years. His mother went sometimes, but his was not a family that took to religion. He tried to remember a prayer. There had to be a prayer.

He could no more remember a prayer than remember where he'd left his mac. He stumbled to his feet, his face still covered. He turned and fled. Halfway up the slope he slammed into a tree. His hands fell away from his face, and he tumbled backward. At the bottom of the hill he opened his eyes, expecting to meet his death. The woman was standing only yards away. Even gripped by the worst fear he had ever known, he saw how beautiful she was.

She stretched out a hand and stroked the air in front of her, again and again.

She was warning him away.

Jamie wasn't certain how he knew the ghost's intent. But at the moment he realized that he wasn't to come any closer, she vanished. He rubbed his eyes and peered through the darkness, but the lady of light was gone.

"Peter!" He found his way to his feet and started up the slope again. "Peter!"

"I'm right here, ye idjit!" Peter materialized out of the darkness. "And what is it yer doing there, when you should be at the burn?"

Jamie told him what he'd seen, or at least he tried to. The words came out wrong. He stuttered. He sputtered. But when Peter tried to push past him, he grabbed his arm. "Ye can no' go that way, Peter. That's what she was saying."

"Saying? She did no' say a thing, did she? She was no' even there! Ye've had too much whiskey and too much rain!" He shook off Jamie's arm and started down the hill.

"Peter. Dinna go that way!"

But Peter disappeared into the rain. As Jamie watched, his brother's dim outline vanished completely.

It didn't take Jamie long to consider what to do next. He started back toward the road at a run. He was completely sober now, sober and determined. He would not remain in the woods, not for all the whiskey in Scotland. He was sorry that Peter hadn't listened, but not sorry enough to follow him and try to persuade him.

He was the thinker and Peter the doer. And now he thought that in the very near future he would become a sober man and a regular at the kirk, as well.

Chapter 8

The entire month of May was stormy, but no night had been as threatening as the one of April's birthday celebration. The burn that wandered lazily from the hills above Druidheachd had risen swiftly, spreading and rushing up the slopes that enclosed it until it had changed from peaceful stream into roaring river.

Peter Gordon had stories to tell about the burn, stories of logs rushing past him as he clung to a root in the frigid water, stories of prayers prayed and promises made. Somehow his life had been spared. His brother, Jamie, had trudged the long road home to discover that Peter hadn't arrived yet. A rescue party of villagers had retraced Peter's path through a field where Jamie insisted his brother had last been seen. They had arrived at the burn just in time to save Peter from the waters.

There had been other damage during the flood, a cottage washed from its foundations, a car submerged nearly to its roof, sheep and cows stranded on rocky knolls and lambs drowned.

But the gossips of Druidheachd spared little conversation for the flood. High waters would come and go, and it was a pity that some people weren't canny enough to stay out of them. What was more interesting was the vision that Jamie Gordon swore he had seen, the ghost who had warned him away from the burn.

"They've come up with a name for her now," Andrew told Duncan one afternoon just outside Andrew's house. "There's a solicitor from Perthshire with a summer cottage on the loch who heard Jamie tell his story. It seems there's a legend in Perthshire about a ghost like ours, a braw lassie with flowing hair and a green satin gown who warns people of impending danger. They call her My Lady Greensleeves. Now some people in the village say she's just changed her place of residence."

Duncan watched April romp with Primrose and Poppy. Never had dogs been less deserving of their names, or more ridiculous because of them. All three of the puppies were mouse brown and shaped like a baker's first loaf of bread. April had chosen names for them after a great deal of thought—christening Iain's puppy Hollyhock in the process. Andrew, with great forbearance, had accepted his fate, but Duncan was afraid that some day Hollyhock was going to conveniently disappear into the loch. Even Primrose, April's puppy, had the grace to appear chagrined whenever his name was called.

April sprawled on the narrow shore of Loch Ceo to be tackled by the hellhounds, shrieking happily all the while, and Duncan turned his attention back to Andrew. "No one is serious about this ghost thing, are they? Jamie Gordon had too much to drink that night, and so did his brother. They both admit it freely. Surely no one is taking a drunken man's word for something so ridiculous."

"There've been other stories. They started about two years ago, you know, long before you came back. And Jamie's story is a bit like the lights you saw the night the lorry nearly smashed into you," Andrew said. "You saw a woman, too, or something that looked like one."

"Something that looked like a woman is a very different thing from seeing a ghost." Duncan looked past April and the puppies to the loch. "But a man who believes in loch monsters might be hard to convince."

"I have no' closed my mind, it's true. I have no' made the mistake of thinking I understand everything."

"And neither have I. Just some things. Like the fact that there are no ghosts and no monsters."

"Some people are saying that the ghost began to appear just after Mara bought her land from Iain. And Mara's from Perthshire herself."

Duncan had only seen Mara briefly in the past weeks. She had asked him for time, and he hadn't rushed her. But he had missed her more than he'd bargained for. Yesterday he'd glimpsed her going inside Cameron's, so he'd invented his own grocery list just to be with her for a few minutes. She had refused his invitation for a drink at the hotel, but she had invited him to bring April and visit today. They would be heading up the mountain after April tired of playing with Poppy.

"They're not saying Mara has anything to do with the ghost, are they?" he asked. "Don't they know a coincidence when one hits them on the head?"

"Some are saying Mara *is* the ghost."

"I'm going back to the hotel and pack my bags."

"It's said with good humor, Dunc, but it does no' help that Mara hides away in her croft and refuses to socialize with people in the clachan. They're suspicious of her. Good humor can quickly turn to bad."

"Do you know why Mara stays away from people?"

"Aye. But should I tell that to the good folk of Druidheachd? That's she's no' a ghost, merely a seer?"

"No. As far as I'm concerned, she's neither."

"And what accounts for her visions, then?"

Since Duncan didn't know, he couldn't answer. "I'll talk to her today. I'll tell her what's being said. And I'll think of something to turn the tide of suspicion."

Duncan considered Andrew's warning—for that was exactly what it had been—as he drove the winding road to Mara's. This was the twentieth century, and even Druidheachd couldn't completely ignore the march of time. But pry off the thin veneer of contemporary attitudes and beneath it there was a deep foundation of Celtic superstition and primal mysticism. If an immediate answer couldn't be found using rational, scientific methods, an answer from the pagan past would suffice.

He silently berated the villagers until he turned onto Mara's road. But during the last mile he'd given up his own magical thinking. Druidheachd might be more in touch with its past than most places. Legends might be more freely bandied about here, stories passed down, the mystical cherished, but Druidheachd was like any corner of the universe and the people here like any other. They wanted and needed answers. They were willing to settle for old ones if new ones didn't suffice.

Primrose scampered up the path to Mara's cottage, and April skipped after him. Guiser came down to greet them, and after sniffing and approving of Primrose, trotted off with the puppy at his heels. Duncan crested the hill and saw Mara beside her house piling wood under a black iron kettle.

He thought of every fairy tale he'd ever been read as a child, every Saturday morning cartoon with black cats and witches. She wore a loose smock to cover her dress, and her hair was pulled back in a long, pale braid. Had she been wearing a pointed hat, he might have turned tail to run—except that she was so incredibly beautiful.

"What on earth are you doing?" He watched April break into a jog. Mara turned and dropped an armful of wood to open her arms to his daughter.

She lifted April and swung her around. "Och, look at you," she said. "All pink-cheeked and bonny from the sunshine."

Duncan lifted his gaze to the sky. If there was sun today, it was the Scottish variety, hiding behind clouds and peeking out just often enough to tease them.

He joined them. "If I were a stranger, I'd think I was about to be turned into a frog. Or added to eye of newt and wing of bat to complete one of your secret potions."

"If you were a stranger?" She lifted a brow. "Dinna you half think that now?"

"What are you doing?"

"I'm about to make dye. I thought April would enjoy helping."

His gaze strayed to the ground by the kettle where suspicious bundles of dried plants were assembled. "You dye with those?"

"Aye. I grow or collect much of it myself. Would you like to see my garden?"

Duncan could see that this was a true source of pride for her. He had no doubt that she had a green thumb. Even though the weather hadn't truly warmed, the rock-lined beds outside the cottage were filled with interesting foliage and occasional bright splashes of color. "I'm renowned for how quickly I can kill a plant," he warned. "My father despaired of me."

"Will you kill my herbs by just walking through?"

"I give no guarantees."

"Do you want to see, too?" Mara asked April.

"I want to find Guiser."

"Then you shall." Mara set her on the ground. "Off with you. And bring him back when you find him."

"She'll be all right?" Duncan asked.

"Guiser will no' have gone far. He's just giving Primrose a tour." She didn't look at him. She watched April until she had disappeared behind the byre.

Duncan put his hand on her shoulder. She turned then and raised her eyes to his. "I've missed you," he said.

"I dinna know what to do about you, Duncan."

The way she said his name did strange things to him. To Mara, he was Doon-kin, a fluid, musical sound that was almost an endearment. "You dinna have to do anything," he said. "Can we no' just see where things lead?"

She smiled at his accent. "I can almost hear the kilt and the bagpipe."

"I come by it honestly, you know. I lived here for the first eight years of my life."

"There's no hint of your Scots blood now except when you feel passion. Usually anger."

"I've been angry too often with you." He touched her braid. It slid through his fingers, fine and soft.

"It's no' your anger that frightens me."

"There's no reason to be frightened."

She shook her head slowly.

"You're just finding yourself. I know. I'm wary of women who need to find themselves. I know that, too. But that's out in the open. We understand each other. We can be careful with each other."

"Is it just care that's needed, then? Is it as simple as that?"

"Give it a chance and see."

"I've missed you, too." She took his hand and linked her fingers with his. "And I was glad to see you at Cameron's yesterday. Were you really so desperately in need of butter that you braved the rain for it?"

"There's twenty pounds in the hotel refrigerator."

She laughed. "Shall I show you my herbs now?"

He leaned forward, hands still linked, and kissed her. She didn't move away, and she didn't move closer. Her eyelids drifted shut, and she sighed against his lips. Sensation spiraled through him. He felt as if he'd been holding his breath for most of a month, waiting for this. But he felt more than relief. Much, much more.

"My herbs?" she said at last.

He heard April's laughter somewhere just behind the byre. He stepped back. "Your herbs."

Her garden was fenced against the animals, a rectangle carved from the rocky soil. "In two years' time, how did you manage all this?" he asked.

"Remember, there was a settlement on this spot once. The garden plot was here. The rocks had been cleared away for a larger garden than this, the soil cared for and replenished. When I moved here there were weeds aplenty, weeds I'd never even seen before. But beneath them, the land was as rich as any in the Highlands. Each year I'll reclaim a bit more." She opened the gate, a modern-looking affair with sturdy hardware. "Now, be careful where you step. I'll no' have you trampling my seedlings to death."

"I'll be drawn to them like magnets."

"Step where I step."

"My feet are twice the size of yours."

She was ahead of him, and she didn't turn. "They are no'. You take a respectable boot and no more."

"And how do you know so much about my feet?"

"I know all about you, Duncan. There's little I have no' noticed."

He wished he could see her face. "All? Nothing left to the imagination?"

"Nowt that my imagination could no' provide."

He laughed softly. "My imagination probably works as well as yours, but apparently I find it less satisfying."

"I did no' say it was satisfying."

He laughed again.

She bent and brushed soil away from a mound. "I grow some plants for sachets to ward off moths. This is camphor. And in the row beyond is sweet woodruff."

He was growing more interested in spite of himself. But in Mara, not her herbs. "How did you learn all this?"

"When I was a wee girlie I had an auntie, a great-auntie, really, who took me to stay with her whenever she could. She taught me to spin and to collect plants for dyeing."

He was relieved to find that someone in her life had wanted her. "Did she teach you to grow things?"

She straightened. "The MacTavish women were always known for their gardens. As well as other things."

"Their great beauty?"

She smiled. "No." She hesitated, as if weighing her answer. Then she shrugged. "For having the sight, Duncan. It's been passed down for as long as anyone remembers. Sometimes it skips a generation or two, but it always reappears. My granny had it, but she died before I was born. My mum tried to hide the truth from me, but my auntie told me before she died. I was no' the first MacTavish woman to see the future. But perhaps I'll be the last."

"Why would you be the last?"

"There are no more in my line. My mum was an only child, and her auntie had no children. And I have no brothers or sisters."

"You could have children."

"But first I'd have to find a man who wanted them with me, would I no'?"

"A man who didn't want your children would be a fool."

"I've married one fool already. It's possible I'd marry another. It's not a risk I'd take lightly, or even willingly."

"You would be a superior mother."

"Did you think Lisa would be a superior mother, too?"

"No. I'm not sure I ever thought about it."

"A superior mother takes a superior marriage. A woman needs support to weather the storms of childhood. A man does, too."

"I'm doing all right alone."

"It takes its toll though, does it no'?"

He almost protested; then he grimaced. "I almost forgot. I'd better go find April."

"She's over there." She pointed to the sheep pen. "I saw her a moment ago."

"Then lead on, MacTavish."

She showed him more of the herbs that she dried for sachets, lavender and pennyroyal, tansy and, in an isolated corner of the garden, wormwood, a herb so powerful its very fragrance was said to inhibit the growth of neighboring plants.

They moved down the rows, and she pointed out plants she grew for dyeing. April joined them, and Mara drew her into the tour. "This is weld, which gives a clear yellow dye, and this is woad, which gives a blue. These . . ." she pointed to a lacy-leafed row ". . . are cosmos, flowers bonny enough to pick for bouquets, but I grow them for dyeing. This is ribwort, this is coreopsis, a lovely golden blossom." She pointed to a quarter of the garden on the edge opposite them. "And that's my dinner for months to come, though I'll be using the skins of the onions for dyeing, as well, and the stalks of the tomatoes."

"Can we dye with onions today?" April asked.

Mara ruffled her hair. "No, today we'll dye with crottal. Do you know what that is?" April shook her head. "It's lichen. It grows on rocks. We'll go for a walk later, and I'll show you a bit I saw yesterday. It's a wonderful dye, April. It's used for Harris tweed, and it turns the wool a russet color. Did you know that fishermen will no' wear a russet jersey? The people of the Highlands say that crottal always tries to find its way back to the rocks it came from. And fishermen are afraid that the crottal will make them sink like a stone if they fall overboard."

April was wide-eyed. "Do they really sink?"

"Hardly," Duncan assured her.

Mara showed April how to hill dirt over the potato plants in the vegetable portion of the garden and supervised as April carefully covered the emerging shoots with dirt. "You've got the touch. You'll be a gardener, unlike your father, who looks as if a rock's fallen on his head."

Safely outside the confines of the garden, Duncan walked with Mara back toward the house, while April, with the dogs at her heels, took a handful of fresh comfrey leaves to feed a trio of baby lambs in a stone pen. "You wouldn't know to look at the garden that you can make dye from any of those plants," he said.

"Are you intrigued?"

With Mara, definitely. Duncan made a sound that could have meant anything and hoped it sufficed.

"You can make dye from so many things. Roadside weeds and the bark of trees. In the next months I'll be picking everything I see. Broom and thistle, goldenrod and dandelions."

"Then you'll be very busy this summer?"

"Aye. Very. But no' too busy, Duncan."

"Not too busy?"

"For you."

He pulled her to a halt beside him. He knew how to press an advantage. "Then come with me to the fair in the village next weekend." She frowned. He could tell she had expected something more intimate. "Come be with me there."

"Why?"

"Because you don't let anyone in the village know you. You've kept yourself a stranger to almost everybody in Druidheachd. It's time you got to know the villagers."

"And why would you care when you hardly know them yourself? There's more to this than you're saying."

She might not read minds, but she was a hard woman to fool. "There's talk, Mara. Some people claim to have seen a ghost, a ghost who unfortunately resembles you."

"A ghost, is it?"

"Fortunately a good one. They're calling her My Lady Greensleeves after some ghost in Perthshire."

"I know the story."

"She's warned several people of impending danger, most recently a young man who was almost caught in the flood." He remembered Mara's warning that night. *There'll be flooding, Duncan. Tonight when they come to ask you for help with it, remember that I told you so.*

Andrew *had* come to ask his help that night. Duncan hadn't been called on to search for Peter Gordon, but he and the hotel's minibus had helped a family evacuate their home.

Mara shook her head. "And now you want me to come to the fair so the village will see I'm no' a ghost at all, but a woman of flesh and blood?"

"They've seen that much before. Now let them get to know you a little. Let them see you laugh and smile and flirt with me."

"You know why I avoid crowds." She searched his face. "At least you know why I *say* I do. Everyone from the village and beyond will be there. How can I come? Can I pretend I'm just like them when I'm no'?"

He rested his hands on her shoulders. "You *are* just like them. You can be hurt by malicious gossip, just like any of them. You can be hurt by too much isolation. You can be hurt by your own fears. Come to the fair."

"You can no' know what it's like, Duncan."

"Maybe not, but I can be there for you. I can be there beside you. And if it gets too bad, I can help you find a place to escape everything for a while."

"You can be so kind."

He pulled her closer. "I can be even more."

"Do I feel like a ghost to you, Duncan?"

"You feel like a woman."

She leaned forward. "Do I taste like a ghost?" she asked softly. She pressed her lips against his.

He enclosed her in his arms. She tasted like the Highlands, seductive and exhilarating. There was a wildness in her as well as a deep serenity. She was all the things he had carefully schooled himself not to want.

But he wanted her.

"Come to the fair with me," he said when he had finally forced himself to step away.

"Aye, I'll come. But I'll no' guarantee that it will have the results you desire."

"Don't wear green." Green was the color that fairies wore, and now the color associated with the ghost. Even if it suited Mara perfectly, he didn't want her to have any strikes against her.

She smiled sadly. "I could wear pink or blue, but it will no' make a difference. If the people of Druidheachd dinna want me here, they'll find a reason other than the clothes I wear."

"I want you here."

"Duncan, have you forgotten you will no' be here long yourself?"

For the first time that thought gave Duncan no pleasure.

Chapter 9

As promised Mara didn't wear green. She wore violet—violet skirt, violet stockings, and a violet body suit, with her hair flowing loosely over it like a golden satin mantle. Her eyes were still green, however, as green as a Scottish summer and as filled with clouds. Early in the morning—or at the skreich of day, as Frances always called it—Duncan contemplated Mara standing in the hotel lobby and knew that she had come only to fulfill her promise to him. She didn't want to be here.

"I half expected plaid," he said.

Sunshine broke momentarily through clouds. "The only plaid I own is nearly all green."

He laughed. "I'm not surprised."

"I did no' want to be My Lady Green Tartan."

"You look lovely."

"And you look bonny yourself, Duncan. More a Scot than an American today."

Her words gave him pleasure, although he told himself that was silly. The local tailor had insisted on fitting him for a jacket of the finest Harris tweed, and he wore it now as a public relations gesture. Frances had given him a tie she'd bought him in Inverness. He held it out now. "The Sinclair tartan," he said with a grimace. "I look like a tourist."

"Have you ever visited Rosslyn Chapel south of Edinburgh?"

"No. Why?"

"It's the burial place of the Sinclairs. And you've more in common with your clan than you might think. Until the seventeenth century was nearly over, the Sinclair men were buried in full armor. Even in death they were no' vulnerable."

He narrowed his eyes, but he laughed, too. "Well, I haven't donned my armor today. And under the tweed and plaid beats an American heart," he said.

"But's it's interesting, is it no', that when you needed refuge, you came back to Druidheachd? Perhaps you have two homes, Duncan. A person can belong to more than one place."

He didn't want to explore that, but he didn't protest. "I wasn't sure you'd come."

"I told you I would."

"Good. Because I need you."

She lifted a brow in question.

"We're going to set up a stand at the fair," he said, "to sell food and drink. Two of my staff got sick during the night, and they won't be able to man it. I could use your help."

"Me?"

"Think about it, Mara. Everyone in the village will stop by. It will give you a chance to see and be seen."

"Aye, I know. That's the trouble."

"Are you afraid? I'll be there with you."

"I'm not afraid. Resigned, I suppose."

"I thought you couldn't see your own future."

"No, but I mind well my past."

He wanted to take her in his arms and reassure her—at least reassurance was part of what he wanted to give her. But people passed back and forth beside them, and there had already been enough furtive glances in their direction. "This is the present. And you're with me. Everything's going to be all right."

"My Lady Greensleeves and one of the Men of Midnight?" She smiled. "It's a wheen of blethers to think my reputation will be improved by the likes of you."

He put his arm around her shoulders and guided her toward the kitchen. "Frances is making enough sandwiches for a Highland regiment. Will you help her? I'll be at the green setting up for the next hour. When the sandwiches are finished, I'll come back for the food and the kegs."

"And what do I get for all the hard work?"

He thought how lucky he was that the question had been asked just then. He pulled her into a dark corner of the hallway. Momentarily at least, they were alone. "What do you want?"

"Undying gratitude?"

"Yours forever. Anything else?"

She surprised him. She rested her hands on his shoulders and drew him closer. Her fingers curled against the back of his neck. Lightly, seductively, she stroked. "No pleas and no promises," she said. "Just a moment at a time. The blink of an eye, then another."

"I can give you that."

"Aye, if you will." She raised up to kiss him. His mouth descended hungrily to hers.

And more than a moment passed.

Duncan didn't know if he had ever been in love. As a young man he had been infatuated with Lisa. They had married young, before they'd had the good sense to look behind their passion to see if they shared anything else. When it had become clear to him that passion wasn't enough, that in fact they no longer shared even that, he had tried to find common ground on which to build a marriage.

But he hadn't tried hard enough. He had been busy building a career. As part of her endless search for meaning, Lisa had gotten pregnant. He, in turn, had worked harder to support his growing family. Lisa, in turn, had looked elsewhere for answers to the mysteries of life. The cycle had completed itself inevitably with divorce. If there had ever been love, or even the potential for it, it had wilted on the vine.

Since his divorce there had been little time to think about the future. He had been left with a daughter who needed all his attention and a lack of faith in his own potential as a husband. He was still bitter about the damage that Lisa had done, and wary about letting anyone get close to him.

Yet beside him today, as close as he had allowed anyone to get in years, was Mara MacTavish, a woman with problems to rival Lisa's and a heart that was entirely different.

"There you go, Mr. Burton," she said. She counted pounds and pence and smiled politely as she did. "All your change and your sandwiches, too. And there's crisps to go with them in the poke."

Duncan watched Carlyle Burton, a man no younger than seventy-five, bathe in her smile. From across the green the skirl of half a dozen bagpipes and as many drums drowned out Carlyle's response, but from the corner of his eye Duncan saw Mara flush. "Cheeky old chap," she said, when Carlyle was gone.

"I gather he likes you."

"I think you asked for my help to stir up business."

She *had* been good for business, but not only because men like Carlyle had succumbed to her charms. Duncan had watched the faces of most of the villagers who'd found excuses to stop by the stand. Mara was a creature under a microscope. She had been silently scrutinized by the cowardly and questioned by the bold. In return, she had presented herself with the perfect mixture of reserve and warmth to even the most judgmental patrons. But Duncan had felt no easing of suspicion as the morning wore on. Mara was an unknown quantity, a stranger who kept to herself and lived alone in a primitive stone cottage she had built with her own hands. And why would a woman live as she did unless she had something to hide?

"It's important for people to get to know you," he said. "How else will they see that you're exactly like them?"

"Am I? Am I exactly like them?"

"Yes," he said firmly. "Maybe you're a little more sensitive to your environment. That's all. I think you pick up clues the rest of us don't notice."

"Is that how you explain my entire life?"

"Yes."

"And that's what you tell yourself? That's how you justify your interest in me?"

He wasn't completely insensitive. He heard frustration and sadness in her voice. "I don't know what you mean."

"It's no' complex. You have to explain me somehow. If you dinna, then you have no way to explain yourself."

He frowned. "Are we having a fight?"

Her shoulders slumped, and for just a moment he saw exactly how difficult the morning had been for her. "I've no wish to fight with you, Duncan."

"Then let's not."

She nodded. As if she needed to put space between them she crossed the straw-scattered ground to talk to Frances. The stand was nothing more than an ancient canvas tent with two sides open to the elements and long tables across the openings piled with food. Behind them Frances and Jessie sold kedgeree, a fish and rice stew, and at the end of their table Brian dispensed beer. There were similar tents strung around the green, manned and womanned by local organizations, but the Sinclair Hotel had the greatest variety.

The midday rush began, and both he and Mara were caught up in the flow of patrons. It wasn't until later that he was able to talk to her again. "I wasn't trying to downplay what you've been through, Mara. I know your sensitivity has made life difficult for you, and I know today's been a trial. I was trying to let you know I understand."

"I dinna think that's it at all. Are you no' asking for reassurance, Duncan? Dinna you really want to know if I've seen someone's future today? Dinna you really want to know if, as I handed out crisps and sandwiches, I had visions of who's destined to die or merely who's going to suffer terribly?"

He didn't answer immediately. He pushed past his initial rush of anger and tried to sort out his feelings.

She spoke first, but she didn't look at him. "I'm sorry."

"What in the hell's going on?"

She was silent for a few minutes. She handed out more sandwiches with a forced smile and made change. He was pulled reluctantly into two separate conversations with villagers. Only when the crowd slacked off again did he turn back to her. "Are you going to tell me?"

"I dinna ken how to tell you."

"Tell me what?"

Her shoulders were pulled back as rigidly as a soldier's, and her chin was lifted high. She shook her head.

He was headstrong and stubborn, and he'd long ago learned how to get what he wanted in situations like this one. But staring at Mara, Duncan knew that this time he'd found his match. He could poke, pry, plead and she still wasn't going to tell him what she didn't want him to know.

"Can I help?" he asked instead.

She seemed to wilt before his eyes. "There's nowt to be done."

"I can't remember feeling this frustrated in a long time."

"I think I'll stroll the green." She untied the white chef's apron that Frances had provided her with. "Can you manage awee without me?"

"Would you like some company? Or would you rather be alone?"

"If the company's you."

He felt the strangest mixture of emotions that he didn't want to dissect. He removed his apron, too, and asked Jessie to cover their table while they were gone.

Outside the tent he took her hand and wove his fingers through hers. He waited for her to pull away, but she left her hand in his. "Shall we just walk around, or did you have somewhere special you wanted to go?"

"I just wanted to walk."

"Then that's what we'll do."

The Druidheachd Johnsmas fair was part medieval market festival and part traditional Highland Games. There was no written record to document when the first one had been held. For as far back into antiquity as anyone could see, the fair had been held on Midsummer Day, climaxing in the evening with dancing and bonfires on the hills just outside the village. For centuries before this one, men in belted plaid and trews had strolled the Druidheachd green with their ladies, bartering for bolts of cloth or bits of ribbon. There had been fire eaters and jugglers, strolling bards and games guaranteed to test the strength and endurance of the strongest clansman. There had been bannocks warm from stone ovens and strong malt whiskey from local stills.

And there had been laughter.

Laughter was noticeably absent in the voice of the woman walking beside Duncan. The Mara he knew was warm and witty. Now she was as brittle as glass, but not nearly as transparent.

"Have you seen April lately?" he asked her. Sally, one of the hotel maids, had offered to take April for the day. She had two young daughters, and April enjoyed playing big sister. The last time Duncan had seen them all, they were enjoying the antics of a clown at one of the two stages set up on opposite ends of the green.

"They may have gone back to the hotel to put the bairns down for their nap."

"April could use a little nap herself. She hardly slept last night, she was so excited about the fair."

"I'm sure they'll return before the tossing of the caber and the other games."

"There's a horse race at three. I know April wanted to see it."

"A race?"

"It's been a tradition in Druidheachd since I was a boy and probably for a hundred years before." He pointed to the center of the green. "There's a ring of sorts there, pounded hard as stone by horse hooves. It's not exactly the Kentucky Derby, but it suffices."

"But it's a wee bittie green. There's no room for a race."

"No one's expectations are high. This is Druidheachd. Half the fun's the anticipation, the other half's the wagers.

No one cares if the horses have to go round and round to log any distance." He pulled her toward one of the stands where local crafts were displayed. "Look at this, you could have sold your wool or your herbs. Let's check out the competition for next year."

Her hand seemed to grow cooler as they walked, and she grew stiffer. She was silent as they perused the hand-knit sweaters and white pottery adorned with thistles and blooming heather.

"You're a braw pair, are you no'?" Andrew asked from behind Duncan.

Duncan faced his friend, his hand still entwined with Mara's. Andrew was dressed in full Highland regalia, from kilt and fur sporran to plaid pinned at his shoulder with a silver brooch. On his right stocking the traditional *sgian dubh*, a dirk in a sheath, peered over the top. He was a splendid sight with his auburn hair gleaming in the sunlight and his hazel eyes reflecting the dark green stripes of his tartan.

"I'd have run the other way, no questions asked," Duncan said. "I wouldn't have stayed to meet you in battle."

"No' to worry. We'd have been on the same side." Andrew extended his hand to Mara. "What do you think of our fair, Mara? Have you seen one to rival it anywhere?"

"Andrew has a natural career in advertising," Duncan said, "but I've never been able to convince him."

"And why would I want to sell things I dinna believe in to people I dinna even know?"

"Aye, why would he?" Mara asked. She smiled. It was a pale imitation of her usual, but it was an attempt.

"I don't think you told Andrew how you were enjoying the fair," Duncan said.

"It's a bonny wee fair."

Duncan watched Andrew search her face. "There's shade over in the corner. If Duncan does no' take you there to rest, I will."

"Mara?" Duncan asked. "Is he right? Do you need to sit down for a while?"

"Maybe a bit."

They started over toward a trio of chestnuts that shaded the grass in a wide circle. It was adorned with the bodies of young and old alike who were temporarily protecting their pale Scottish complexions.

"I was thinking of Fiona just a moment ago," Andrew said. "I mind a Johnsmas fair where we were lads and she was a bit of a thing."

"Fiona?" Mara asked.

"My sister," Duncan said.

"She was a canty wee lassie, all spirit and laughter. She leaped up on the stage and tried to dance the fling." Andrew fell silent.

"That was a long time ago," Duncan said.

"Aye."

Mara and Duncan settled themselves in a quiet spot, but with a wave Andrew wandered off toward the stage. He played in a pipe band that was scheduled to perform soon.

"Did something happen to your sister?" Mara asked.

He was so glad for a change of subject that he was even willing to discuss Fiona, a subject he usually avoided. "There was a fire at the hotel when she was just three. I was eight. I don't know if anyone ever really determined what caused it. A carpet too close to the fireplace; a spark that probably smoldered for hours until everyone was fast asleep. Unfortunately the fire started in the room that Fiona and I shared. I was away that night, staying with Iain and Andrew at Fearnshader. Fiona was alone in our room with our parents asleep in the next. Maybe if I'd been there I'd have woken up at the smell of smoke. But Fiona always slept deeply. By the time my father awoke to her screams and rushed in to rescue her, the draperies had caught fire and her bedcovers, too. If the hotel weren't solid stone, it might all have gone up."

Mara reached for his hand and covered it with hers. "How terrible to lose her that way."

He felt connected to Mara again; she was no longer a million miles away. "She didn't die, but we all lost her anyway, or we lost the person she would have been. Andrew's right. Fiona was all spirit and sass, and he and Iain loved her as much as I did. Her burns were serious, and for a while no one knew if she'd recover. I remember my parents fighting constantly for those weeks. My mother wanted to fly Fiona to America to a burn center there, as soon as she was stabilized, but my father wanted her to stay at the hospital in Glasgow. Finally my mother got her way. She was an American citizen, so there was no red tape. She and Fiona and I flew back to the States, and the two of them have never returned to Scotland. My father insisted that I come back for a month each summer, and my mother allowed him that small victory. But Fiona's never been back, not even for my father's funeral. He left her half the hotel, but she refuses to make any decisions about it. She's put me in charge."

"And where is she now?"

"She still lives in New York with my mother." He debated how much more to say. He had already bored her with the story of his marriage. But Mara seemed genuinely concerned, and Fiona's story seemed to have taken her mind off her own problems.

"She's never really grown up," he said. "She went through terrible pain, skin grafts and treatments all the years of her childhood. I'm sure that changed her, but the worst part was my mother. She smothered Fiona until there was almost nothing left of the little girl we'd all known. Mother felt so guilty about what had happened that she devoted her entire life to making things easy and safe. Now Fiona doesn't seem to be able to function without her."

"That's very sad."

"You want to hear the real irony? Fiona's writing children's books. She's been successful, because she's still a little girl at heart, a little girl who may never grow up."

Mara was silent for a while. "Did you ever think," she asked at last, "that what happened to Fiona might explain a bit about why you did no' interfere with the way that Lisa was raising April? Were you afraid you might turn out to be as overprotective and smothering as your mum?"

He hadn't thought about it. He had *never* thought about it, even though it seemed perfectly clear to him now. But he couldn't absolve himself of guilt that easily. "Even if it were true, it would hardly be an excuse, would it?"

"We're too old to need excuses, Duncan. But perhaps, if it is true, it might help explain something that obviously bothers you."

A month ago he would have been angry; a month ago he *had* been angry when he'd believed she was trying to analyze him. Now he leaned over and kissed her lightly on the lips. "You're always trying to get me off the hook, aren't you? You're determined to make me feel good about myself as a father."

"Is that so bad?"

She really wanted to know. He read her own questions in her eyes, questions deep inside her, formed by the life she'd been forced to live. "Nothing you could do would be bad, Mara." He was all too aware of a green filled to capacity with gossiping villagers, of her reputation and his, of customs and superstitions and centuries of Sinclair men who had probably sat at one time or another in this very spot with the women they loved. "Nothing."

He kissed her again, aware of everything, but most especially, of her.

She didn't know what would happen or to whom. She'd had no clear visions, no glimpses of the future. She just knew that something *was* going to happen, and soon.

Mara watched Duncan cheering for Andrew in the caber toss. The caber, nearly eighteen feet long and weighing more than a hundred pounds, was to be lifted and tossed so that it lay across the ground in front of the competitor like the hands of a clock at midnight. The crowd hushed in anticipation and Andrew hoisted it, ran the required steps and heaved it into a nearly perfect position.

The crowd roared. Duncan, who had swung April to his shoulders for a better look, strode over to congratulate his old friend. Mara saw a cluster of young women eyeing Andrew with longing. Andrew liked the ladies, and in turn they liked him twice as well.

Her vision swam for a moment, as it had on and off since midmorning. She felt suddenly clammy, and her head began to pound. The scene before her vanished; transposed over it was another that was much the same. She saw the village green and the people thronging it. The sun still shone—although it was lower in the sky—but even as she felt its rays warm her skin, she heard the roar of thunder. Horror gripped her. She struggled to move, but her limbs were weak and uncoordinated. She struggled—

"Mara?"

She felt a hand on her shoulder. She swallowed, then gasped for air. The vision dimmed, then disappeared. Duncan was beside her, and it was his hand she felt.

Heat flooded back into her body, but her head pounded harder.

"Mara, are you all right?"

She shook her head. She couldn't speak.

Duncan swung April off his shoulders and pointed her toward Sally, who was standing in a line at a nearby stand. "Sally's buying currant buns for you and the girls. Better go help, or little Fanny will eat them all before you get yours."

"Is Mara going to be all right?"

"Sure. She's just not used to the sunshine."

April patted Mara's hand, then she skipped off to find Sally.

"It's not the sun, is it?" Duncan asked when they were alone.

She shook her head.

"Do you want to tell me what's going on?"

"You would no' ken."

"You could try me."

She tried to focus on his face. Little by little her vision cleared until she could see every nuance of his expression.

And she realized she couldn't tell him. He was wary, already suspicious that her behavior had something to do with the second sight he didn't believe in. She could share herself with this man, share her feelings, even the story of her life before Druidheachd, but she couldn't share her visions. Because the visions would stand between them.

"I've a bad headache," she said.

"And I wouldn't understand that? I've never had one myself?"

"Duncan, dinna push me. I can only tell you what I can."

"Maybe you ought to go home. I'll drive you if you don't feel well enough. Or better yet, let's go back to the hotel. I'll put you to bed in my room. You can sleep this off, then we can have a nice supper together."

"No."

"No?"

"I have to stay here."

His tone grew sharper. "Why? You didn't even want to come in the first place."

She left him standing there with his questions and his suspicions. She started back toward the hotel stand, paying just the minimum attention to her surroundings. Somehow she had fooled herself into believing that she could keep her visions separate from her relationship with Duncan. She had almost believed that she could allow him into her life and her heart.

But they could not be separate.

"Mara!" She felt a hand on her arm, and she was jerked unceremoniously out of the path of a sturdy chestnut mare.

"Iain." She put her hand to her throat. Her pulse beat wildly beneath her own fingers.

"You were about to get trampled. You certainly weren't watching where you were going. Are you all right?"

"I seem to have all my body parts intact. Thank you."

He was dressed much as Andrew except that he wore a white shirt with his black-and-red kilt and a black velvet jacket instead of a plaid across his shoulder. He grimaced as she surveyed him. "It's expected," he said. "The laird of Druidheachd always shows up in his kilt."

"And you dinna like it?" She certainly liked what *she* saw, and she knew that the other women at the fair would, too.

"I don't mind the kilt. I mind being the laird who has to show up."

He walked beside her, still holding her arm. Two more horses trotted by. She saw them clearly now, and she stayed out of their way. "You were deep in thought," he said.

"Aye."

"Trouble, Mara?"

"I came here to find peace, Iain, but there's no peace to be found."

"There might be a message in that."

"What do you mean?"

"Maybe peace isn't what you need." He squeezed her arm before he dropped his hand. With a wave he disappeared into the crowd gathering to watch the horse race.

She was torn about what to do. She had only rarely felt this lost. She wanted to go home, to her mountain and her cottage. She wanted the solace of a peat fire and Guiser lying contentedly at her feet. But she had to stay.

She felt warm arms come around her. She knew they belonged to Duncan. She shut her eyes and leaned against him. And despite everything else she felt, she no longer felt lost.

"Don't run away from me again, Mara," he murmured close to her ear. "Maybe I don't understand everything, and maybe I don't even want to. But don't run away. Let's see if we can find some compromises."

She covered his hands with hers in answer.

"Come on. Let's go watch the race."

She let him lead her to the edge of the crowd. The oval where the horses were to race was large enough that there were enough places along their route so that everyone could see. Posts had been set up and ropes marked the boundary so that no one would stray onto the course. The horses waited at a makeshift gateway. There were only three of them, the chestnut that had nearly trampled her, a heavyset white gelding that looked as if it belonged behind a plow, and a bay that danced nervously from side to side each time a bugler summoned the crowd to the race.

"I've got a pound on the chestnut," Duncan said. "Iain wants the white and Andrew the bay. What'll you take?"

"I've no talent for this," she said too sharply.

He ignored her tone and its implications. "Well, which one looks like a winner to you?"

"I'll take the chestnut, too."

"Good girl. You can pick a winner."

She tried to smile, but her face felt frozen. The pain in her head was nearly unendurable; she knew that worse was coming.

She could hear Duncan making soothing conversation; she could hear her own polite responses. The bugler finished and the horses came through the gateway to line up beside each other.

"They go around five times, I think," Duncan said. "I'll bet the white doesn't even go four."

Someone fired a shot into the air and the horses were off. They streaked by, their hooves pounding the earth just in front of her. Mara closed her eyes, but she could still see them. The chestnut was out in front, the white in second, and the bay, who was tightly reined in by its rider, was a close third. The rider would keep the horse in check until nearly the end of the race. Until...

The horses thundered by again, but Mara barely heard them. She opened her eyes but it wasn't the present she saw. She saw the fifth and final lap, and as she watched, the bay's rider gave the horse its head. But instead of surging forward, the horse jerked to one side, and before its rider could compensate, the horse plunged into the crowd.

Exactly into the spot fifty yards from where Mara stood. The spot where two little boys stood beside their mother, who was holding high a chubby, laughing toddler, so that she could see the race.

She jerked away from Duncan and began to push her way through the crowd. The horses were on their fourth lap now, at least she thought they were. Time was confused and confusing. It stood still and sped forward in the same instant. There was no time. She was alone in a timeless void, and she had to reach the children.

She pushed harder, ignoring the disgruntled noises of those she trampled. The crowd was dense here, too dense to easily pass through. She made a path for herself with both hands, concentrating only on what lay ahead.

She could hear the horses rounding the bend, although she didn't have time to spare a glance. She was only ten yards from her goal, ten impossible yards.

"Please, let me through!" She pushed, and at last the crowd parted. She launched herself forward. The children were almost within reach. She could see their faces, eyes huge and glowing with the excitement of the race.

She saw those same eyes, sightless eyes staring from a wooden kist in the old stone kirk across the green. "Let me through!"

She made a final push and grabbed the closest boy by his collar, flinging him with nearly superhuman strength into the crowd behind her. The second boy screamed in protest as she grabbed him and flung him after his brother. Their mother whirled, shock, then fury written across every feature. She lunged at Mara, and Mara circled her with her arms. She could feel the baby between them, still safely cocooned against her mother. She launched herself backward, taking them both with her. Pain shot through her arm as she fell, and her head exploded into a million shards of light as it hit the ground.

She blacked out just as the bay broke through the ring and charged into the empty space where a mother and three small children had just been standing.

Chapter 10

There was a moment as Mara fell when she cried out silently against fate. She felt no regret for trying to save the children, but she knew as she heard the thunder of horses' hooves closing in on her that her vision had come too late. She had not been warned in time. She had not thrown the boys completely clear and she had not protected their mother and the baby. She had been taunted with their fate, but she had not been given the strength or time to prevent it.

How much better not to have known.

As fireworks exploded in her head, then darkness closed around her, she felt an agony that surpassed physical pain. She had battled fate and lost, and in the process she had lost Duncan, too.

"Mara."

Pain shattered the darkness, and she tried to retreat, but a man's voice called her name once more. "Mara. Wake up. Mara, can you hear me?"

She tried to retreat further. She lay very still and willed the voice to go away.

"What I dinna understand is how she knew the horse would bolt," a different voice said.

"Why does that matter now?" the first replied.

"It does no' matter, it's just a subject of some interest in the village."

"Damn it, Angus, the only thing I'm interested in right now is if she's going to be all right!"

"You're a man who will no' take telling, are you no'? I've told you she's going to be fine. I've told you more than once. It's a nasty bump, but I've seen nastier."

"We're talking about a brain here. She hit the ground hard, and it's been over an hour. She still hasn't come to!"

"She's waking up now. After nearly fifty years I know the signs. Her head will ache for days, and she may be a wee disoriented. But her arm will give her more trouble than her head. She'll be in a sling for weeks at the very least. She'll no' be milking cows or doing chores."

"I don't care about her cows! Her cows can be damned. It's Mara I'm worried about."

"Listen to me, Duncan Sinclair, Jeanne whacked your wee bottom nearly thirty years ago in this very room, and now I'll do it myself if I must. Stand back and give the lass room. She'll no' come round a' tall with you breathing all her air."

Putting the men's words together in some sort of logical order made Mara's head hurt worse, but she struggled to make sense of their conversation.

A woman's voice sounded from faraway. "Angus, the lads are all patched and ready. The bittiest one's climbing the walls, and I can nae contain him any longer."

"Let me check them over again, Jeanne. Then they can go."

"And nae a moment too soon!"

Mara felt someone take her hand. "I'll call you if she wakes up, or if there's any change."

"Then you'll be calling me soon. She's awake now. She just does no' want to be." Mara heard a door slam.

"Mara, is that true? If you're awake, will you please open your eyes and let me see for myself? For God's sake, I can't tell if this old quack knows what he's talking about or not."

Everything was clearer now. Mara willed it to be even clearer. She opened her eyes and saw gray. Gray stone, gray light, the grayish pallor of Duncan Sinclair's face. Her eyes closed.

"Mara." Duncan's voice was close to her ear. She could feel the warmth of his breath against her cheek. "Do you know where you are? You're at the hospital in Drui-dheachd. You've been here about an hour."

"The . . . children?"

"They're fine. A few scratches, that's all. Their mother's all right, too. You got her out of the way just in time. The horse was so close it caught the heel of her shoe when it plunged past, but she wasn't touched. The baby just had the wind knocked out of her when all of you fell."

Mara didn't know if she dared to believe him. Then, from somewhere in the distance, she could hear the whooping of children's voices, and she knew he was telling the truth. She began to cry.

"Don't cry. Mara, don't. Please. For God's sake, don't cry."

She cried anyway. She could feel his fingers stroking away her tears. They trembled against her cheek. "I thought . . ." She couldn't form the words.

"You thought you were too late? You weren't. You got there just in time."

"So I was right. She's awake." The door slammed once more.

Mara opened her eyes again. Old Dr. Sutherland swam into view. "Aye."

"Well, it's no' every day I treat a heroine, lass. I'm honored to have the good fortune today." He came over to stand beside the bed. He lifted her wrist and felt for her pulse. "You had a bad bashing, and your head will ache for a while yet. But it's your arm that'll give you the most trouble."

Their earlier conversation was beginning to make sense to her now. "Arm?"

"Your right arm. You did no' break it, but it's a nasty sprain. We'll have to keep it immobilized for a while. You can no' do a thing except have the good grace to accept it."

She attempted to move the arm in question and discovered it was tightly bound against her chest. Panic began to fill her. "I can no' manage without my arm. I can no' keep it in a sling."

"You've no choice. It'll be too painful to use, even if I allowed it, and I will no'." He dropped her wrist. "Mara, there's a question I'd like you to answer, if you're able. How did you know, lass, that the horse was about to break through the ropes?"

The panic spread. She was vulnerable in a way she had never been before. Her arm was bound to her side; her head pounded as if the crew of the Royal Scotsman was trying to lay new track through her brain. She was surrounded by people who were suspicious of her, who thought her a ghost or a witch, and there was no place more remote that she could run to. She was trapped. Her throat closed around the truth that might have her drummed from the village. She couldn't speak.

"Damn it, Angus, she didn't know," Duncan said. "She was trying to get a better view, that's all. We were watching the race together and Mara told me she couldn't see from where we were standing. So she headed for a free space at the rope. The horse bolted just as she got there. She was so close she saw instantly what was happening, and she grabbed the kids and their mother. It wasn't anything more mysterious than that. Don't tell me all these rumors about Greensleeves are getting to you, too."

Angus was silent. "Where do you want to go, lass?" he asked at last. "You'll have to stay here tonight, and maybe tomorrow. But after that you can no' go back to your cottage alone. Someone has to look after you while you recover. Shall I make arrangements with someone in town to take you in as a boarder for a week or two?"

"She's coming home with me," Duncan said, before Mara could answer. "She's coming home with me if I have to carry her like a sack of oats down High Street and tie her to my bed."

"Now that would be a muckle show," Angus said. "There'd be no more rumors about witches and ghosties, I'm thinking. The rumors would be far more interesting." He patted Mara's good hand, and laid it gently on the bed. The door closed behind him.

"Duncan..."

"Hush, Mara. You're coming home with me."

"Duncan, I did no' tell you I was going to the rope...to get a better view."

"Hush. Save your strength. All you have to worry about now is getting better."

"Duncan..." Tears filled her eyes and frustration, her heart.

He smoothed her hair back from her forehead. "I know, Mara," he said softly. "I know. Just close your eyes and rest. You did a good thing today, a wonderful thing. No matter how it happened, you saved those children. Just close your eyes and rest now."

"My sheep... And my cows need milking."

"Jessie and Roger will see to everything. They've already promised me. Please, just rest so I can take you home tomorrow."

His hand was so soothing. Her eyelids drifted shut. Pain continued to pound through her head, but it was growing more bearable.

"When I fell," she said softly, "I thought..."

"What? What did you think?"

"I thought I'd lost you."

His hand paused. Then she felt his lips against her forehead. "You haven't lost me," he said. "Now rest. But don't fall asleep. We're going to have to watch you carefully for a while. What would you like me to talk about to keep you awake?"

"Tell me...about growing up in Druidheachd."

Duncan chose a room for Mara on the wing where his apartment was located. He had rejected one with a view of the green—because of obvious reminders—and chosen another with a view of a small enclosed garden where guests sometimes took tea. Jessie's husband, Roger, the hotel gardener and handyman, tended the flowers with a loving hand, and fragrant stock and bright-eyed daisies bloomed in profusion under Mara's window, along with the early roses.

Duncan filled Mara's room with the choicest blossoms and asked the maids to take special care with cleaning and airing it before she arrived. April donated her favorite doll and a lace-edged pillow embroidered with teddy bears and rainbows. By the time Dr. Sutherland was ready to release Mara, they were more than ready for her.

"Now don't forget, Springtime, you can't jump on Mara when she gets here. You have to be quiet when you're around her. She bumped her head pretty bad, and it still hurts."

"She'll be glad to see me," April said, with a serious face.

"I'm sure you're right. But you still can't jump on her."

"Lolly says Mara's a ghost."

"Lolly's wrong."

"You can see through ghosts, can't you?"

"There are no ghosts." He kissed the top of her head and sent her on her way.

He could walk to the cottage hospital in minutes, but he took the hotel's minibus instead because Mara certainly wasn't going to feel like walking back. She was doing much better, completely out of danger now, but she was still pale and in a good deal of pain. She'd made light of it when he'd visited early that morning, but he had seen the pain's effects.

This afternoon she looked tired but pleased to be leaving the hospital. She was sitting in a chair beside a window, dressed and ready. "Duncan." She rose to meet him.

"Now, you're sure you feel well enough to go?"

"Please get me out of here."

He frowned. "What's wrong? Haven't they been good to you?"

"Oh aye, the care's been wonderful." She bent and picked up the small suitcase that Frances had packed for her. "But may we go now?"

Hospitals, even cottage hospitals in scenic Highlands towns, were not places where anyone might want to linger. But Duncan was mystified at her hurry. Mara said her goodbyes to the staff and even accepted a hug from Jeanne Sutherland before they stepped out into the fresh air. She seemed to relax visibly as they walked toward the parking lot.

"Did you know that Jeanne and Angus were married about six months after I was born?" Duncan asked. "They claim that delivering the wee laddies of midnight brought them together."

"They're both past seventy, are they no'? But Jeanne says Dr. Sutherland will no' give up the hospital."

"The new doctor does most of the work, but Angus keeps an eye on him. He wouldn't be happy if he had to leave it all behind."

"There's been much sadness there."

"Where? The hospital?"

She didn't respond.

"Is that why you were in a hurry to go? You found it depressing?"

"It would be hard to explain."

"You could try."

"And I could no'."

He took her arm to guide her to the minibus. He didn't say anything until they were on the road. "Did you sense things there that you found disturbing?"

"Does it matter what I say, Duncan? Are you saying you'd believe me?"

He was silent until he pulled into a space behind the hotel. "I don't know what I believe," he said, as he turned off the engine. "But I'll tell you what I don't. I don't believe you're crazy. And I don't believe you're making any of this up. You saved lives at the Johnsmas fair because you sensed something that the rest of us were completely oblivious to. I'd be the crazy one if I didn't acknowledge that much. So, if you tell me the hospital was a hard place to be because you were picking up vibes or having visions, or whatever it is you do, then I'll believe you. I won't understand it, but I'll believe you."

"Duncan . . ."

He cupped her chin and turned her face to his. Her eyes were moist with tears. "I believe *in* you," he said.

He didn't add that he was beginning to believe in them. Them together. Them in each other's arms. Them giving and taking pleasure. He had begun to believe the moment that he found he hadn't lost her forever.

He touched her lips with his thumb, lightly brushing it back and forth. "And now I'd better get you inside, so April can see for herself that you're okay."

She smiled. Something very much like hope bloomed in her eyes. He felt it deep inside him.

Mara had never been idle, not in her entire life. She let Duncan, Frances and April fuss over her for exactly two hours, then as soon as they left her to rest, she began to prowl the hotel.

She immediately found the room where Duncan's sister had been burned. She couldn't see the past clearly—not nearly as clearly as her occasional glimpses of the future—but she could sense residues of deep sadness. True tragedy resonated for centuries in the places where it had occurred, and the more tragic the event, the more deeply she could experience it.

Her room at the cottage hospital had oppressed her almost beyond endurance. At first she had tried to screen out her impressions. She'd told herself that certainly people had died there, but death was as natural as life and no reason to make her feel distraught. Still, she had slept little, and by the end of her stay she could no longer block her own misery. Something sadder than death had occurred in the very bed where she slept, something within recent memory but not something that either Jeanne or Angus Sutherland had witnessed.

She had been almost hysterically grateful to be discharged.

Her impressions about the room where Fiona had been burned were much clearer. She sensed fear and terrible pain when she stood at the door—thrown wide open so that Sally could clean it later—and when she stepped over the threshold, she could almost hear the screams of a child. She turned and came face-to-face with Duncan.

"You're supposed to be in bed," he said.

"I've been in bed much too long already." But even as she said it, she knew he was right. She was suddenly exhausted.

"Why'd you end up here?"

"I was just exploring."

"This was my room as a child."

"I know."

He cocked his head in question. She shrugged in answer.

"Shall I escort you back to bed?"

"Aye." She was stiff with tension. She could still hear a child crying.

He frowned. "Shall I carry you?"

"Of course no'!" She hadn't finished speaking before he swept her off her feet and started down the hall. "Duncan, we'll be the talk of the village. Put me down!"

"Don't be silly. We're the talk of the village anyway."

The feelings vanished as they moved away from the room. "You've a wee daughter who'll wonder what's wrong if she sees this!"

"My wee daughter is at Jessie's house playing with Lolly."

Duncan turned down the corridor where Mara's room was located. He pushed her door open with his knee and strode to her bed. He bent and laid her carefully on the coverlet, protecting her arm as he did. He didn't straighten. Instead, in the blink of an eye he was lying beside her.

She stared at him. "The door's open."

He said a few choice words that spanned the gap in slang from Scotland to the U.S. But he didn't rise to shut it.

"I'll be known as a fallen woman," she warned.

"That might be an improvement."

She laughed. Her good arm curled around his neck. His face was only inches from hers. "Is this why you volunteered to have me here, Duncan? So you could have your way with me anytime you pleased?"

"You mean it would be that easy?"

"You could try it and see."

His eyes darkened. "I don't know if I could live with the disappointment if you said no."

"And if I said yes?"

"I don't know if I could live with the joy."

"Then I suppose you'll be forced to live with indecision."

He laughed, a low, sexy rumble that seemed to vibrate between them. "I know my decision. Do you know yours?"

In an instant they were no longer teasing. Mara could feel Duncan's response to having her so close. He was a leopard ready to spring. If they were truly alone and naked, skin-to-skin, he would be ready to sink deeply inside her. And the pleasure would be unbearable.

"I want you, Duncan," she said. "I want you when the moment is right and we can no' be interrupted. I want you no matter how it turns out, because someday when I'm an old woman, I'd like to know that this once in my life I reached out for what mattered to me."

"Mara..." She felt the pressure and warmth of his lips. She felt the strength of his body pressing her against the mattress. His hand crept to her breast. She could feel the imprint of his fingers through her dress and wild pleasure streaking through her body.

She was only dimly aware of noise in the hallway, but Duncan pulled away abruptly. In a moment he was on his feet staring down at her. "When the moment's right," he said in a low voice. "And damn it, it's not right now." He lifted her hand to his lips. "Get some rest, Mara. Sleep, and when you're well, we'll find the right moment and the right place. And I'll be there when you reach for me."

By the end of the day Mara knew she would go mad lying about for a week or two and watching the world go by without her. She prided herself on her independence, and the forced inactivity gave her too much time to think. After Duncan had deposited her back in her room again she had counted all the reasons why they could never have a future together, and she had allowed herself the luxury of sadness. Then she had begun on the lives of others, sifting through the impressions that came her way as they passed in the hall. By supper, she knew that something had to be done.

She dressed with difficulty. The slightest movement made her arm and head throb, and she couldn't will the pain away. She had no choice but to keep the arm completely immobile and to move like a tortoise mired in treacle. By the time she had changed she was frustrated, exhausted, and all fantasies of returning immediately to her cottage had vanished. But something still had to be done.

Something presented itself when she started toward the dining room to wait for Duncan and April at their special table. She found a frustrated Duncan standing in front of the reception desk along with Nancy, the thoroughly intimidated young woman who womanned it.

Mara caught most of their conversation as she approached.

"It's sorry I am, Mr. Sinclair. Truly 'tis. But what can I do? My granny's sick, and there's no one to leave the babies with in the afternoon. No one a' tall. And my Harry won't be back from London for a fortnight, so there's no hope he'll be able to help until Granny's better."

"I understand, Nancy. I just don't know what I can do about it. With three of the maids leaving on holiday we're short staffed as it is and we've got twice as many guests as we had last month. I can't spare anyone from their usual jobs to take your place. I'm sorry, but I may have to hire someone to replace you."

Nancy looked as if she were going to cry. She was a plump woman in her late twenties with a sweet face that didn't take well to tears. "I know. I'd do anything I could to stop that from happening, but what can I do? My babies have to come first."

"I'd be the first to agree with you."

Mara stepped forward. "I'm sorry, but do you mind if I ask what's wrong?"

Nancy looked too choked up to speak, and she edged away subtly as Mara moved closer. Duncan shook his head in frustration. "Just the usual joys of being an innkeeper. Nancy's going to have to take afternoons off for a while, and I don't have anyone to replace her with."

"But you do. I can do it."

"Mara, you're here to rest and recover, not to work."

Nancy found her tongue. "But it's no' hard work, Mr. Sinclair. I could take care of all the paperwork in the mornings. I'd have time aplenty. Miss MacTavish would only have to answer the telephone and speak with the guests."

"It would give me something to do, Duncan." Mara saw she wasn't reaching him. He was as stubborn a man as any she'd ever met. "It's either work here or go back to my cottage," she said firmly. "And as weak as I am, the cottage seems very faraway."

He narrowed his eyes. "I'll think about it."

Nancy tossed away caution; she grabbed Mara's hand and squeezed it. "It's true what I've heard about you," she said.

"And what's that?"

"That you probably dinna wish any of us harm."

Duncan glowered at Nancy, but Mara touched his arm to keep him silent. "Thank you, Nancy."

Nancy beamed. She took off for the reception desk, sensing, Mara imagined, that she should leave before Duncan had a chance to add his own comments.

"Well, it's nice to know that no' everybody thinks I'm the devil's tool," Mara said.

"Why on earth did you volunteer to help? Nancy's not your problem, and neither is the hotel."

"I did it for myself. I've got to have something to do, or I'll be as daft as a sheep in a shearing pen before I'm all healed. This is something I can do with one good arm." She saw indecision in his eyes, but she knew how to get around it. She smiled and stepped closer. "And dinna you ken? It will put me in the public eye. Maybe everyone who comes through the hotel will see that I'm just flesh and blood and relatively harmless.''

"Unless you start saving lives in the lobby."

"You're going to let me do it, are you no'?"

"There's nothing I'd refuse you."

Her smile broadened. "I'll hold you to that, Duncan. I will most decidedly hold you to that."

Chapter 11

Sometimes it seemed to Mara that in the two weeks that she had been at the reception desk the entire village had paraded through the hotel lobby. She kept a private collection of her favorite excuses. Some were almost reasonable, others so far-fetched that April would have been able to see right through them. One man sat on a sofa just in front of her day after day and claimed when asked that he just wanted to see if Duncan was maintaining the same high standards as the Sinclairs before him. A woman was curious as to whether the lobby furniture had been rearranged recently—she checked every afternoon at four. Still another woman asked—unsuccessfully—for the guest book to determine if her neighbor to one side was using the hotel for trysts with her neighbor to the other.

Mara responded politely to all of them. She allowed herself to be examined and judged, and she didn't flinch from questions. By the time she was nearly ready to return to her own cottage, she realized that she was going to miss the hotel. She had begun to make friends, a benefit she hadn't expected. Some of the same people who had come to investigate had stayed on for the duration. The couch-sitter now brought flowers from his garden every morning, and the furniture arranger had agreed to Mara's suggestion that together they draw up a new plan for the lobby that would facilitate the flow of traffic while at the same time provide cozy seating groups.

There were others, as well. The woman who delivered fresh sheets each day had a son in Dublin and loved to talk about her visits there. The greengrocer sought out Mara every afternoon to discover whether she had been pleased at supper on the previous night with whatever fruits or vegetables she'd selected from the menu. Most touching of all, Sarah MacDaniels and her children—whose lives Mara had probably saved—had come in at the end of the first week with a basket of fresh blackberries and a promise of a winter's supply of jam.

"How did you know about that horse, Miss?" Sarah had asked as she and the children were leaving. "Just how did you know?"

Mara shook her head. She couldn't make up a story for Sarah. Of all people she deserved to know the truth. "I wish I could tell you, but I can no'. I just did." She smiled warmly. "Have you no' had that happen yourself, Sarah? Have you no' felt something deep inside you, then watched it come true?"

Sarah nodded. "Aye. Once I woke up from a sound sleep and got out of bed for no reason to check on my weans. Something told me to do it. My oldest had a high fever, even though he'd been well before bedtime. I dinna know what would have happened if I had no' awakened."

"Then you understand."

"But no' everyone would."

"Which is why I keep the truth to myself."

Sarah nodded again. "And why I'll keep it to myself as well."

There had been other benefits, too. April to play with and read to and cuddle. Hot water and indoor plumbing, a view of a garden she didn't have to work herself, meals prepared by Frances Gunn, the finest cook in the village.

And Duncan.

Mara had wondered at the beginning how it would be to have Duncan so close at hand. At first Robbie had found her fascinating, too. Her second sight had been as attractive to him as her trim body and long golden hair. But after they had married, Robbie's enchantment had ended abruptly. The reality of living with her visions had eclipsed the novelty.

She was not married to Duncan. He had never been awakened in the middle of a night by a wife trembling and crying from nightmares of things to come. He had never been asked to leave a party because she was overwhelmed with impressions and had to retreat. He had never been forced to purchase the quietest house on the quietest street, never given up a holiday in bustling Rome for one at a lonely seaside villa, never abandoned the idea of having children because he couldn't bear the possibility of passing on her handicap to future generations.

Duncan had never had any of those experiences. But in her two weeks at the hotel, he'd had others. He had been there when she'd realized that Mrs. Robbins, a warm, witty pensioner who came to the hotel each Wednesday and Saturday for tea, would not last out the year. He had learned to tell when she was becoming engulfed in images, and he'd learned to help her avoid those times. He found quiet places for her to retreat and often went with her. He drove her up to her cottage every night so that she could see for herself that all was well.

And he had yet to ask anything of her that she couldn't give him.

That changed on what was to be her last Friday afternoon at the hotel. Her arm was out of the sling now, although it was still tender. She had begun to exercise it more, and it promised to be good as new eventually. She still had headaches occasionally, but the severity had decreased. Best of all, her recovery had coincided with the return of Nancy's husband from London, and next week Nancy would be ready to take back her afternoon shift.

"I'll just be going," Nancy said, when Mara came to relieve her after the midday meal. "But before I do, you should know something.'' She lowered her voice. She and Mara were coconspirators now. Over the weeks Nancy's feelings had progressed from hesitant gratitude to outright affection. ''April's mum called this morning. She tried to get me to put her through to April, but, of course, I did no'. I've strict instructions to put her through to Mr. Sinclair when she calls.''

Mara knew about those instructions. Nancy had warned her repeatedly the morning she'd trained Mara to take her place.

''She'll be phoning back,'' Nancy continued. ''Mr. Sinclair was out when she phoned the first time. And when she hears a different voice at the desk, she'll ask you to put her through to April. I likely can guarantee it.''

Mara felt suddenly chilled. ''Thank you for the warning.''

Nancy chattered on. Her granny was better. Mara should come over some evening to meet her Harry now that he was back. Did Mara think that Mr. Sinclair was going to let her rearrange the lobby furniture?

Mara made all the correct responses, but her mind remained on Lisa. After Nancy had gone, she settled herself at the desk and finished the paperwork that Nancy hadn't gotten to, but her distress increased. And when the telephone rang at half past two, she knew who was waiting impatiently across the Atlantic.

She picked up the receiver. ''This is the Sinclair Hotel. How may I help you?''

There was a slight pause. ''Excuse me? Did you say this *is* the Sinclair Hotel.''

''That's correct. May I be of service?''

''Umm ... Yes. I'd like to speak with April Sinclair, if she's there. This is ... a friend of the family's. From the United States.''

Mara knew that Duncan was back. She had eaten dinner with him at noon. They had exchanged a few hurried kisses in a dark hallway and promises of more. Now he was in his office, and April was playing with Primrose in the garden outside Mara's room.

"Hello?" Lisa sounded puzzled that there had been no reply.

"I'll connect you. It might take a moment. She's outside. Please dinna hang up."

"Oh, I won't. I promise I won't!"

Tears filled Mara's eyes, but she didn't know exactly whom they were for. She put the call on hold, then started down the hallway closest to the garden and her room. She beckoned April inside and when the little girl came in, she unlocked her own door. "There's a call for you. Somebody I know you'll want to talk to. Take it in here, April," Mara said. "Just hang it up when you're done. Then come and find me. I'll be at the front desk."

Dread had replaced tears by the time that April ran through the lobby. Mara held out her arms, and April leaped into them. Mara held the little girl tightly against her.

"That was my mommy!"

"I know, dearest."

"She wanted to talk to *me!*"

"Of course she did."

"She says she misses me."

"Of course she does." Mara rocked back and forth in her chair. "I'm certain she misses you very, very much."

"She wanted to know about school and my friends and my room. She wanted to know everything!"

"And did you tell her everything?"

"I told her about Primrose and Uncle Andrew and Iain, and about the dead toad we found in the garden."

"The important things."

"And I told her about you."

Mara went very still. "Did you, April?"

"She said she thought you were nice, too, for letting her talk to me. What did she mean?"

"I suppose she was just glad that I did no' mind going outside to look for you."

"Oh." April was already beginning to sober a little. "Daddy doesn't know I talked to Mommy... Lisa. Does he?"

"No, I dinna think he does."

"Are you going to tell him?"

Mara had been asking herself the same question. The answer had to be yes. But when and how were different matters. "Would you like to be the one to tell him?" she asked.

April frowned. She didn't answer.

"I can tell him if you'd rather."

The frown began to fade. April's phone call had been too wonderful and too important to let anything spoil it. "Do you think she might come to see me? Do you think Mommy might come?"

She would come. Mara knew it as surely as she had ever known anything. Lisa would come, and she would bring pain and turmoil with her. Mara hugged April, then set her firmly on the floor. "What I'm thinking right now is that a certain wee puppy might just take it in his head to run out in the road if you dinna go find him."

April ran off in search of Primrose. The lobby was silent. For once no one was watching. Mara put her head in her hands and closed her eyes.

Duncan waited for Mara to walk through the door of his apartment. He had been moved to cook supper for her himself, as moved by the fact that April was going to Lolly's for a sleep over as by his desire for pasta—which Frances rarely served in the dining room.

He had steamed and marinated vegetables overnight to serve over fettuccine, and he had chilled a bottle of vintage French Chablis, purchased on his last trip to Fort William. Frances had sent up a loaf of her best oat bread; he'd made a salad of local lettuce and glasshouse tomatoes. There were two servings of the hotel's special trifle in glass bowls in his refrigerator and fresh, thick cream to serve over it.

And there was dark roast coffee to savor after everything else had been eaten. If he and Mara were thinking about coffee right about then.

Having Mara at the hotel for two weeks, within reach at all times, had been torture. He had walked around in a perpetual state of temptation. He had told himself again and again that Mara was still wary, that she had been hurt too deeply to take sex lightly, that she was still physically weakened and emotionally vulnerable.

And each time he'd seen her, he'd wanted to take her to his bed and explore every secret of her mind and body... particularly her body.

Familiarity hadn't bred contempt; rather it had bred desire, and along with it, respect and admiration. Mara had faced up to the problem of her reputation in Druidheachd, and she had held her head high, enchanting and charming a fair number of the locals along the way. Duncan was enchanted and charmed himself. He couldn't sleep at night without dreaming of her. He couldn't walk through the hotel halls without hoping he would run into her. He couldn't work at his desk without seeing her face on the papers in front of him or hearing the musical cadences of her voice on each breeze that drifted through his window.

Tonight there were no breezes, but a bracing wind that announced a storm was to follow. He had almost adjusted to the cold Scottish climate again, to penetrating mists and smirr, the fine rain that was a step beyond fog. He had learned to look forward to lengthy summer nights and iridescent clouds that adorned the blue noonday skies, to spectacular views of distant treeless peaks and an unpolluted loch one brief stroll away.

He didn't want to live in Druidheachd, and he didn't know how that might affect his growing desire for Mara. But for now he was happier than he had ever expected to be.

The wind carried April inside with it. She had been outside most of the day, and her cheeks were as pink as Primrose's ridiculous lolling tongue. The puppy squealed happily—Duncan was resigned to the fact that Primrose would never learn to bark—and skidded across the floor to his water dish where he landed headfirst with a splash and another squeal. Duncan, experienced by now, already had a dishrag in hand.

"It's going to rain, rain, rain." April danced in circles. "Rain, rain, rain..."

Duncan rose after setting Primrose back on all fours and mopping the water. "Let me guess. You think it's going to rain."

April tackled him, wrapping her arms around his hips. He stroked her hair. "Did you see Mara downstairs?" he asked.

"She's coming. Coming, coming, coming."

"Let me guess. You think she's coming."

"Daddy is silly. Daddy is silly!" She began to dance around the floor again. He couldn't remember seeing her so happy. She was growing into the little girl he had never expected to see but for whom he had wished desperately. At the moment she wasn't worried about anything. She had nothing to do except be herself.

For the first time he wondered if perhaps someday he might be forgiven for being a bad father after all.

There was a soft knock on his door, a tentative knock. He crossed the room and threw it open. Mara's expression was serious. She assessed him, and he had the strangest feeling that she wasn't sure if she was satisfied with what she saw. "Shall I come in?"

"No. I thought I'd serve you supper in the hallway tonight." He grasped her arm and pulled her inside. "Welcome to the madhouse. April and Primrose are competing to see who's crazier."

April tackled Mara, then she grabbed her father, too. They were cocooned together in one little girl hug. Duncan could see a faint sprinkle of freckles across Mara's nose. He was close enough to kiss them and just disciplined enough to resist.

Instead, he lifted April off her feet and swung her to his hip. She was almost too large now to be held that way; she was definitely growing up. "Look, Springtime, you've got to get yourself together. Jessie's going to be up in a few minutes to pick you up for the sleep over."

"I'm all ready." She clasped his neck in a death grip. "Ready, ready, ready!"

"I think she's ready," he told Mara.

"And excited about it," Mara said.

"Is that why you're so silly tonight?" he asked. He tickled her, and she giggled and kicked to get down.

"I had a wonderful day," she said. She began to dance around the room again.

"Did you? I'd say all that fresh air and sunshine agrees with you. Or was it the walk over to Cameron's for ice cream?"

"No. 'Cause I got to talk to Mommy." She stopped spinning.

For a moment Duncan didn't register what she'd said. He was busy watching Mara. It was the change in her expression that brought him to attention. "What did you say, April?"

April stood very still now. "I got to talk to Mommy." She looked up at Mara, as if asking for help.

"Mrs. Sinclair called this afternoon and I put her through to April," Mara said. "They had a nice chat, did you no', dearest?"

"She misses me," April said. "Just like I miss her." She still didn't look at her father. "I told her everything."

"Did you know who was calling?" Duncan asked Mara. He kept his voice neutral, but it took considerable effort.

"Aye, I knew."

There was nothing he could say that could be said in front of April. He gazed out the window until he could control his tongue. "Did you remember to pack your toothbrush, Springtime? And how about your seal?"

"My seal and my lamb." April relaxed again and beamed at Mara. The lamb had been a birthday gift, lovingly sewn by Mara from scraps of her own fleeces.

"And how about Primrose?" Mara asked. "Did you pack him, too?"

"Silly! He has to stay here." April wrapped her arms around Mara's waist. "Can I pack you?"

"Will I fit?"

April's giggle was interrupted by a knock. Duncan opened the door and ushered Jessie and Lolly inside. There was a flurry of greetings, followed by a flurry of goodbyes.

Finally he and Mara were alone, and the apartment was as silent as suspicion.

He crossed the room and poured himself a whiskey. He kept his back to her. "May I get you a drink?" His voice froze the air between them.

"I dinna think so. I dinna drink with anyone who is angry with me."

"Angry is a pale word for what I'm feeling."

"Then tell me what you're feeling, Duncan, and let's have it on the table. Dinna pretend that nowt's happened."

He faced her. "You let my daughter talk to her mother. I put an ocean between Lisa and April. I put thousands of miles between us. I'm living in the most godforsaken part of a godforsaken country just so Lisa can't have any interaction with April! And you let April talk to her!"

"Aye."

He slammed the glass down. Whiskey sloshed over the rim. "Who do you think you are? It's my decision if and when Lisa ever gets to talk to April! Goddamn it, I paid enough to have the right to make that decision, didn't I? And then you come along, with your bleeding heart and your conviction that you know what's best for everyone, and you take that decision out of my hands! And I'm the one who has to live with it! I'm the one who has to watch that woman ruin my daughter's life again!"

"You're right, of course. I had no right. But I'd do it again, Duncan. Because you're right about something else. Lisa is ruining April's life. But no' in the way that you think. She's ruining it by no' being part of it."

He covered the distance between them, towering over her. He wanted to shake her. He wanted to grab her shoulders and shake her until the rage inside him subsided even a little.

But he didn't touch her. He had never touched anyone in anger, and even this, even this betrayal would not alter that.

"You weren't there," he said softly. "You weren't there when I unlocked a bedroom door and found my child, *my* little girl, huddled in a corner screaming her heart out. There wasn't even a light on in that room, Mara. Lisa hadn't even had the decency to leave a light on! April's still afraid of the dark. To this day she's still afraid!"

"I'm no' defending Lisa, Duncan."

"Then what are you doing? What in the hell are you doing?"

"I'm interfering. Because I love you both."

"Love?" He took a step back and folded his arms in front of him. They were safer there. "What is this? Do you love us both enough to ruin April's life and mine, too? Is that the kind of love you practice? Is that the kind you know? Has your life been so devoid of love that you don't know what to do with it?"

"My life may have been short on love, but it's been long on watching people suffer. And your daughter is suffering, and I could no' stand by and watch her suffer more."

"I think you'd better go."

"No' before I show you something."

"What? What could you possibly show me that would change what you did today? You encouraged Lisa. And now she may take it in her head to find Druidheachd and her beloved baby girl. She's just exactly unstable enough to become fixated on seeing April now that she's talked to her. Finding April can become her newest obsession. Who knows where it will end!"

"Obsession is exactly what this is about." Mara moved past him and to the doorway leading into the hall. "Do you want to see, or no'?"

He wanted her to leave. He had been crazy to let himself become involved with her. He had known, from the very beginning, that she was trouble, yet despite his own experiences, he had allowed her to take over a portion of his heart.

She disappeared into April's bedroom. He had no choice but to follow. He would see whatever she wanted to show him, then he would ask her to leave.

She opened April's toy chest and began to rummage. "I dinna even know if it's still here. She may have taken it with her to Lolly's. I dinna think she often lets it out of her sight."

"What are you talking about?" He stopped in the doorway.

She continued to rummage, removing toys and piling them on the floor beside the chest. Finally she stood and gazed around the room. Regret colored her eyes a darker green. "She took it. And now I can no'..." She stared at the bed, then she shook her head. "No, there it is." She walked to the bed and lifted April's pillow. "She must have planned to take it with her and forgotten in the hurry at the end." She held out a carved wooden box.

He knew the box. It had once belonged to Lisa. She'd kept crystals in it or candles or incense. Something magical and absurd. He didn't know how April had gotten hold of it, but it hardly seemed to matter. "So?"

"Look inside, Duncan. Have a good look at obsession."

Reluctantly he took the box and lifted the top. He stared at the contents. Time passed. He didn't know how much time. He heard Mara's footsteps fading from the room, and moments later he heard the apartment door close softly behind her.

He didn't move. He stared at his daughter's memories and the sad, discarded mementos of the mother she was not allowed to see.

And when his eyes finally closed in defeat, he still held the remains of his marriage tightly in his hands.

Chapter 12

The day had been warm, but the storm had brought with it chilling winds, and Mara was glad for the peat fire burning on her hearth. She had made herself tea when she'd arrived home, and even as simple an act as that had left her feeling tired. She closed her eyes and rested, willing herself to concentrate on the familiar sounds of the croft instead of the voices in her head.

But the voices were louder.

She loved Duncan Sinclair, and she had told him so. But the revelation had made no difference to either of them. What did love matter when there was no trust with it? She hadn't trusted him enough to go to him immediately and tell him what she'd done. He hadn't trusted her enough to wait for her explanation.

Guiser stretched out at her feet. He had been pathetically grateful for her return. Jessie and Roger had taken excellent care of him during her absence, but he was a one-woman dog. She inspired mindless devotion in animals and exuberant growth in plants. And in humans she inspired mistrust and anger.

Guiser shifted, and his ears perked up. She didn't know what time it was, only that hours had passed since her return. She knew she ought to go to bed because tomorrow her life would resume its usual course and she would rise at dawn to begin her chores. She was two weeks behind in her gardening and dyeing, and she didn't know how she was going to manage to do everything in the few warm months still left to her.

Guiser got to his feet and started toward the door. She followed, throwing it open to watch him dissolve into the darkness. The storm still thundered somewhere in the distance and rain fell hard enough to obscure whatever view she might have had. She wanted to follow him, to run through the darkness and keep on running. She did not want to face her life alone again. The croft that had once seemed like a prayer's answer now seemed like a prison.

"Mara?"

She stepped back, startled. Duncan stood before her, and she hadn't even sensed he was there.

She didn't know what to say. She hadn't expected him to come. She had tried to glimpse her own future, and she had seen a void.

"Mara." He stepped forward. He reached out his hand.

She backed away. "Why are you here?"

"May I come in?"

She realized he was standing in the rain. His mac had been no match for a summer thunderstorm. His dark hair was plastered to his forehead and raindrops traced his cheekbones. She stepped to one side and let him in, but she didn't move away from the door.

"May I stand by the fire?"

She gestured toward it, giving permission. He took off his mac and hung it on a peg, then he crossed the room. "It was hell coming up the mountain in this. But at least I didn't see any ghosts."

She didn't answer.

"I forget sometimes that I'm not in California anymore. I forget it can be so damned cold in July."

"We're in the most godforsaken corner of a godforsaken country. Dinna you tell me that earlier?"

"Are you going to stand there, or are you going to come over here?"

"Say what you've come to say, Duncan. Then please go."

"Do you think I'm going to hurt you?"

"You've already hurt me. I'm no' in the market for more."

"Mara..."

She closed her eyes. His voice wrapped around her heart and squeezed mercilessly. "I was wrong to go against your wishes today," she said. "But I never deserved such anger. Do you think I did it easily? Do you think I was no' torn? I knew you'd be upset, but I thought you'd give me a chance to explain. I was only waiting until we were alone."

"You had all afternoon and evening. You could have found a time and a place."

"I did no' want you to be hurt by what I had to show you, and I knew you would be. But I should no' have waited. You're right about that."

"And I should have known you had reason to put Lisa through to April. I'm sorry."

She opened her eyes and he was standing just in front of her again. "So you've said what you came for."

"Mara..." She tried to turn away, but he cupped her face in his hands. "I was wrong. I had no idea what April was going through. I shut my eyes to it, just like I shut my eyes..."

"To what?"

"To what you said to me when we were fighting."

"I said a lot of things."

"You said that you loved me."

"I love easily, Duncan."

He dropped his hands. "Is that right?"

"Aye. I dinna know how to protect myself."

"Then I'm just one of a series. Is that what you're saying?"

She just stared at him.

"I don't think so," he said softly. "I think you've built walls as thick and as solid as the walls of this cottage. And I think you've isolated your heart the way you've isolated yourself on this mountain. But you weren't meant for any of this. You were meant to love and be loved."

"That's what we were all meant for. But no' all of us succeed, do we? And for some of us, it's better if we stay in our stone cottages and isolate ourselves on mountains."

"Not for you." He pulled her close and turned her face to his. "Not for you. You were meant for this."

She tried to pull away, but his lips took possession of hers and his arms circled her. He claimed to be cold, but his body was as warm as fire against hers. She was enveloped by his warmth. Some part of her that had long been frozen began to thaw, and she knew she couldn't let it.

She slid her hands to his chest and pushed. "I want you to go. Please go. I've nowt to offer you."

"Just yourself." He dropped his arms, but he didn't move away. "I'm asking for that, and nothing more."

"You dinna know what you're asking!"

"I do know." He took her hands and held them to his heart. "I know who you are, and I know what you suffer sometimes. And I'm telling you it doesn't matter. I want you the way you are, Mara. I'm not asking that you be someone you're not."

"Please, Duncan." But she didn't know what she was begging him for.

"I've made a million mistakes in my life." His hands tightened around hers. "A billion. And I'll go on making them. And I want you anyway because I can't help myself. If I was any kind of man at all I'd walk through that door and leave you here because I'm not good enough for you."

"No' good enough?"

"I don't know how to be the man you need. I couldn't be enough for Lisa. God knows I tried, but I just couldn't be everything she needed. And if I could have been, maybe she never would have gone off the deep end."

"It was never your fault." She wasn't sure when her fingers had woven with his. He was no longer holding her hands. They were joined by mutual consent. "How can you blame yourself?"

His eyes were the color of peat smoke. "And how can you think you have nothing to offer? You're the kindest woman I've ever met, and the most perceptive. There's nothing small or mean about you. From the first moment I saw you standing in that meadow I knew there was going to be something between us. And that something is this."

He bent his head lower. She knew she should move away, that this time he would take nothing from her. He was giving her time, teasing her with her own need. He was asking for a commitment, a mutual expression of longing.

And she wasn't strong enough to deny him. She groaned as his lips found hers, because suddenly lips weren't enough. She had been hollow too long, and she had yearned for Duncan all of her life. There were no walls thick enough, no mountain high enough to keep him from her any longer.

"Oh, Mara." He breathed her name against her hair. "For once let's stop fighting what we both want."

She couldn't fight. She stroked instead, stroked the damp dark silk of his hair, the warm skin of his neck, the rough-textured wool of his jumper, the cool, slippery cotton of his shirt. She stroked and she tasted the secret flavors of his skin and lips and the deeper recesses of his mouth.

His hands were as eager for sensation as hers. They skimmed her hair to close tightly over her shoulders and propel her even closer. Restless again they edged to her breasts, to her waist, to the narrow flare of her hips. He was hard against her, aroused and ready to forsake the pleasures of foreplay and slide deep inside her.

But he didn't move toward the bed. "Tell me you want this, too."

"Aye." There were better ways to say it. She grasped the hem of his jumper and tugged it toward his head. "Aye Duncan, I want this and I want you. And I'll have what I want."

His eyelids drifted shut. His hands moved over his head and in a moment the jumper lay on the stone floor. She had been a nurse, used to dressing and undressing men of all ages, but her fingers were suddenly clumsy. He stood completely motionless, taut and brimming with tension, and let her fumble with the buttons. He made a soft sound, a moan of raw pleasure as her palms skimmed his bare chest at last. She savored the sensation of the wide expanse of skin, of broad shoulders and muscular arms. The shirt joined the jumper on the floor and firelight turned his torso to bronze.

"This is a favor I can return." He sounded like a man lost somewhere between pleasure and pain. His fingers trembled as he guided the zipper of her dress to its lowest point. Her skin seemed to smolder every place that he touched it. She felt as if she were expanding inside, winging to some uncharted place with only the boundaries of her skin to keep her grounded on the earth. The dress fell to the floor and pooled at her feet and her bra followed it. His hand closed over her breast, and she had never felt such pleasure. She melted against him, pressing herself closer. She heard a moan and didn't know if it was hers or his.

His lips found her ear; her hands found his zipper and the bulge beneath it. She freed him and felt the fire of his arousal against her abdomen. The bed seemed a light-year away, a journey through impossible terrain. He swung her off her feet, kicking his pants away, and strode there. The soft mattress gave willingly beneath her back and his weight was welcome and heavy on top of her.

She wasn't sure when the last of their clothes had disappeared. They were naked together now, but there was no time to explore or to note. She was driven by a purer need than curiosity. She had been created for this moment, for the merging of her being with Duncan's, and he had been created for her. She knew, without knowing how, that they would both be changed by what was already an inevitable conclusion. They would be separate again, but never quite as separate. This moment would always be between them, no matter what the future held.

They were two, then they were one. She took him inside her and felt the power of their merging shake the foundations of everything she had ever known. Time, which had so often moved in mysterious ways for her, stood absolutely still.

And the pleasure, the raw, mindless pleasure, stretched into eternity.

Mara was sleeping. Her thighs skimmed his, her arm was draped lightly over his chest. The scent of herbs, of lemon balm, lavender and mint perfumed her hair and tickled his senses in ways he had never imagined they could.

There was an owl hooting somewhere nearby, hooting blatantly, shamelessly, now that the worst of the storm had passed. There were other sounds. The distant bell of a wandering sheep. Mara's soft breathing. The sizzle of peat on the hearth. Wind sighing through the waltzing branches of trees.

He couldn't remember feeling this way before. He couldn't even find a word to describe the interplay of emotions that had assaulted him while making love with Mara. And afterward, afterward he had brimmed with feelings. He envisioned a dam as thick as the walls of Mara's cottage and a slow, steady leak that could never be plugged again. He had believed himself to be a man with few emotions. Now he knew that he had built his entire life on a myth. He was emotional, wildly, furiously emotional and passionate beyond comprehension.

And he had met his match in Mara. She had set him on fire, wringing passion from him and returning it in full measure. How could two people who had been so terribly careful for so long ignite on contact? How had they found each other when there was so much that should have separated them? That still could?

She cuddled closer and he drew the blanket higher over her, although he hated to block his glorious view of her body. She was more beautiful than he had imagined—and he was a man who was long on imagination. Her legs were showgirl length and wickedly agile. Her waist was as slim as a reed, her breasts small but beautifully rounded and softer than anything had a right to be.

She stirred again, and this time her eyes opened. She smiled and touched his cheek. "What time is it?"

"I have no idea. You don't seem to have a clock."

"Umm ... That's right. I dinna."

"Why don't you?"

"What would I need one for?"

"Moments like this. When you wake up and want to know what time it is."

She smiled. Something sparkled in her eyes. "Ask *me* what time it is, Duncan."

He shifted, so they were face-to-face. His heart began to beat faster. "What time is it, Mara?"

She circled him with her arms. "Come a little closer, my love, and I'll show you."

Mara was up before Duncan. He was sleeping so soundly that he didn't stir when she dressed to go outside. Roger had moved the cows to his own croft to make them easier to care for, so until she got them back—if she did—there was nothing to do for them. She was considering the possibility of selling them to Roger if he was interested. She realized now that she had bought them as much to tie herself to the land as for any other reason. But she had moved beyond needing excuses for anything that she did. And if Roger took the cows, she could buy her milk from him and turn the tables nicely.

The sheep were another matter. She had become a fair shepherd since she had moved to the mountain. She could vaccinate and lamb and do a hundred other less appealing tasks now, but she would never get used to breeding lambs, then selling them off at the end of each summer. The mourning cries of their mothers rang in her ears for weeks after the ewes themselves had adjusted, and thoughts of the lamb's fates weren't to be tolerated. No, in the weeks since she had been away from the croft she'd had time to contemplate her life. And what she'd seen hadn't necessarily pleased her.

She walked to the barn, Guiser at her heels, and opened the door to let the sheep out for the day. With Guiser's assistance she herded them to the section of pasture where they would graze for the next few weeks. She closed the gate behind the last one and trekked the circumference of the fence, to be sure that no stones were out of place. Then she leaned on the gate and watched the lambs at play.

She kept two different herds, although she grazed them together. One was an ancient breed, the Shetlands, whose wool ranged from white to black and included a shade called Moorit, a deep, rich, reddish brown. The other she kept were the Highland Black Face, a sheep with a beautiful long fleece and a tendency to fatten quickly for meat. The Shetlands were her favorite because their wool was so unusual, suggesting endless combinations for a creative spinner, but the wool of the Highland sheep took color beautifully.

"What are you doing? The sun's hardly had time to rise."

She turned to find Duncan right behind her. She put her arms around his neck for a good morning kiss, savoring the taste of his sun-warmed lips. His hair was endearingly tumbled and the shadow of a beard adorned his jaw. He had never looked sexier. "I had to get the sheep to pasture."

"Do you rise this early every morning?"

"Earlier when the cows are home."

"And in winter?"

She made a face. "It's harder."

He put his arm around her shoulders and stood with her at the fence. She didn't know what she had expected to see this morning when they were face-to-face. Regret, perhaps. Astonishment. Distress. But she had seen none of it. Duncan simply looked like a satisfied man.

"I've liked the sameness of all this," she said, sweeping her hand in an arc. "I've liked the chores and the primitive conditions, working with the animals, even sometimes, the bleakness of the weather."

"You've been testing yourself."

She was pleased he understood. "I needed to begin at the most elemental level. Does that make any sense to you?"

"Yes."

She was pleased again. "We have a saying here, to 'dree yer ain wierd.' Do you know it?"

"It means to face up to whatever's ahead of you. My father used it often."

"I suppose I've thought this croft was my way of doing just that. I thought to make a life for myself, to face up to who I was and learn to accept solitude as my lot."

"And now?"

"You were right when you told me I had to spend more time with people. After I divorced Robbie I was convinced the only thing left to me was retreat. Now I'm no' so certain."

"You've got a fan club at the hotel. They're a hard bunch to win over, but they've already formed ranks around you."

"They're a dear group of people."

"So, what will you do?"

"Simplify a bit, I think."

"Sell this place and move into the hotel with me?"

She turned to him and smiled. He had said the words lightly, but she suspected there was something more than humor behind his request. "I'm going to sell the cows and some of the sheep. Downscale instead of grow. I dinna like raising lambs for meat, so I'll stop that first. I'll only breed the ewes whose lambs I'll likely want to keep. And I'll keep all I can for shearing. Without so many lambs, my work will be easier, and I can spend more time with my plants and my dyeing and spinning."

"Aren't the lambs an important source of income?"

"I'm fortunate. I've no real need for the money. But I think I've more need for time . . . and freedom."

"Freedom?"

"There's a wee shop on High Street that needs a tenant. The stone house that's part of the old mill?"

"I know it."

"I've a mind to lease it myself and run it as a gift shop. I could sell my wool and my herbs and lease space to others to sell their handicrafts. There's no place in Druidheachd to feature the work of local craftsmen or artists, and we have enough tourists to support one."

"There's a capitalist under this beautiful hair." He wound a long lock around his finger. "But it's not money that's driving you, is it?"

"No. I need to spend more time off the mountain."

"You need to spend more time with me."

"Aye. I do." She rose on tiptoe and kissed him and desire heated her blood. When she had come to Druidheachd she had locked away desire, along with every other emotional need except survival. Now, after one night together, Duncan seemed as important to that survival as the air she breathed.

His arms closed around her. "What do you have in mind for the day?"

"Do you have to go right back to the hotel?"

"No. April's not due back until this evening, and the hotel can run itself. I don't care."

"Stay with me, then. Have a look at the way I live. Gather herbs, mend fences, perhaps even go with me to collect peats if the good weather holds."

"Mara, you're just getting over a nasty fall. You shouldn't overdo."

"Oh, I will no' overdo. It's supervising I plan. Have you ever used a *toirbhsgir* to cut peats yourself? It's a nasty, sharp blade, but it gets the job done. You should have the experience, you know, if you're going to live in the Highlands even a little while."

"Have you ever read *Tom Sawyer*?"

"Aye, and I've no' a fence in sight that needs whitewashing. Just a bothy that'll need a good peat fire come autumn."

"I'll donate a whole truckload of coal if it means I don't have to cut or haul peat today. Besides, I've got another idea for keeping you warm this winter."

She wrapped her arms around his neck. "Have you now?"

"Come back to the bothy, and let me teach you a new strategy."

She knew her eyes were dancing. She couldn't remember ever being happier. It didn't take second sight to envision the future only minutes away when she would be in Duncan's arms again. "I've always believed in education and progress. Can I refuse?"

"Not if I have my way."

"And do you always get your way, Duncan?"

"Never as gloriously as last night. Do you suppose my luck has changed?"

"I'd have no way of knowing that. But I do know something."

He lifted a brow in question.

"My luck changed one cold night in a meadow just across the ridge, and I've Geordie Smith to thank for it."

He cupped her face in his hands. "My beautiful Lady Greensleeves."

She pulled his face down to hers and brushed her lips across his. "*Your* lady, Duncan. Your lady for as long as you're here."

Chapter 13

There were half a dozen crows perched on the stone fence that surrounded Mara's garden, eyeing her cornstalks with undisguised ardor. They ignored Guiser's barking and Mara jabbing at them with her hoe and politely waited for her to depart. As soon as she left the garden and closed the gate behind her, they would take her place.

"My old auntie could make a tattie bogle that scared away every crow for a hundred miles," Mara told Duncan as she stopped to wipe her forehead with the back of her hand.

"Yours is smiling. Everybody knows a scarecrow is supposed to look fierce." Duncan made a terrible face. "Like this."

She pressed her hand to her heart. "That would certainly do it."

"I could be persuaded to improve on yours."

She smiled. "Oh? And what would I need to do to persuade you."

"I could think of a thing or two."

Her smile widened. "Oh, could you now? And what if I reminded you that I've a million and one things to do today and dinna have time for your foolishness?"

"Foolishness? I could swear that's not what you were calling it last night."

Her cheeks grew pink, and not because the sun was shining on them. "You're a scunner, Duncan Sinclair. You've no right to come here today and tempt me away from my work."

"Now I'm a temptation?"

"You're a trial."

"Put up your hoe and come with me. It's a gorgeous afternoon and we're going to Iain's this evening, anyway. Spend the rest of the day with me."

"But I've two months' work to do in one, and the first frosts will be coming soon. I can no' spend such a braw afternoon trauchling after you when I've my own work to do."

He crooked his finger. "Come over here and let me persuade you."

More than two months had passed since Mara and Duncan had become lovers. The heather had bloomed; the largest part of a small tourist population had come and gone; the creature said to live in Loch Ceo hadn't shown itself for yet another summer.

Mara had sold her cows and the lambs she couldn't keep; she had spun her fleeces and dyed her yarn in hues as variegated as the gorse and bracken of the hillsides and the unpredictable blues of a Scottish summer sky. Duncan had seen his own changes. The repairs to the hotel were nearly finished and with Mara's help and only a small outlay of cash, he had remodeled and brightened the lobby and dining room. Best of all, surrounded by love and security, April had bloomed into the child he'd been afraid he would never see. She had regular conversations with her mother now, and spoke more openly about her. He was comfortable with neither, but he had seen the improvement in April, and he was willing to do what he had to just to keep the smile in her eyes.

He'd had no hopes for his months in Druidheachd except the most basic. He had wanted to escape from Lisa. He had wanted to refurbish and sell the hotel. He had wanted to rebuild his relationship with his daughter.

Instead, he'd gotten so much more.

"If I come over there, I'll no' be going back, will I?" Mara asked.

"That's a distinct possibility."

"You'll steal me away, like a fairy king. And when you return me, I'll be old and withered and good for nowt."

"Now, that part I doubt very much."

She came within kissing distance. "What exactly do you have in mind?"

"April's at a birthday party until six, then Sally's agreed to watch her at the hotel until Frances can take her home. I've got my jacket and tie and a clean shirt in my car."

"And?"

"And I thought you might like to spend some time together. Your choice."

She leaned over the fence and planted a kiss on his lips. "My choice? Really?"

"Anything you want to do."

"You'd pull weeds if I asked?"

"Along with perfectly healthy plants, I imagine."

She put a finger to her nose and wrinkled her forehead. "You'd dip sheep or help me breed the black face ewes to Roger's prize tup?"

"If you think I could stand the excitement."

"I know just the thing."

"If it's along those same lines, you need some help in the imagination area."

"I have some seeds to gather before the frosts come. You could help."

"Where?"

"No' here. I'll show you." She kissed him again, then followed the fence to the gate and let herself out. The crows cawed in anticipation. "About that tattie bogle," she said.

"I'll put the plans on the drawing board."

He escorted her to the door, and then he began to wander. When he visited Mara he never asked her permission to do chores around the croft. He knew if he asked she would say no, so instead he worked on the sly. It had become a game to find places where his labor wouldn't be noticed right away. She was so fiercely and rightfully proud of all she'd accomplished. He was sure she didn't want to give up even a shred of her independence.

While she changed her shoes for hiking and packed a snack for tea, he walked down to the spring behind the house. It gushed from the earth to form a small, crystal clear basin, and Mara had hauled stones to line it. He had noticed the first time that he'd gone for water that stones were needed at the source of the spring, too, to keep silt from washing into the basin.

He crouched beside the spring and began to feed stones into the places where they were missing. When he had used up the ones within easy reach, he stood and ranged farther, hauling them back and setting them in place. He became so involved in his project that he forgot to watch out for Mara.

"Now that's something I've had on my mind to do for months," she said.

He stood and faced her, chagrined. "I was just killing time."

"And why should anyone want to? We've so little of it as it is."

"You've done such a good job with the spring. I was just playing with it a bit."

"You were helping, and you've been helping for months. Did you think I would no' see?"

He smiled. "I don't know what you're talking about."

"You're beginning to like this place, Duncan. It's weaving its spell around you."

"You've got a better imagination than I was giving you credit for."

"You like my croft, and you like the village, and you're beginning to grow fond of some of the people here, even though you find it hard to admit." She walked toward him and stopped. She stroked her palms up his chest.

"I am definitely fond of certain people." He put his arms around her and drew her closer.

"You still have Scotland in your blood."

He was beginning to believe he had a certain woman in his blood. Every day since they had become lovers he warned himself to be careful. He would not be staying in Drui-dheachd, and Mara would not be leaving. All they could ever hope to have was a brief, passionate love affair. But no matter how many times he told himself to slow down and step back, he couldn't stay away from her.

"You know, it wouldn't be hard to channel this water into your house," he said. "With a pump and some pipe you could have running water."

"Aye. I've thought of it more than once."

"And there are ways of running electricity in from the road that wouldn't ruin your views."

"And telephone, too?"

"Sure, and we could hook you up to a computer network and buy you a fax machine and a satellite dish and get you on the information superhighway in a jiffy." He snapped his fingers.

She laughed and reached up to kiss his nose. "I want to keep the cottage just the way it is. But I've other plans for this property. Shall I show you?"

He clasped her hand in his. "You have my undivided attention."

He learned soon enough that her plans were extensive. The cottage that she lived in now was someday to be a dormitory for schoolchildren who would come to learn the ways of their ancestors and the history of the Highlands. She wanted to build more cottages like it, to have the older children do it themselves as part of their learning experience. With the right kind of help and supervision they could learn to construct walls and thatch roofs. She believed it would give them the same sense of pride and accomplishment that building the cottage had given her.

"But I dinna need to live this way forever," she said, swinging Duncan's hand in hers. "I'm going to build a bigger, more modern house for myself. One with water and electricity and proper plumbing."

"I definitely vote for the plumbing."

She stopped and pointed to a place just beyond them. "There."

He could imagine a house on the spot she had chosen. It was a wide, level site with a view that on a clear day like this one probably couldn't be topped. He whistled softly and his imagination took flight.

"You like it?"

"It's outstanding."

"I knew when I saw it that I wanted this property. That's why I bought it. I started small so that I could learn what I needed to. Now I think I'm ready for this."

"You're not saying that you're going to do the work yourself?"

"No. Some, perhaps. But I'll be well prepared to supervise."

He wondered if he would ever see the finished product. He could imagine the house, nothing large or ostentatious, but small enough to be cozy and roomy enough not to feel cramped. There would be wide windows on every side, double paned and tightly sealed against the wind. And Mara, with an artist's sensitivity, would design a flawlessly simple floor plan with an eye for the best of traditional and contemporary.

"It'll be wonderful," he assured her.

"Do you think so? I'll show you my plans someday. You might have suggestions you'll want to make."

He didn't know how to remind her that he wouldn't be in Druidheachd much longer. His suggestions would be worth nothing because he wouldn't be here to see them implemented. He had always been honest about his plans to sell the hotel and leave Scotland, but now he felt reluctant to mention them again.

She led him across the site and down a path where he had never been. The path narrowed at the edge of a sheer drop of fifty feet or more, then it seemed to stop. She stood beside a large boulder, a chunk of mountain that probably had fallen from some higher peak hundreds of years before. The boulder was covered with a fine, lacy moss, some of which was in flower. Brambles grew in a thicket just beyond them and vines twined and slithered along the ground. "You must swear never to tell any secrets you might learn here," she said. "You must promise."

"This is where you keep all the men who've fallen hopelessly in love with you, isn't it? I've wondered where you put them."

"Duncan," she said severely. "You must promise."

"On my honor."

"Hold up your hand."

He did.

"I suppose you can follow, then." She turned and with her back to the boulder, she slid along beside it, carefully watching every step. When she was halfway around she beckoned. "Just watch your feet, and you'll be safe."

"Dipping the sheep is beginning to sound more and more appealing."

"Are you afraid of heights, Duncan?"

"No. Just of breaking my neck."

"You will no' fall if you pay attention. And if you do fall, I have a sturdy rope. Somewhere." She smiled. "I think."

He followed her and discovered that the ground at the base of the boulder was solid rock and wider than it had looked. Mara took his hand on the other side. "Welcome to Lon an Sith."

"Lon an Sith?"

"Fairy's burn. Look below you. What is it you see?"

The path dropped sharply for a hundred yards or more, then widened. Beyond that he glimpsed paradise. He didn't know what to say. The area was completely unspoiled, as if no one had ever stepped foot there before. A variety of foliage covered what was probably a three-acre glen. A brook bubbled over stones to one side and pooled between two large rocks, then narrowed once more and flowed out of sight.

"It's magnificent."

"It's a hard climb. Are you willing?"

He had already started.

Five minutes later they were standing at the entrance.

"I've seen red deer here, and the first year I lived on the mountain a fox made her den just over there." She pointed.

"There are ptarmigan and blackcock and other types of grouse, and I've seen wild swans swimming in the wee lochan."

"It's unbelievable."

"It's protected from man and sheep, and from the worst of the elements. There are plants growing here that I've yet to see anywhere else in the immediate area. Those are the seeds we'll collect today."

"What do you plan to do with them?"

"Spread them to other places where they might find some protection. In time, perhaps they'll colonize. Man has no' been kind to the earth here. We brought in the sheep and cut down nearly all the trees, and now we're planting our bens and braes with species that were never meant to grow in the Highlands. It's our task to restore what we've destroyed."

"And this is your way of doing it?"

"It's a wee small thing."

"Enough wee small things can make a great big difference."

"Aye. I think so, too. Now we must be canny, Duncan, when we take seeds. Only a few at a time. We've no right to destroy the balance in this place."

Her tone was reverent. She might as well have been praying in the village kirk. He was enchanted with Lon an Sìth, but more so with her. "I don't know a thing about collecting seeds. Are you going to show me how?"

"I'll show you." She led him to a smattering of plants he recognized as a local wildflower, spikes of purple bells that he'd often seen cultivated in cottage gardens. "Do you know this one?"

He hedged. "It's familiar."

"I'll make a gardener of you yet, Duncan." She knelt beside it and motioned him down. "Now there's nowt rare about this. It's foxglove, found all over Scotland. But there are few plants that can match it for beauty. I'll tell you how it got it's name."

He crouched beside her, and watched the way the sun set her hair aglow. "It's truly lovely," he murmured.

"Long ago the flower was called Folksglove, the glove of the fairies. Do you see the wee spots inside it? That's where the fairies have placed their fingers."

The petals were velvety and surprisingly sensual to the touch. He brushed his fingers over them lightly. "The fairies had a good thing here. Is that why you named this place Lon an Sith?"

"No. I'll show you why later. You've heard of digitalis? The drug used for heart disease?"

"Sure."

"This is where it comes from. The Latin name of this plant is *Digitalis purpurea*. We'll just take a few seeds now. It hardly needs our help to flourish, but it's a bonny plant to demonstrate on."

He watched her caress the plant gently. Desire stirred inside him. He could imagine her hands touching him the same way.

"Different plants sow their seeds in different ways. Some store their seeds in pods that burst open when they've dried and seed flies out like wee cannon balls. Some, like this one, have pods that ripen a bit at a time, and as they dry they open and spill their seed, so it's best to collect them each day. Like this." She twisted off one of the withered blossoms at the bottom of the stalk. Then she took a white tissue from her pocket and spread it on the ground and gently shook the bloom. Tiny seeds fell to the tissue. She gestured to the plant. "Now you try it."

He selected a blossom, but she put her hand over his. "That one's too new. The seed probably has no' had time to develop enough. Try one farther down."

He selected another, and she nodded. He twisted it as she had done and waved it over the tissue. Several seeds fell out. "How's that?"

"Truly brilliant." She smiled, but her eyes turned a deeper green as he bent his head to kiss her.

Her lips were as soft as the flower petals. The fragrances of the earth surrounded her and entwined with the scent of her hair and skin. He wanted to fill his hands with her hair and hold her there forever. They had been lovers for months, but he couldn't seem to get enough of her. Each time he touched her, each time he made love to her, he found himself wanting more.

"Shall I show you some of the other plants?" she asked.

He didn't trust himself to answer. He stood, and she took his hand and led him between trees and stones, stooping to show him the plants she wanted to collect seeds from today and teaching him how to collect as she went. She identified a rare white lousewort along with butterwort, its leaves spotted with insects entrapped by the plant for a leisurely dinner. In the deepest of the woods she showed him wild orchids and white habenaria, varied species of violets and saxifrage. She took seeds when she could until finally she put her carefully marked collection safely in a bag and stored it back in her pocket.

"That's all for today. This will give me plenty to do. I'll have to find places for each seed with conditions nearly the same as I have here." She put her hands on his chest, and he put his arms around her. "Would you like me to show you why I call this the fairy's burn?"

He could think of a thousand things he wanted her to show him, none of which had to do with the landscape, but he smiled. "I'd like to see it."

"You're a game chappie, Duncan. You've stood up to this well."

"It's really a lovely place. Why haven't we come here before?"

"I've never brought anyone here. It's my very own dell. I'm no' even sure that anyone else knows it exists. I come here when I'm loneliest, or when I have a problem to solve. I can sit beside the burn and listen to its song, and when I go back home, I'm stronger."

He was touched that she had shared her special place with him. He let her lead him to the brook. They walked beside it until they came to the place where the water flowed out of the rocks. "This is the source," she said. "And this is where I come to sit." She stepped across a series of boulders to a wide grassy mound. The sun fluttered through leaves and dappled the ground. "Come join me."

He didn't need another invitation. He followed her path and sprawled on the grass beside her. There was a distinct chill in the air, but the earth was still warm. Duncan lay on his side and propped his head with his arm so he could watch Mara.

"Now, are you listening?" she asked.

"To what? To you?"

"No' to me. Close your eyes. Put everything from your mind."

"I'd rather look at you."

"Close them. Go on, now. Do it, and listen carefully."

His eyelids drifted shut. Warmed by the sun and lulled by the murmuring water, he let his mind go where it would. There were birds singing somewhere close by. He couldn't remember the last time he'd listened to them. And bees humming, preparing, he supposed for a cold, damp winter.

Unaccountably he heard laughter and knew it came from inside him. He remembered another day, one so long ago that he couldn't say what year it had been, when he had gone walking with his father and Fiona. Fiona had been tiny then, a laughing, chirping baby-child, and his father had carried her on his shoulders. Now he could almost hear her laughter, and his father's, too.

His father had laughed. As a young man, Donald Sinclair had laughed. Duncan had forgotten that until now. And once, Fiona had been afraid of nothing.

What an enormous burden of guilt his father must have borne to change from that youth joyfully carrying his beloved daughter, into the stern, brooding man Duncan had known in later years.

He didn't want to examine that memory too closely. He opened his eyes, and saw that Mara was watching him. "This *is* a magic place," he said.

"What did you hear?"

"Laughter."

"That's as it should be."

He turned to his back and closed his eyes again. He could feel the sun against his eyelids and deep inside him. Mara lay down, and he could feel the length of her leg against his, the dip of her waist and the soft pressure of her breast against his arm. He reached for her, pillowing her head against his shoulder.

And then he heard the music.

At first he thought the sound was coming from his memory, just as the laughter had. But the song that resonated from the earth was like nothing he had ever heard before. It was the sound of the Scottish countryside, pipes and fiddles and an accordion, too, but played with such artistry that it seemed to fuse with the air he breathed. It was made up of sunshine, of the clearest, cleanest air, of the scents of late summer and lacy flakes of winter snows. He listened and saw the wildflowers Mara had picked so carefully, the glisten of Loch Ceo in misty moonlight, snow-covered, barren peaks and an endless stretch of unruly sea.

"Do you hear it?" Mara whispered.

He listened harder. There was a minor note, too. Battle cries and the weeping of women. Screams of defeat from Culloden Moor, the hand-to-hand clatter of dirk and sword as clan battled clan, the voices that still sounded today, demanding separation from the remainder of Britain. And there was the babble of languages, the soft guttural sounds of Gaelic, the sharply accented burr of the lowlands, the lyrical, poetic speech of the highlands.

The sounds, the music, clutched at his heart. He opened his eyes and stared at the sapphire Scottish sky. For a moment he couldn't breathe properly. "What do *you* hear?" he asked.

"Fairy music."

"Is that what it is?"

"We're on their roof right now, you know. They live in this hill. And the music is their gift to us."

"Is it?"

She turned so she could see his face. She was smiling. "You can no' tell anyone, Duncan. No one else would understand. The local folk are afraid of the fairies."

He managed a smile, too. "Shouldn't they be? Don't fairies carry away mortals and imprison them until they're very old?"

She laughed. "And how would you know?"

"I've read the book you gave April."

"*Duncan and the Fairies*? Aye, that's what happened to poor Duncan, I'm afraid. But he had cut away the fairies' roof, after all, even though they'd warned him to take his peat from another place."

The birds were singing louder and the burn was bubbling merrily as it emerged from the stone. He knew the birds and the brook were all he had heard, and yet... He threaded his fingers into Mara's hair and turned to her. "Then they won't be angry with us for lying on their roof?"

"Does it sound as though they're angry?"

"Will they mind if I kiss you here? Will they spy on us?"

"I dinna know what they'll do. I've never kissed a man here before."

He pulled her a little closer. "Shall we try?"

"I think we should. For the sake of fairy science."

He brushed his lips against hers. Once. Twice.

And the music began again.

Chapter 14

Fearnshader was too Gothic for Duncan's tastes. Had he come across it on a New York City street, he would have assumed Fearnshader was a church where every Sunday morning a stern message of sin and redemption was trumpeted to shivering parishioners who wished they were home in bed reading the *Times*.

On a rambling, tree-lined Scottish wynd miles from the nearest village and a stone's throw from the hulking remains of Ceo Castle, Fearnshader could only be a country home built by a humorless laird and lady of a past century. Castellated, parapeted and foreboding, Duncan loved Fearnshader still. He wondered if Mara, who was cuddling beside him with her hand on his knee, would sense the happy hours he had spent here. Would the laughter of three young boys still hang in the hallways for her to hear?

"There's been much unhappiness here," she said instead, as he parked beside the gatehouse. There were other cars there already.

"That's a safe bet. What old house hasn't known unhappiness?"

"It's no' always the first thing I feel."

"Why haven't you been here before? I can't believe Iain hasn't invited you before this."

"He knew I preferred my own company."

Something occurred to him, and he wondered why he'd never thought of it before. Iain had reassured him before Duncan had even met Mara. But he wondered... "Did Iain..." He tried again. "Did you and Iain ever think about having a relationship?"

She smiled. "What are you asking, Duncan? Do you want to know if Iain and I were lovers?"

"No. Of course not." He considered his own answer and frowned. "No, I really *don't* want to know if you were."

"Well, we were no', so you can rest your mind. He's always been a friend, and nowt more. I was too much in need of solitude, and Iain, despite the face he turns to the world, is too much in need of distance to choose someone like me."

"Like you?"

"Iain chooses women who will no' feel badly when he moves on to another. Have you never noticed?"

It was almost exactly what Iain had said. "Iain plays the field, but he's no different than a lot of men. He's just not the type to settle down."

"No, there's more to it than that."

"What do you mean?"

"I dinna know." She must have seen the doubt in his eyes, because she shook her head. "I really dinna know. He's afraid of something."

He leaned over and kissed her nose. "And well he should be. How many happy marriages have you seen?"

"Aye, it's always a gamble. But Iain's no' a coward. There's something more."

"You look beautiful tonight." He touched her hair. She had pulled it off her face and confined a portion of it in a sleek roll at the back of her head in honor of Iain's dinner party. He wanted to take out the pins and watch it tumble over the lace collar of her dress.

"You look fair handsome yourself, Duncan. Harris tweed suits you well." She laughed at her own pun. "Aye, at moments like this you look a Scot through and through."

"We could make this a short evening. I could use April as an excuse."

"And what did you have in mind?" Her eyes sparkled. "A stroll beside the loch? An evening of chess or gin rummy by the fire?"

"There's nearly a full moon. We could haul some more peat." He watched her cheeks color. They had gone to the peat bog one evening and ended up instead making love between mounds of earth on the open moor. They had found a hidden spot where the grass-covered ground was as soft as feathers, and as a sliver of moon had peeked at them between clouds, they had taken possession of each other's souls. He had felt part of something ancient and lasting that night, just as he had this afternoon at the fairy burn, sealed somehow to the land where he had been born and to the woman in his arms.

"I'll no' be hauling peat with the likes of you again," she said. "You're all play and no work. I'll be cold all winter because of you."

"There's always a warm fire at the hotel."

She stroked his hair back from his forehead. "I know how warm *your* fire is, Duncan."

The *car* was suddenly too warm. He'd believed on the night they first made love that the passion between them would one day burn itself out. Now he wasn't sure of anything except that he walked around in a state of continuous desire, waiting impatiently for the moments when they could be alone. "We'd better get inside."

"Aye, it would no' do at all to have you zipping your pants and me straightening my hair when Iain comes to the door."

He burst into laughter. She blinked innocently at him, and he grabbed her for one final kiss before he got out of the car.

Roses scented the air, old roses with pedigrees as ancient as Iain's own. He stooped for a sprig of sweet william to tuck in Mara's hair and one for his buttonhole. The air was growing cooler with the onset of fall, and he used the chill as an excuse to put his arm around Mara to keep her warm.

Iain didn't answer the door. An elderly woman in a starched gray dress answered instead. "You were always late, Duncan Sinclair. Never as late as Andrew, mind you, but late. You always had the idea that whatever it was you were about was too important to interrupt for politeness sake. The good Lady Ross nearly gave up on you a time or twa." She turned to Mara. "And you have no' reformed him, I see?"

"I'll confess I did no' realize he had such a major failing."

"Then he's on time when he comes to see you?"

Mara shrugged. "Always."

"It must be love then, pure and simple."

Duncan cleared his throat. "If you don't mind, Gertie, I'd like a kiss on the cheek."

Gertie blushed like a schoolgirl, but she did as he'd asked. "So you remember me, do you?"

"How could I forget? But I thought you'd retired and gone to Glasgow to live with your sister."

"Och, I dinna need all the noise and thrang of a city. And the sister had no notion how to keep me happy. If she told me once no' to clean under her bed, she told me a thousand times."

Duncan shook his head in mock disapproval.

"So I'm back, and I'll stay here, thank you. Master Iain needs me, and he does no' complain if I take the dust mop to his room every morning."

"Well, he's lucky to have you. If he doesn't treat you right, you can come to the hotel and live with me."

"And are you going to introduce me to your lady friend?"

"Mara MacTavish, this is Gertie Beggs. Renowned for having a worse bark than a bite."

Gertie ignored him. "And you'll be the lass they're saying is the ferlie."

"Aye."

"Ferlie?" Duncan asked.

"You've been away too long," Gertie said, shaking her finger at him.

"Something out of the ordinary," Mara translated.

"Something strange and wonderful," Gertie said. "And I can see it applies here."

Iain, dressed in a dark suit, came up to stand behind her. "Are you going to let them in, Gertie? Have they passed muster yet?"

"Master Iain, you have no' changed enough in the years I've been away!"

"But now that you're back, you'll see that I do."

"No' likely," she said. "No' likely a' tall." She strutted back down the hall. Even with her back turned to them, Duncan was sure she was inspecting for dust motes.

He ushered Mara in and followed close behind. He watched Iain compliment her and kiss her cheek and felt something stronger than gratitude that Iain and Mara had never been lovers.

"Everyone's here but Andrew," Iain said.

"I pity him. Gertie will tear him from limb to limb."

"She'll just whack him a bit. She always had a soft spot for Andrew." He started toward the drawing room. He kept his voice low. "I can't guarantee the company tonight. I have business dealings with both of the men you're about to meet. They're pleasant enough on the surface, but sharks underneath, both of them. Watch that you leave with your wallet."

"How kind of you to invite us," Duncan said dryly.

"I asked you because you'd better get to know them both. They're looking for investments in this part of the Highlands."

"What kind of investments?" Mara asked.

"Nothing much, really. They want to market the life we've always been privileged to lead."

"Exactly what do you mean?" Duncan asked.

"Let them tell you. And listen carefully."

There was a fire in the drawing room, what the Scots called a stick fire, with logs as thick as the caber Andrew had tossed at the Johnsmas fair and flames leaping from the cavernous fireplace. Two women stood beside it, one with silver hair arranged in perfect waves and a pale blue dress that skimmed the middle of her calf. The other was much younger, with sleek black hair falling from two combs at the side of her head and a red cocktail dress that was one step to the left of immodest.

The men were less diverse. Both were in their fifties and balding. One was overweight; one obviously spent the requisite hours at the gym. But neither of them seemed comfortable relaxing in the environs of a Scottish country home.

Iain made the introductions. The overweight man was married to the elegant woman with silver hair. They were Martin and Sylvia Carlton-Jones from a town just outside of London. The slimmer man, Nigel Surrey from Birmingham, was partnered for the evening—and for as many nights as she'd have him, Duncan imagined—with the brunette, Alicia Cox.

"Iain tells me you're from the States," Nigel said.

Duncan accepted a glass of Iain's finest whiskey and took his first swallow. He felt unaccountably irritated. "I was born in Druidheachd," he said.

"And you've come back to stay?"

"No."

"Duncan owns the Sinclair Hotel, along with his sister," Iain said. "And he'll soon be putting it up for sale."

"Will you?" Martin asked, moving closer to take part in the conversation. "I know the building. I've admired it, actually. It's quite . . . Scottish."

"Quite," Duncan said. He downed the rest of his drink, but he didn't take his eyes off Martin. Both men seemed completely ineffectual to him, hesitant and not particularly bright. But he was a good enough businessman himself to know how important it was sometimes to put on an act. And he trusted Iain's judgment. Iain could spot a shark well before it began to circle.

"Are you in the area on holiday?" Mara asked.

Nigel's pleasantly vacuous eyes focused for seconds on her. Duncan watched him scan Mara with the efficiency of a radiologist. "We'll be heading east in a day or so to shoot grouse."

"The grouse dinna stand a chance," she said.

Duncan had rarely heard a nip in Mara's voice. Now he was surprised that Nigel wasn't dripping blood.

"But while we're here," Martin said, "we thought we might look around. We're always looking for property to invest in. The idea of a hotel in the Highlands intrigues me. Druidheachd's a lovely little village, and your loch is so un-spoiled."

"And will remain that way," said another voice. Duncan smiled at Andrew, who had come to join them. Introductions were made all around, and Andrew gripped the necessary hands.

"Andrew knows every inch of Loch Ceo," Iain said, as if introductions hadn't interrupted the conversation.

"It's a perfectly wonderful little lake," Alicia said. "And there are the dearest little cottages around it. I'd like to have one myself." She slipped her arm through Nigel's.

"I dinna think there are any for sale," Andrew said. "The families who live on the loch have lived there for centuries and passed their homes down from generation to generation."

"Andrew has one of those dear little cottages himself," Iain explained.

"But everything has a price," Martin said. "Or at least I've always found that to be true." He turned to Duncan. "We might discuss the price of your hotel, Mr. Sinclair. Would you be willing to give us a quick look at it tomorrow?"

Duncan met Iain's eyes. Iain gave the slightest, almost imperceptible shrug. Duncan switched his gaze to Mara. Her face showed no expression, and her eyes were carefully blank.

Duncan had taken a dislike to both Nigel and Martin, although he hadn't had time to analyze exactly why. But it seemed they might just give him what he had hoped for most. Freedom and a chance to start over. "I can show you around," he said. "Will ten be convenient?"

"It will do nicely."

"And now I'd say we should start toward the dining room before Mrs. Beggs comes in and leads us there by the ear. I've been told that the cook's outdone herself." Iain held out his arm to Mara. The others paired up and Andrew and Duncan were left to walk in together behind them.

Andrew held Duncan back. "Does it no' feel odd, Dunc, to sell your birthright?"

Duncan felt a flash of anger, made more potent, he supposed, because the same thought had occurred to him. "No odder than it must feel to spew guilt so blatantly, Andrew."

"I dinna like these men."

"Am I supposed to wait for a buyer you approve of?"

"You belong here."

"I don't!" Duncan took a deep breath. "You don't know me anymore. You don't know what I want or need."

"No? Then that makes two of us, does it no'?" Andrew started for the door.

Duncan grabbed his arm. "Look, I can't stay here. What's here for me?"

Andrew shook his head. "If you can no' figure that out alone, there's nowt to be done about it."

Duncan dropped his hand. "Why are we fighting about this? We're not kids anymore. We're both adults. I don't tell you what to do, and you've never tried to tell me what to do before this."

"I'm no' telling you what to do. I'm asking you to look at yourself and your life, Dunc. That's a wee thing to ask."

"I've looked and I've thought, and I'm leaving. Just as soon as I can. I owe it to April, and I owe it to myself."

"I mind the day you left Druidheachd. We were eight years of age. You sobbed as if your heart would never be whole again. And it has no' been whole since that day. And it will no' be whole until you cease trying to run away from who and what you are.''

Duncan stared at his friend. He had never seen Andrew so serious. "I don't even know what to say."

Andrew jammed his hands in his pockets. "Will you make my excuses to Iain, please? I dinna think I can eat tonight. And certainly no' with this company."

Andrew left Duncan standing in the hallway.

Mara had felt uneasy all night, although she hadn't been sure why. Fearnshader, with its medieval gargoyles and shadowed corridors, was a house with terrible secrets, but once there had been laughter there, too, and that balance had kept her from being overwhelmed.

She had disliked Iain's guests, and at first she had believed the dread growing inside her was related to them. But as the night wore on she realized that Martin and Nigel were only part of the problem. Her feelings were much more closely related to Duncan.

"So, you'll be showing Mr. Carlton-Jones the hotel tomorrow," she said in the car as she and Duncan drove back toward her cottage.

"I suppose so. He seems interested."

She wished, as she often had, that she could read Duncan's thoughts. "Did you like him, Duncan? Did you enjoy your conversation?"

"I didn't like him."

"But business is business?"

He glanced at her. She couldn't read his expression, either. "I've never thought it was necessary to like the people I negotiate with."

"And you feel no different when it's your da's hotel you might be selling?"

"You know, it's possible you've ended up with the wrong man of midnight, Mara. You and Andrew may be more suited to each other."

She was hurt clear to the bone. She stared out the window at darkness.

He was the first to break the silence. "Look, I'm sorry. I just don't want another guilt trip, okay? I may have a buyer for the hotel, and that's what I've been working for since I came here, so I'm happy about it. Maybe Martin won't make an offer, and maybe he will. But even if he doesn't, I'm going to sell the hotel to someone, and I'm not going to ask the villagers for yea or nay votes."

"You have no attachment to it?"

"None. And no attachment to Scotland."

"I see."

He smacked his hand against the steering wheel and pulled off the road at the next passing place. He turned off the engine. "Look, I didn't mean that the way it sounded. I didn't mean there's nothing here that I want or care about."

"It does sound that way." She still didn't look at him.

His tone softened. "You know I care about you, but we've both known this was coming. I've always been honest about my intentions."

"So you have."

"I would take you with me if you'd only go."

"You've never asked, have you?"

"Because I know what your answer will be."

"Perhaps you do, or perhaps you only tell yourself I'd no' consider following you."

"Would you?"

She heard a dozen conflicting messages in his voice. Even through her own pain she could hear his longing. He was a man with a deep well of emotion inside him, even if he rarely acknowledged it. He wanted and needed her desperately, and that was in his voice. But there were other messages, too. Fear. Distrust. A stubborn resistance to what he needed most. He had made up his mind what was best for them both, and he wouldn't reconsider.

"I would follow you anywhere if I thought I was truly wanted," she said. "But I will no' be following when you go."

He touched her hair, as if to reassure her. "Could you really be happy in New York or London or even a smaller city? What kind of life could you live where you were over-whelmed by impressions of the people all around you? You would be a prisoner."

"What kind of life will *you* live when there are *no* im-pressions of the people around you because they are all strangers?" She faced him. "Is that no' a prison, too, Duncan? Will you leave the people who love you most to go live among people who dinna even know you?"

"People do it all the time. People change jobs, move on, make new friends."

"And the new friends will be the same? You'll learn to love them as you love Andrew and Iain?"

"And love you?"

It was as close to telling her he loved her as he had ever come. She swallowed. "And me."

"What else can I do? I can't stay here. You can't go."

She saw that in his mind there were no other answers, no compromises. "Why can you no' stay here?"

"There's nothing here for me. I have to live in a city to be a success in advertising or any business. And I want to be a success again. Lisa took something precious from me, and I want it back. Druidheachd is a prison, and Martin Carl-ton-Jones may very well have the key to help me escape."

"There is no prison except the one you've made for yourself."

"Don't talk in riddles."

She saw that he really didn't understand because he wasn't going to listen to his heart. And there was no way she could make him. "It's getting late. I think you'd better take me home."

"Mara, don't do this. Don't let anger spoil the time we still have together. Let's make the most of it."

"It truly is getting late."

He shook his head and turned back to the steering wheel. In a moment the car was climbing again.

There were so many other things she wanted to say to him. But there were no words for any of them. There were so many things keeping them apart, and the very least of them was his need to live in a city.

They were almost to the turnoff to her croft when she spotted a car on the side of the road. Duncan's car was warm, but inadvertently, she shivered. "Isn't that Frances's car just ahead?"

He didn't answer. Instead, he pulled over and parked behind it. She started to get out when he did, but her growing dread slowed her limbs and pounded through her head. She closed her eyes for a moment, but it didn't help. She tried to envision walls as thick as a fortress, but that didn't help, either. Nothing helped; she'd had a lifetime to learn that lesson.

The conversation drifted toward her.

"Frances, what's wrong?"

"Oh Duncan, it's glad I am you came along. I've a tire that needs changing. And I can no' seem to get it off."

"Then I'm glad I came along, too." He peered inside the car. "Where's April? I thought she was going home with you tonight?"

Frances, who had been examining her woefully flat tire, straightened. "April? But I've no' seen her all night. I went up to check on her just after you'd left, and she was no' there. Sally'd been keeping an eye on her out in the garden, as you asked, and Sally said she left with someone and we thought—"

"My God, and you didn't call me to check?"

"But there seemed to be no need! Sally said it had all been arranged, that the woman said—"

"Woman?"

Frances was becoming agitated. "Aye. It was a young woman that April left with. And she told Sally she'd met you and April in Inverness at the hotel supply company there, and that when you heard she was going to be in town you'd asked her to take April out for the evening since you were going to be away. She said you must have forgotten to mention it. Sally thought it odd, but April seemed so glad..." She stretched out her arms. "No! I never thought.

We had so many guests for supper, and I was so busy. And Sally...!''

"What did this woman look like? Did Sally say?"

"No, except that she was bonny."

"Sally knows better! Somebody should have called me!"

"But it could no' be April's mother. She must have spoken like a Highlander, Duncan, or Sally would have been suspicious. How could Mrs. Sinclair have spoken like a Scot?"

"She can sound like a Frenchwoman or a German or an upper class English aristocrat! She's an actress. She can be whatever a role requires!"

"Oh Lord, forget me, Duncan. Go back to the hotel. Someone else will come along, and I'm no' that far from home."

"I'm sorry, but I'm going to have to leave you." He started back toward the car. "I'll phone Roger when I get back to town."

Frances wrung her hands. "It's my fault. I should have thought. Sally's so young, and she would no' think the worst of anyone. And she said she was watching from the window when the woman went to get April, and April seemed so glad..."

Duncan slammed the car door behind him. He swung around in the narrow space and started back toward Drui-dheachd.

"It's Lisa," he said after he'd left Frances far behind.

"Aye."

"Damn it, I knew if she started talking to April on the telephone, she'd start thinking about trying to see her! I know her. I know what she's like!"

"She's a mother, Duncan. Had you no' let her talk to April she might have come sooner."

"You don't have any idea what you're talking about!"

"I know more than you think."

"What?" He was terrified, and he was covering his terror with anger. "What could you possibly know?"

"I know that April's all right, and that Lisa has no intention of stealing her from you. She's taken her somewhere so that you can no' stop her from visiting, but she plans to bring April back."

"Oh really? I feel better now. Thanks!"

She told herself not to be hurt. She told herself he was suffering. She was bleeding inside for him. "I know you have little faith in my gift. But listen this time, please. Lisa's intentions are good."

"If you can see all this, just tell me where she's gone, why don't you? I'll go wherever you say. Just tell me where that woman's taken my daughter!"

"I can no'."

"Can't or won't?"

"I can no' see the fate of anyone I love."

"You can see just enough to stop me from worrying, but not enough to tell me where she is?"

"I can no' *see* anything that I can understand. I can feel this in my heart. Lisa loves April, too. She wants the best for her, and she wants to show you she can be responsible."

"She has a strange way of showing me, doesn't she? She's kidnapped my daughter! She doesn't have any right to her at all."

"She has a mother's right to see her own child."

She could see the muscle jump in his tightly clenched jaw. She wondered what terrible words he was trying to repress.

She felt nauseated, and her head continued to pound. Visions had filled her head as soon as they'd encountered Frances; indistinct pictures she couldn't understand, and a cacophony of indistinguishable sounds. She had seen as if through a fog, and every image she could glean was unfamiliar and mystifying.

The only thing she knew for sure was that Lisa had no desire to hurt either Duncan or April.

They were both silent until they got to the hotel. Sally was gone by then, and Mara listened as Duncan spoke to her on the telephone. He hung up with great care, as if afraid that if he gave in to his impulses, he might tear the phone from the wall.

"It was Lisa," he said. "It could only have been Lisa." He called the police constable who served Druidheachd alone and explained the situation to him, then he hung up again. "There's not much he can do, obviously. But he'll be over in a few minutes."

"Might she have left a note?"

He ran his hand through his hair. "I doubt it, but I can look."

"I'll phone Roger and then I'll check the desk. Perhaps you should have a look around your flat?"

He left for the second floor without a word. She told herself he was distraught, that his anger was for Lisa, not her. But she knew it wasn't completely true. She was the one who had convinced him to allow Lisa back into April's life. She was the one who had slipped behind the barriers Duncan erected to protect himself from his own feelings. And she was the one who understood most what he was going through.

Minutes later she knocked on his door. When he didn't answer right away she let herself inside. He was sitting beside the window. In answer to her unspoken question, he held out a slip of paper. She took it. Written in a delicate, feminine script was Lisa's plea for forgiveness, and her promise that nothing would happen to April. She would return her on Monday.

"Please believe me. She wants only the best for her," Mara said. "There's no malice here."

"I'm going to have every police officer in Scotland out looking for them!"

"I dinna think that will help matters. Can you no' wait until Monday before you begin to search? Can you no' have that much faith in her?"

"I have no faith!" He got to his feet. "You don't know what she's like! If she takes it into her head to steal April forever, she'll do it. Just like that!"

"She means April well."

"Stop it! For God's sake cut it out, Mara! You don't know! You can't know, despite what you think your intuition is telling you. You don't know her!"

"And neither do you." She saw the truth now. With blinding clarity she saw the truth. And it didn't take second sight. "You dinna know her either, do you, Duncan? You never took the time to get to know her. And that's what's been destroying you since you parted. You never really gave her a chance. Oh, it was no' your fault, no' completely. She was insecure and fragile, and when you made the effort, she did no' know how to respond. But when you could no' get through to her, you stopped trying."

He started to pace. "I've told you all that. Stop pretending that you're reading my mind."

"But there's more that you never told me. When you realized how badly Lisa needed your help, you took April and ran instead. You were afraid to reach out to her, even then, even when she was vulnerable and you knew you might have made a difference. Because reaching out terrifies you. You could have helped her. You could have gotten Lisa help, but you paid her off and took April and you vanished."

"Stop it!" He started toward her. "Who do you think you are?"

"I'm the other woman you're running from."

He stopped just in front of her. "You know, you're more like Lisa than I thought." His voice shook with anger.

"And yet you've loved us both, have you no'? You've loved us both because we're no' afraid to feel. And we're aware, both Lisa and I, that there's more to the world than anyone can see and touch. And that's why you've loved us both, and that's why you're so afraid now. And that's why you're going to run again."

"I never loved Lisa the way I've loved you!"

"Loved, Duncan?"

He stepped back, as if he couldn't bear to be so close to her. "I think you'd better go."

She saw his anger; she saw his distress, and she felt as if a hole had opened up inside her. There was nothing more she could do or say. "Aye. Perhaps I'd better."

"I'm going to get my daughter back, and then I'm going to sell this place!"

"And vanish again," she said.

"I know how to cut my losses, Mara. Apparently that's something you've never learned."

"For which I'm thankful." She turned and started for the door. Her hand was on the knob when she spoke again. She didn't look at him. "And I'm thankful for something else. I'm thankful I've loved you, Duncan, despite everything that's happened here tonight. Because loving someone is worth all the risk. No matter how it ends."

When he didn't respond she stepped into the hallway and closed the door softly behind her.

Chapter 15

Duncan needed a shave and a clean shirt. He was an adept
businessman who knew the value of appearance and pres-
entation, but he was also a father, frantic at the thought that
he might never see his daughter again. He tucked the shirt
in tighter and splashed water on his face, then he left the
Gatwick Airport restroom and headed for the next of half
a dozen ticket counters that he hadn't tried yet.

The airport bustled with travelers coming in and going out
of London. Flights were continually announced over the
intercom and toddlers wailed as their weary parents hauled
them through the foot traffic.

Duncan stood in a long line and waited his turn. He had
plenty of time to scrutinize all the clerks, and by the time his
turn was next, he had singled out the one most likely to help
him. When he was called, he passed up his turn and waited
for the clerk he'd chosen instead. She finished with her customer and the moment the old man stepped away from the
counter, Duncan took his place.

The clerk was pretty, blond and blue-eyed with the classic English milk-and-roses complexion. He had watched her

carefully. She had been uniformly polite to even the rudest customer, and she hadn't rushed anyone. Now she smiled and asked how she could help.

"I'm looking for my daughter," he said. He handed her April's most recent photograph. "She may have come through here with her mother. I have custody and three days ago her mother kidnapped her." He pulled out the documentation that proved the courts were on his side. Then he pulled out Lisa's photograph, the one that April had kept in her wooden chest of secrets. "This is my ex-wife. Do you remember selling her a ticket?"

She frowned, obviously not happy to be involved.

He glanced down at her hand and saw a wedding ring. "Do you have children?" he asked.

She nodded.

"Then maybe you can guess how I might be feeling? The court gave me custody because my ex-wife isn't fit to raise a child. And now she has our daughter, and I may never see her again."

She took the photograph of Lisa, but she didn't look at it. "Hundreds of people come through here every day, sir."

"I know. I know this is a long shot. But I'm desperate. Please. Just look at it. And show it to your colleagues. That's all I ask."

"Do you have reason to think she came here?"

"I don't know. I've already been to Prestwick and Heathrow. No one remembers her."

The clerk sighed and shook her head. Then she looked at the photograph. "Well, she's quite lovely. She has a memorable face."

"Yes. I see it clearly in all my nightmares."

"But I'm afraid she doesn't look familiar." She picked up April's photograph again. "And neither does your daughter. She favors you, doesn't she?"

"Will you show it to your colleagues?"

"I'll just be a moment."

"Take all the time you need."

Duncan had learned patience in the past three days. He had learned to stand and wait, and he had learned that disappointment left the taste of ashes in his mouth. He watched the young woman show the photograph to first one clerk, then another, and he watched them shake their heads. As she moved steadily down the row, he realized that he had chosen her to be his emissary because in appearance she reminded him a little of Mara.

He hadn't seen Mara since the night April had been kidnapped. Mara had been gone for only minutes when he regretted everything he'd said to her. But he hadn't gone to find her. He didn't know how she'd gotten home, and he hadn't inquired. He had let her slip out of his life without ceremony.

There'd been little time since to think about her and no time to grieve. He had to concentrate on finding April. Too many days had passed already, and by now Lisa and April could be living anywhere in the world. But Lisa was a creature of impulse, with little talent for long-range planning. He was counting on that to help him. Perhaps Mara had been right and he'd never known Lisa well, but he did know enough to guess how she might proceed.

Snatching April was probably as far ahead as Lisa had been able to think. Now that she had April, Lisa would begin to make plans. She had money. She could fly anywhere and settle down, but she would need a passport to get out of Great Britain, and April would have to have one, too. Lisa probably wouldn't chance using her own name, in case the airports were being watched, and April's passport was under lock and key at the hotel. So she would have to get false papers. And false papers took time.

If he could just get one lead, one possible sighting, it might not be too late.

The clerk returned. She looked genuinely sorry. "No one recognized the photographs. But if you have copies to leave?"

He left her several copies of each photo, along with his thanks, his name and the number of the Sinclair Hotel. Then he headed for the next counter.

By the time there were no more counters to try, he was exhausted. But a new shift would settle in after the dinner hour, and he planned to make the rounds of the counters all over again then. Now he headed for the closest restaurant and waited for a table. Once he was off his feet with a drink in his hand, he let exhaustion overwhelm him. He leaned back and closed his eyes, and he wondered what more he could possibly lose.

"Can you squeeze in another invitation to this affair?"

He opened his eyes and saw Iain standing beside the table. He leaned forward. "What in the hell are you doing here?"

"Looking for you." Iain held up his hand. "No, we haven't heard anything."

Duncan slumped back in his chair and gestured to the seat across from him. "I'm surprised you found me."

"I thought you'd probably stay on until you could interview the evening shift."

Duncan nodded. "Why are you here?"

"To take over. I've got you a seat on a flight back to Prestwick in about an hour. Then you're to go home and get some sleep. And have a shave, for God's sake. You look like a barbarian. Your car's there?"

Duncan was so tired he could hardly make sense of it all. "You're going to take over for me?"

"I'll stay for this change of shift and the next. Andrew's checking all the other routes out of the country. Ships, ferries." He shrugged. "It hits me every once in a while that we live on a great, huge, bloody island."

Duncan's throat felt tight, the way it had as a boy when he'd needed to cry but known he was too old. "I don't know what to say."

Iain made a face. "Then please, by all means, don't say anything."

"Nobody's heard anything back at the hotel?"

"Not exactly."

He was almost too tired to pick up on Iain's words, but not quite. "What do you mean?"

"Mara came by to see me this morning."

"Mara?"

"You remember her?"

"Cut the crap, Iain. Has she heard something?"

"No. But she still thinks Lisa is sincere. She still thinks she's planning to bring April back tomorrow."

Duncan didn't say anything.

"I gather the two of you fought," Iain said.

"Is that why she came to see you?"

"No. She's having disturbing dreams. Apparently she's been having them since Lisa took April."

"Then we still share that much, at least."

"She's afraid that despite Lisa's intentions, she's going to be prevented somehow from returning April."

Duncan rapped his fingers on the table. "I'd thought better of Mara than that."

"What do you mean?"

"Can't you see what she's doing? She's talking out of both sides of her mouth. She's making completely different predictions so she can't possibly be proved wrong. Whether Lisa returns April or not, Mara's hedged her bets."

"Do you think so?"

"Well, what do you you think?"

"I think you're a fool." Iain got to his feet.

Duncan reached across the table to stop him from leaving. "Why am I a fool?"

"Because Mara has no need to prove herself to you or anybody. She's not selling her talent, Dunc. She doesn't need a perfect record."

Duncan realized just how low he had sunk. Now he was trying to invent a case against Mara when all she had ever tried to do was help. And why? Because even this tenuous connection to her was too painful. "Sit down."

Iain must have heard something promising in his voice, because he sat. "What can I do?" Duncan asked. "What should I do?"

"Go to her. See what she can tell you."

"I don't know if I can face her."

"You know, I've always envied you."

"Me?"

"Does that surprise you? It shouldn't. You have April."

"You forget. I don't have April anymore."

Iain shook his head. "And then Mara came into your life. And for a while you had her, too. And what man wouldn't count himself fortunate? There's nothing she wouldn't share with you if you'd let her."

"So what are you trying to say?"

"You're in danger of letting them both slip through your fingers. And then you won't be a man to envy."

Duncan held out his hand. Iain took an envelope from his inside coat pocket and handed it to him. Duncan shuffled through his ticket, noting the gate and time of departure. "Do you remember the day I left for America? We were just eight."

"I remember."

"Andrew reminded me of it when we were at Fearnshader the other night."

"Our Andrew can be ruthless."

"I hadn't thought of that day in years." Duncan gave a harsh laugh. "I was sure my world was ending."

"It did."

Duncan looked up. "I guess it did. I felt like I'd been ripped out by the roots. And I didn't transplant well until I stopped caring about everything."

"Do you need something else to think about?"

Duncan didn't answer.

"In your absence I took Martin through the hotel and showed it to him. He's made a bid for it. With some negotiation, it should do. It's rather generous, actually."

"Why are you telling me now?"

Iain gave a sad smile. "Because somehow, it's all connected, isn't it?"

Mara was waiting at the hotel when Duncan, weary beyond imagination, walked into the lobby after his drive back to Druidheachd from the airport. It was already past midnight, but his own exhaustion seemed insignificant when he saw her. She looked pale and drained, as if she hadn't slept in days.

She didn't smile when he approached, but she rose and nodded in greeting. He wondered how she had known when he would be arriving.

"Iain told me what time your plane would be getting in," she said, as if to set the record straight immediately.

"He told me he'd talked to you."

"I dinna want to take up much of your time." She hesitated. "For what it's worth, Duncan, I did no' want to take up *any* of it. I'd hoped that Iain would speak to you for me, but he refused."

He was too tired to fight his own feelings. Regret as deep as the bottom of his heart surged through him. "I hope you feel you can always talk to me."

She met his eyes, and he saw her answer. She was a woman willing to risk almost anything, but she was not a fool. She, too, knew how to cut her losses. "I will speak to you about this because I'm afraid for April."

"Let's go upstairs." She appeared to consider, as if she didn't want to be alone with him. His regret dug deeper. "Mara, come upstairs. I'm not going to hurt you. And we can't talk privately in here."

Her nod was almost imperceptible. He led the way and she trailed after him. He ushered her into his apartment and turned on the lights. She went straight to the couch and sat down, as if her legs were too tired to hold her.

"I'm going to make some tea," he said. "We can both use it. Just sit tight."

Her eyes were closed when he returned, but she held out her hands for her cup. She wrapped her fingers around it and hugged it to her chest as if she needed the warmth. The night was unusually cold for September, and the hotel hadn't yet turned on the heat for the season. Duncan didn't think about his next move. He picked up a soft wool afghan from the end of the couch and draped it over her shoulders.

"I'm quite capable of looking after myself," she said.

"I know."

She opened her eyes, but they might as well have stayed closed because there was no expression in them. "I've told you from the beginning that I believe Lisa means no harm by what she's done. I think she has every intention of returning April."

"So you've said."

"What I have no' told you is that I've been plagued with . . . other feelings? Sensations? I dinna know how to explain. I can only say that there is something else very wrong."

Duncan took a seat beside her instead of one across the room. She shifted subtly, as if she didn't want him to touch her. "Tell me more," he said. "Tell me whatever you can."

"I've had nightmares, and waking dreams, too. The images are frightening. They make no sense to me, and they get no clearer with time. It's as if I'm seeing everything through a fog. The mists swirl, then there's a brief opening. I see a face or a figure and then the mists swirl over them again."

"Do you recognize anything or anyone?"

"No. And the orra thing is that no one I see looks . . . as they should?" She lifted her shoulders in question. "I dinna ken why."

"All right. Maybe we should start there."

"Start?"

"Yes. Start trying to pin it down a little. Maybe we should start with why they don't look the way you think they should. What's strange about them that you haven't been able to put your finger on yet?"

"I've never been able to pin my visions down, as you put it." She set her tea down and stood, as if she couldn't stand to sit beside him. She began to pace. "I have no control over what I see or when I see it."

"Why are you pacing?"

"I'm more comfortable this way."

"Mara..."

She stopped pacing. "I'm here because I'm afraid for April. Dinna make this into something else, Duncan, or I'll be forced to leave."

He dropped his hand to his lap. He hadn't even realized that he had reached out to her. "Can you describe what you see?"

She began to pace again. "Faces. Mist." She shook her head.

He watched her pace. "What about the faces? Men's? Women's?"

"I dinna know." Suddenly she stopped and faced him. "I can no' sleep, because when I do, the dreams begin. And I wake up with a scream in my throat."

He felt wrenched by the emotion in her voice. She was struggling not to let him see how deeply she had been affected by the visions, but the struggle was there for him to hear. "Is that very unusual?"

"Aye. I've often had prophetic dreams, but never ones that repeat themselves over and over."

"When you wake up, what do you feel? You must feel fear if you're ready to scream."

"No' fear. No' for myself." She began to pace again.

"Then for someone else? For April?"

"I dinna think it's April in the dream. But it's about her."

"I don't understand."

"Neither do I."

"Mara, you're wearing yourself out. Please sit down before you drop."

She continued to pace. Faster, if anything. "There's a feeling of such betrayal—"

"Betrayal?" He sat forward.

"Terrible, terrible betrayal."

He thought of his own betrayals and shame filled him. "Well, there's not much doubt where that comes from."

"What do you mean?"

He stood and intercepted her, resting his hands on her arms. She pulled away as if she couldn't tolerate his touch. "I betrayed you," he said softly. "I used you, and I betrayed you. And you were right, I did the same thing to Lisa, even if the circumstances were entirely different."

"This is no' about you and me."

"I think it is. What you believe to be a nightmare about April is really about us, Mara. You gave so much of yourself, and I gave so little. And when you wanted more, when you reached out to me, I shoved you away."

"This is no' about you and me. The dream is about your daughter!"

He reached out to her, and she backed away. "Dinna touch me, Duncan. Dinna touch me again or I'll leave and no' come back."

He saw how agitated she was becoming. He had never seen her this way. He nodded, afraid she would do exactly as she threatened. "All right."

"Please, move away from me."

He walked to the window and looked out over the village green. He struggled for something to say, something ordinary and soothing. He didn't struggle long. "It's snowing." He slapped his palm against the windowsill. "I knew it was cold, but I had no idea it was that cold."

"They've been predicting storms in the Highlands all day."

He could tell from her voice that she was doing exactly what he was, struggling for normalcy. It almost seemed insane. "Then it's not just a flake or two?"

"At the highest elevations it might be several feet."

He turned slowly. "Maybe your dream isn't about me and you, but that doesn't make what I said any less true."

"Does it no'?"

"I've closed myself off from everyone for so long that I don't even know when it started. But you got too close, and it scared me."

"You've never trusted me. No' from the beginning, and no' now."

"What do you mean, I don't trust you now?"

She began to pace again. "I've told you this dream is about your daughter, yet you persist in calling it something else."

"I'm trying to tell you I'm sorry!"

"And will that change anything? You've suddenly realized that you're at least partially to blame for the problems between us, but you still dinna see what you're doing."

"What am I doing?"

"You have no' really changed at all. You see me and everything I am as less than whole. You see the sight as a regrettable handicap, and me as a hysterical woman whose own psychological needs are coming out in dreams and visions. It's a wonder you're taking the time to speak to me at all!"

He stared at her. He saw her pain, and the self-respect that she had somehow managed to cultivate anyway. And he realized that she was right. At no time during their reunion had he truly taken her visions seriously. He had used them as an excuse to be with her.

From the beginning of their relationship he had ignored the abilities that she had used so often and so well. He had seen her predictions come true time and time again, yet he had pushed her successes out of his own narrow mind. And when he had been forced to confront the evidence, he had sought other explanations. Any other explanation.

He had never trusted her. Not the way that she needed someone to trust her. Not the way that she needed *him* to trust her.

"How could I have been so blind?" he asked. "I haven't understood. I still don't understand. But you're right. I couldn't understand, and so I denied what's so obvious."

She faced him. "And what is that, Duncan?"

He had to push his answer from his throat. He still didn't want to believe it. Even as he said it, he didn't want to believe it. But he knew now that it had to be true.

"You can see the future," he said. "You really can."

"Aye. I can see the future. And it's nearly destroyed my life."

"And you're seeing the future now. In your dreams. In your visions."

"Aye." She lifted her chin. "And it's nearly destroying me."

"How could I have been so stupid?" He moved toward her. She didn't move away. He moved slowly, so very slowly. "Only one of us has behaved irrationally, and it hasn't been you." He stopped an arm's length away. He stretched out his hand. "My mind has been closed. You've proved yourself to me again and again, and I've simply ignored everything I didn't want to see."

She closed her eyes. He uncurled his fingers. He touched her cheek. Lightly. A feather's touch. This time she didn't move away.

"And there's so very much I didn't want to see," he said. "And now I'm beginning to."

Chapter 16

Mara closed her eyes. She could feel Duncan's fingertips against her cheek. She could feel his words in her heart.

And she could feel the boundaries that separated the present and the future begin to shift.

"Dinna touch me," she gasped. "Get away from me, Duncan!"

She stepped backwards. Suddenly she was trembling so hard she was afraid her legs wouldn't hold her. She opened her eyes and saw the shock in his. Then shock turned to hurt and finally to anger. "All right. I won't," he said quietly, but the pitch of his voice was deceptive. He might as well have slapped her.

"You dinna understand!"

"That's possible. Or maybe I do. Finally."

She struggled to find a way to explain. "When you touch me..."

"What? It disgusts you? I'll remember, and I sure won't do it again."

"No!" Dizziness overwhelmed her. She couldn't hold off the inevitable. It was like trying to stop a raging river. "Move away from me. Please!"

"Mara? What in God's name is wrong?" He stepped closer. His expression changed again. Anger disappeared to be replaced by concern.

Her knees gave way and she slumped to the floor. She put her head down, but it only made the dizziness worse.

Then she saw the mists. Thick, swirling mists, and she shivered because suddenly she was so cold, colder than she had ever been in her life. But this *wasn't* her life, nor anyone's that she had ever known. She was somewhere she had never been, and layers of time were crashing one into the other.

She heard screams and nausea gripped her. She wanted to move toward the screams, to help somehow, but she was rooted to one place and could not move at all.

Someone was running toward her in the mist. She could hear the sound of footsteps crunching on the snow. There was snow at her feet. She saw it now. And the mist wasn't mist at all but a snowstorm. A woman's face materialized in the midst of it. She was young and obviously terrified. Her hair streamed out behind her as she ran and a bruise darkened her cheek. As Mara watched a hand closed over her hair and the woman screamed.

"Mara! Are you all right?"

She was jerked back to the present. She could sense Duncan kneeling beside her. She heard a pounding somewhere behind her, but she couldn't open her eyes. With a curse he got up and went to the door. She heard voices.

Duncan's: "No, damn it, I don't know if everything's all right or not."

A woman's: "Is it Miss Mara? I heard her scream. Is she ill?"

Duncan's again: "Will you go get Dr. Sutherland, please? Ask him to come immediately if he can. And get *him*, not his partner." He slammed the door.

She took a deep breath. Her voice came out a whisper. "Stay away from me, Duncan," she said. "Don't come any closer."

"For God's sake, tell me why! What's happening?"

But the mists were closing again. She couldn't speak. She whimpered as they cut off the present again. There were men talking. She strained to understand their words, but they were nearly incomprehensible. She recognized a word, then another. The language was a mixture of a deeply accented English and another language. "Gaelic." She wrenched out the word, but it didn't take her back to the present. Instead the scene cleared. There was smoke mixed with the snow now, thick, smothering smoke. She began to cough. She tried to move away from it, but she was trapped. The smoke stung her eyes, and she began to cry. Then she heard a child screaming.

"April!" She tried to run. She was able, somehow, to get to her feet. Her eyes opened, and she saw Duncan.

"Move away from me," she gasped. "Move away!"

He backed away. "*I'm* the trigger, aren't I? You're seeing the future, and I'm the trigger!"

She shook her head. She could almost feel her mind clear with each step he took. "No' the future..." Her head began to pound, but she was, for the moment, firmly back in the present.

"What then?"

"I dinna know!"

"What do you see?"

She shook her head again. Images swam there, but the feelings were even more terrifying. "Betrayal. Terrible..." She began to cry again.

"I want to put my arms around you!"

"No! Please!"

"I feel so helpless!"

She made it to the couch. But the moment she sat, the visions began again. She heard laughter. Maniacal, inhuman laughter. A man in belted plaid, trews and bonnet, appeared in front of her on horseback. The horse reared and the man lifted a sword above his head. She saw it come crashing toward the earth.

There was blood on the snow.

She felt herself falling through space. There was nothing now except darkness. No visions. No screaming. As she fell she thought she heard the mournful wail of bagpipes. Then, silence.

The silence seemed to stretch into forever. She only truly became aware of it when it ended. She could hear men's voices again.

"I tell you I don't know what's wrong exactly! But I think she's having visions."

"Hallucinations?"

"No! Visions of the future. Mara has second sight. That's how she knew the children were going to be trampled at the Johnsmas Fair. And she's predicted other things. More than I can tell you."

"I thought as much, Duncan. I guessed it when she was at the hospital. But why did you no' tell me before this? Why did you try to hide it?"

"Why? Because most people are stupid and unreasonable if they don't understand something!"

"Most people?"

There was a pause. "Me," Duncan said.

"Ah, I see, lad. It's you who did no' understand."

"And you do?"

"Of course. Have I no' see it before? There was an old woman in Druidheachd, old when I came here to practice medicine. She lived many more years after, and she saw the future until the day she died. The week of her death she chose her own kist and told us to wait until the rain stopped before we put her in the kirkyard. It rained the day she died, of course, and three days after. We waited, you can be certain. Auld Margaret was no' always right, but she was right often enough."

"Margaret Henley."

"Aye."

"Mara's suffering."

"No. She's resting now. Whatever it was she saw became too much for her."

"I think when I'm near, particularly when I touch her, I trigger the visions."

"Then they must concern you somehow. Have they to do with April?"

"Apparently. Mara says that my ex-wife plans to return April tomorrow." He gave a harsh laugh. "Today, I guess it is. But something is going to interfere. She doesn't know what."

Mara tried to speak, but her throat was so dry the sound that emerged was nothing like a word. She felt hands at her wrist. They were soothing hands.

"Get her some water, Duncan, but don't bring it here. I'll come in the kitchen and get it."

Mara opened her eyes and saw Angus Sutherland.

"Do no' even try to talk. Just stay here. I'll get the water," he said.

He returned a few moments later with it. She was sitting up by then, and Duncan hadn't reappeared. "Drink it all," Angus commanded.

Mara's hand shook, and she spilled drops on her dress. But she managed to drink most of it. He took the glass and set it on the table. "Can you talk?"

"Now you know," she said.

"I've suspected for a while." He sat beside her. "May I?"

"Aye."

"How long has this been going on?"

"Three days."

"Have you slept? Eaten?"

She shook her head.

"You're wabbit, lass. Trauchled. Exhausted. I've a mind to put you back in the hospital."

"No!" She put her head in her hands.

"How long can this go on?"

"Till I know. Till I can see clearly."

"I see." Dr. Sutherland patted her knee. "Has this happened before, then?"

"No. Never like this."

"Do you ken why it's different this time?"

"I can no' see the fate of those I love. I've never been able to."

"And this time?"

"I must!"

"Ah." He was quiet for a while. "Duncan says that he triggers the sight."

"This time. Aye." She felt gratitude that Duncan finally understood.

"What happens?"

"I dinna know. He comes close or he touches me and the visions are stronger."

"And that's a bad thing?"

"They're so terrible!"

"Poor lass."

"But I must see! April's safety depends on it."

"Aye. I think you must. And I think Duncan must help you see this to conclusion."

Fear shot through her. She didn't know if she could continue to survive the horror.

"He loves you, you know," Dr. Sutherland said. "And even if he triggers the visions, he'll be right here with you to help you through them. And so will I."

"I dinna think Duncan loves me."

"He's no' a man who can say it easily, Mara. He's like his father that way. I saw what happened to his da when his mother took Duncan and Fiona to the States to live. Donald Sinclair withered, like the moors without rain. He was never the same man after they left Druidheachd. And the saddest thing was that Donald could never tell Duncan how much he loved him. He was cruel to the lad when he visited each summer, and he would no' even let the wee lass come back. Donald cut both of them from his life because he could no' stand the pain."

Tears slipped down her cheeks. He handed her a clean handkerchief. "Will you try now?" he asked. "We must get this over with."

"You'll stay?"

"Aye. I'll no' even write this up for the medical journals."

She tried to smile, but tears filled her eyes. "Call him," she said.

She closed her eyes and tried to prepare. She felt Angus leave the couch. She heard soft voices in the kitchen. Sometime later she felt the couch sag beside her.

"Mara, I'm right here," Duncan said. "I won't leave you, no matter what happens, unless you tell me to or Angus thinks it's best."

She opened her eyes and turned to him. He held out his hands. She lifted hers, and he took them. "I wish, my lady," he said softly, "that I could be the one to suffer."

A blast of frigid air buffeted her, and she closed her eyes to protect them. She was so cold. The temperature in the room had plummeted. She breathed out and her breath crystalized. And then snow swirled around her. Noise swirled around her. Screams and curses and the clang of swords, the firing of muskets.

A woman, the same woman, with dark hair streaming behind her, was running toward Mara. Mara tried to reach out to her, but she couldn't move. The woman's bruised face was contorted with fear. She pleaded for help in a language that Mara couldn't understand. Then a hand closed over the woman's hair, a man's hairy fist.

Mara looked up and saw the man through the snowstorm. He was large and red-faced, and he was on horseback. He dragged the woman beside him until the horse halted. Then he sprang to the ground, his belted plaid flapping around his knees as he did, and dragged her up against him. He lifted a dirk.

"No!" Mara opened her eyes. Duncan gripped her hands harder. "He's going to kill her!"

"What, Mara? Who?"

But she was floating by then, floating like the snowflakes. Except that she was drifting toward the heavens instead of away from them. Below her she heard screaming.

She saw a child running toward a stand of trees, followed closely by a woman carrying an infant. A man passed close by on horseback, but he didn't pursue them. The child knelt in the snow. The mother knelt beside her and covered her with her own cloak. And the snow settled over them and hid them in the darkness.

She floated higher. She saw smoke and the remains of a house, its thatched roof still smoldering. Animals, the shaggy black Highland cattle and sheep with fine, dark wool, ran wild in the steading, chased by men in uniform.

She drifted higher. She could see mountains now, mountains rising in sharp peaks toward the sky. Her view had been so conscribed she hadn't realized she was in the mountains, different mountains than she knew.

The carnage was no less terrible here. She began to spin. Slowly, so slowly. Everywhere she was forced to look she saw fires and blood on the snow. She saw people trying to hide, some successfully, some not. She saw men and women, and children too, clambering through the drifts, up the frozen sides of mountains, into caves between jutting rocks. She tried to look away, but each view was as filled with horror as the one before it.

And then the screaming stopped. Blessedly, the snows began to melt. As she watched, the fires died. Graves appeared and new cottages rose from the ground.

Somewhere a piper began to play. It was a mournful tune, a lament for those who had died. Foxglove, cowslip and willow herb grew in the braes and beside the lochs, and badgers and foxes hunted for prey. Clouds cast their long shadows over awe-inspiring peaks and rocky glens, but there was a longer shadow over the place where the murders had been committed, a shadow that would never vanish in the brightest sunlight.

And the piper played until the lament was finished.

Mara opened her eyes.

Duncan was gripping her hands. Tears ran down her cheeks. She couldn't tell him what she'd seen. There were no words to describe it. She began to hum the lament, tentatively at first, then with more assurance. She remembered it all.

"Do you know the tune?" Angus asked when she had finished. "Do you know what you were humming?"

She shook her head. She couldn't take her eyes from Duncan's. He had not been where she had been; he had not seen what she had seen. But he had suffered for her. She gripped his hands tighter.

"It's *piobaireachd. Ceol Mor*. The classical music for bagpipes. My father was a piper. If I'm not mistaken that's 'Lament for Glencoe'."

"Glencoe." She breathed the word, and it chilled her to the bone.

"Glencoe?" Duncan asked. "I don't understand."

"You've forgotten your history, lad. Glencoe was the scene of a terrible massacre," Dr. Sutherland said. "1692 it was. The Highland clans were told they would be pardoned for their loyalty to King James if they swore an oath of allegiance to William. One by one they did, but MacIain of Glencoe waited 'til the last moment and was kept from making his oath by a storm until the deadline had passed. He did finally swear his allegiance, but it did no' matter. He and his clansmen were attacked by a government regiment that had accepted their hospitality for most of a fortnight. The regiment rose up one night and slaughtered all they could, burned their houses and set their livestock free. Some of the clan escaped into the hills. Many did no'. There's no' been a waur day for Scotland."

"I saw it." Mara took a deep breath. "All of it."

"The massacre?" Duncan squeezed her hands. "But you called out April's name, Mara."

"I heard a child screaming."

"Was it April?"

"No. But she's there. That's where she's gone, Duncan."

"Glencoe? I don't understand."

"Lisa took her there. It's no' that far, an easy drive."

"But why? Is there anything there to see now?"

"I dinna know." She saw his frustration. She felt it. She could feel every emotion that coursed through him.

"She's exhausted," Dr. Sutherland said. "Let her be now. She must rest or I dinna know what will happen to her."

"No. I have to finish this." There was no feeling in Mara's hands they were held so tightly in Duncan's, but she didn't pull away. She had to have the connection to him if she was to see more.

"Maybe you'd better listen to him," Duncan said. "I don't want you hurt."

Mara shut her eyes. For a moment she was afraid there was nothing else she could learn. She could hear Duncan's breathing, the soft crunch of tires against snow in the street below . . . the wild screech of an eagle.

She was floating again. The worst of the images had vanished now. But the wildflowers she had glimpsed were gone, replaced by a soft carpet of snow. She could see a highway and a glen with modern buildings and a vast car park at its edge. Then she was far from civilization, in a mountain pass. The snow was thicker here, a golden eagle soared above her searching for prey against the undisturbed white drifts.

Below her, mountains walled in a canyon. She glimpsed cattle, dozens or more of them, shaggy and broad, penned in by the mountains, too. Then the cattle disappeared.

She heard a child crying. She heard the soothing voice of a woman, then a scream. And she understood.

She pulled her hands from Duncan's. She would see no more. She took a moment to open her eyes. She let the vision stay in her mind as long as it would; she drifted with it, noting everything she saw.

Then she opened her eyes. "They're tenting. They are off by themselves in a wee clearing between two peaks. Lisa did no' want to be with other people, in case you searched for her. So she took April to an isolated place, and they made a snug camp. But she did no' guess that snow would come, and she was no' prepared for it. When she tried . . . or when

she tries..." She shrugged helplessly. She couldn't be sure
if what she had seen had happened or was about to.

"Go on," Duncan said.

"There'll be an accident, or there has already been one. I
can no' tell which. Lisa is hurt and she can no' get April to
safety. And they are in danger because of the cold and the
snow."

"How do you feel, lass?" Dr. Sutherland asked.

She shook her head, but she didn't look at him. "Duncan?"

His voice was gentle, as if he was afraid he was going to
hurt her. "I'm sorry, lady, but Lisa has never camped or
backpacked in her life. Her idea of roughing it is settling for
a motel instead of a four-star hotel."

"Lisa's changed." She saw doubt in his eyes. She had felt
completely drained of emotion. She would have believed she
was incapable of more, except that dread was beginning to
build inside her again. "Duncan, you have to believe me.
That's where April is, and you must find her."

"I know you saw something, Mara. I don't doubt a word
you've told me, and I know it's been terrible to put yourself through this. But you've got to understand. This is
completely unlike Lisa. Completely. You don't know her or
you'd see I'm right. She wouldn't even consider taking April
camping."

"She did."

"Do you need me, lass?" Dr. Sutherland asked. "Do you
want me to bide with you awhile?"

"There'll be no more visions now," she said. She held out
her hand to him. "Thank you so much."

He took her hand and held it for a moment. "Have you
ever been wrong? Have you ever seen a vision that did no'
come true?"

"I've never before seen women and bairns slaughtered in
front of me," she said. Her voice caught. "Am I to believe
I saw them for no reason?"

He squeezed her hand. At the doorway he turned. "Listen well, Duncan," he said. The door closed behind him.

"Will you listen, Duncan? Or will you no' trust me again?"

"I trust you." Duncan touched her cheek, her hair. In a moment she was in his arms. He clasped her against him and his lips found her hair, her cheek, her lips. His arms tightened around her. "Mara, I trust you. I do. And I'm sorry you had to go through...such a terrible experience. But this is unlikely. You just don't know how unlikely it is!"

She pulled away, although it took every ounce of strength she had. "Then you lied when you said you believed I could tell the future?"

"No. I didn't. It's just that this time—"

"I've found April for you, Duncan."

He framed her face with his hands. "Can you say where she is exactly?"

"No. I'll have to go with you."

"You can't go anywhere. You're exhausted. You heard Dr. Sutherland."

"I'm the only one who can find her. I'll know where to go when we get there." She covered his hands and removed them from her cheeks. "If you dinna go, I'll go without you."

She saw a change come over him. He was torn; she hadn't expected anything different. As he battled with himself she knew what she was asking of him, but she couldn't ask less.

"We'll need help," he said at last. "Iain and Andrew are gone. We're going to have to find some other men to help. I'm sure we'll have to fan out when we get there."

She sensed resignation more than acceptance. She was disappointed, but right now the only thing that truly mattered was finding April. "We'll have to tell them why."

"Are you sure? You're willing?"

"Aye. If the people of Druidheachd can no' accept me the way I am, then I'll need to move on. But I can no longer pretend to be something I'm no'."

"I can think of half a dozen people who might help." He stood. "Roger. Geordie Smith—he owes us both, doesn't he?" He named men in rapid succession.

"Did you know you had so many friends in Druidheachd, Duncan?"

He lifted her chin and bent closer. "Will you promise you'll get some rest? It's going to take a while to gather everybody together. Then I'll come back for you, and we can leave. It should be nearly dawn by the time we get to Glencoe. We'll see if we can find something for you to change into. You can't hike into the mountains in what you're wearing."

She knew she wouldn't rest until April was home, but she nodded. He turned to go and the telephone rang. He nearly ripped the receiver from the cradle. "Yes?"

He took a deep breath as he listened to the voice on the other end. She watched his face, but she couldn't read it. He got a pen and scribbled as he listened. He repeated a number and a time. "And the flight hasn't left yet?" He waited for an answer. "Not until then?"

The conversation made no sense to her. She stood on strangely weak legs and went to the window. Snow was still falling.

She knew he had finished when she felt his hands on her shoulders. "That was a woman I spoke to yesterday at Heathrow. A woman matching Lisa's description just bought two tickets to L.A., and she has a little girl with her. The tickets were issued in the name of Elizabeth Sinclair."

"I see."

"Do you?" He turned her gently. "It sounds like it could be Lisa, Mara. The agent says she's the right age, dark-haired and pretty. She didn't get a good look at the little girl, but she was crying and tugging at her mother's hand like she didn't want to go. Lisa's name isn't Elizabeth, but it's close enough that no one would question the difference, not at that point."

"What are you going to do?"

"Their flight doesn't leave for another four hours, but there's no way I can drive to Prestwick and get a plane to London in time to catch them there. But I can take a flight out of Prestwick to L.A. myself. There's one that goes straight through without a layover and Lisa's . . . Elizabeth Sinclair's flight lays over in New York for two hours. I'd beat them to L.A. by about an hour. I could be waiting when they step off the plane."

"Aye. You could."

He rubbed his palms up and down her arms. "It could be Lisa, Mara. And if she gets April back to L.A., she could disappear with her. Who knows where she'd take her from there? For all I know she's had this set up with that crazy cult she was involved with. They've got branches all over the world, and they could keep me from ever seeing April again."

"Your daughter is at Glencoe, Duncan." She gripped his hands. "Elizabeth Sinclair is no' Lisa."

"You're tearing me apart!"

"No. I'm giving you back your child. And if you do no' take her back, if you do no' go and find her with me, I can no' say what will happen."

"I never thought you'd do this to me! You're asking me to choose what I think is right over your ability to see the future."

"Aye. But no' to test you. I've never been surer of a thing in my life. You've said that you trust me. You must trust me now!"

It had come to that. She saw it clearly. Somewhere echoing inside her was a child's scream. She could do no less for April than make this, the ultimate demand on Duncan.

She could feel the tension in his body against her palms. He was a man ready to fly into a thousand pieces. Tears sprang to her eyes, but she kept silent.

"Glencoe," he said. He pulled away from her. "I'll go with you to Glencoe."

"You will no' be sorry."

He walked to the telephone table. He picked up the receiver and dialed a long series of numbers, and he didn't take his eyes off of her as he did. He put the receiver to his ear and waited. "Let me speak to Sam, please. This is Duncan Sinclair. Yeah, I'm calling from Scotland. What time is it there?'' He waited, then he began to speak again.

She listened as he outlined briefly what had happened. She understood from the things he said that the man on the other end was his American attorney. ''I need you to meet a flight that will be arriving there in about seventeen hours. Lisa may be on it with April. If she is, you'll need to get April away from her, and if you can't do that, you'll need to follow them. I'll pay whatever I have to. Use a P.I. if you think it's better. But you've got to be there to identify her.''

He listened again. ''Yeah, I've got all the flight info.'' He picked up the paper he'd scribbled on. He gave the man the same information the ticket agent had given him. ''You can do it? You're sure? Okay, then I'll talk to you after the plane arrives. Sam, thanks. I don't know what I would have done if you'd said no.''

He hung up. ''This has nothing to do with trust.''

She didn't speak because she knew there was nothing she could say that would change anything.

''You've asked me to believe in you,'' he said. ''I do. Now I'm asking you to believe in me. I have to take every precaution.'' He turned without another word and left her standing there.

Chapter 17

Glencoe at dawn had an unearthly beauty. Snow outlined its rugged peaks and ice glistened like diamonds on trees and trails alike. Duncan parked in the lot of a hotel several miles outside the village, but the region bounded by rivers, lochs and mountains was so vast that it would take days to cover the parts that were even moderately accessible.

Duncan laced his boots tighter and pulled on an extra sweater for warmth before he zipped his jacket. The other men were doing the same. Not one of them had blinked an eye at his request. They had nodded sagely and asked when he planned to leave. And they had each been outside his house waiting when Duncan came to pick them up.

Beside him Mara zipped her jacket, too. She was bundled from head to toe, but Duncan was still afraid she was going to suffer from the cold. She was as pale as the snowfall, and her eyes were shadowed. He hadn't asked how she planned to lead them to Lisa and April because he was afraid to hear the truth. She had gone through hell already; he was sure there was more of the same ahead.

"I brought an extra scarf." He offered it, but she shook her head. She had said very little since leaving the hotel. He had hoped she would sleep as they traveled, but instead she had stared out the window. He wondered if she was afraid to sleep, if she was afraid the dreams would return as she neared the site of the massacre.

She had endured so much, and he wanted to tell her how sorry he was that April's disappearance had led to her visions. But Mara had cut herself off from him. From the moment he had made the call to L.A., she had removed herself from his presence, even when she was sitting beside him.

"Are you going to be warm enough?" he asked now. "You're already so run down, a chill could be serious."

"Bring everything extra that you have for Lisa and April." She turned away from him.

"Duncan, do you think we'll need ropes?" Roger asked. "I've brought a good one and an ice axe."

Duncan watched as Mara walked over to the group of men to confer with them. "It won't be a bad idea to have them along," he said.

"You dinna think the woman did any climbing, do you? Not with the child?"

"I don't think they're here," Duncan said honestly. "But if they are, they're just off a trail somewhere. Even if Lisa's taken up mountain climbing, April's too young to climb with her."

"We've food enough for the day, and water. But we'll have to be back here by the time the sun goes down. We're no' equipped to spend the night out."

"We'll be back on the road by then."

They joined the others. Mara was speaking. "I've asked Duncan to stop here because I saw this hotel in my... dream."

The men nodded. Not one of them seemed surprised.

"I also saw cattle huddled in a mountain pass. They were Highland cattle, the old ones." She paused. "I dinna know what that meant, but as soon as I'd seen them, they were gone."

"I'm from here, ye know," Geordie Smith said. He was sober this morning, had been sober for months, and he had been particularly pleased to be included on this expedition. "Well, me mother's people are from Ballachulish, anyway. And I spent me holidays here often enough as a lad."

"Does what I've told you mean anything?"

He shook his head.

"The pass was walled in by mountains. Perhaps someone here at the hotel will know."

"Walled in, ye say?" Geordie scratched his head. "I wonder, could it be Coire Gabhail of which yer speaking?"

"What's that?" Duncan asked.

"It's a corrie below here a bit. It's an odd place, that. It has a floor as level as the counter in your pub, Duncan. Gearr Aonach rises to one side of it and Beinn Fhada the other."

"Coire Gabhail means the corrie of capture," one of the men, a teacher in the village, said. He shrugged when Duncan cocked his head in question. "My family's from Skye. I learned Gaelic as a child," he explained.

"Aye, that's it," Geordie said, slapping his leg. "The corrie of capture. That's where the Glencoe men kept the cattle they stole, or so the tale's told. In those times it was no' so uncommon for one clan to steal from another, but the men of Glencoe were fair fly about it. They would drive the cattle in the corrie and hold them there, and none could be retrieved."

"Mara?" Duncan asked.

"There were mountains on each side, like walls. And it was lonely."

Duncan heard tension in her voice. He wanted to put his arms around her, but he knew he would be rebuffed. "Do you think Corrie Gabhail might be the place you saw?"

"Aye. It might."

"We'll need to get back in the bus, then," Geordie said, taking charge. "And drive up the road a bit. Then there's a footbridge over the Coe, or there was when I was a lad."

"How long will this take?" Duncan asked.

"With the snow and the cold?" Geordie shook his head. "Most of the day?"

"Aye."

"Mara, this will be our only chance." Duncan didn't care if she did pull away from him. He reached for her hands and chafed them in his own. "By the time we're in and out, there probably won't be enough daylight left to look anywhere else."

"I have one chance then?"

"It's not up to me. It's the weather that will limit us."

"I say we go to the corrie."

As one, the men headed back toward the bus. Duncan was surprised by their easy acceptance of her decision. Mara didn't follow, and neither did he. He didn't drop her hands. "They're good men," he said.

"They believe in me." For a moment at least, all that was wrong between them vanished. "They've accepted this as if the sight is a talent like playing the piano or painting still lifes. I've worked all my life to hide who I am, and they've accepted me without question."

"Mara..."

"We'd best go, Duncan. If we have only this chance, then we've got to make the most of it."

"You don't have to go. You could stay here, at the hotel. Now that we know where we're going, you don't have to come. You could rest, maybe even take a room and sleep until we get back. It's warm there and dry."

"I have one chance, and if that's all I'm to be given, then I'll be there for all of it."

"My stubborn lady."

She pulled away then, as if the intimate tone of his voice might be her undoing. He watched her cross the lot to the minibus.

* * *

Mara was less certain than she appeared to be. She had stared out the window on the trip to Glencoe, clearing her mind and opening herself to visions that might lead her to the exact place, but nothing had come to her. Now as she and the men walked she only felt fatigue.

She was in the middle of the line, a place the men had silently chosen for her. She sensed their desire to protect her. They had encouraged her when the walking had gotten difficult, sung to her, told her stories. She couldn't remember a time when she had been the recipient of so much goodwill.

She had found a home in Druidheachd. She had never believed such a thing possible. At best she had hoped for a place where she would be left alone. Instead she was slowly, surely being pulled into village life. It had begun at the Johnsmas Fair. She had exposed herself to anyone canny enough to understand why she had grabbed the children. Then she had faced half the village over the reception desk of the Sinclair Hotel, and what questions there were about her integrity had apparently been answered.

In the midst of an isolated Highland village with its roots firmly planted in the seventeenth century, with its superstitions and its fears of ghosts, goblins and things that went bump in the night, she had found a home.

And a man she loved.

Duncan walked behind Geordie at the front of the line. She could watch the proud set of his shoulders, the masculine thrust of his hips and ramrod straight line of his back. She loved him, this arrogant, stubborn Scot-American who refused to see anything except what was put squarely before him. And perhaps it was that quality—or fault—that she loved best about Duncan, because he was a man who refused to compromise anything. When he believed in something, he believed in it with all his heart, and when he loved . . .

"It's time we took a break," he said now.

Duncan turned and searched for her with his eyes. When he found her, he frowned. "Mara, you look like a snowflake would knock you to the ground. Sit on that rock over there and take a break."

"No, we have to keep going."

"You're not going anywhere. Not until you've rested." He advanced on her, passing Roger who had walked between them as if to shield them from one another.

"We must keep going or we will no' find them in time."

"It's taking longer because every step is like ice-skating, and *because* it is, you're completely done in." He put his hands on her shoulders. "Please." He lowered his voice. "Mara, don't do this to me. I've got enough to worry about."

They had hiked beside a wide burn for what seemed like miles. The burn tumbled through a gorge fringed with birches, and their path was narrow and slick. At some point when the sun had risen high enough to be seen above the mountains, they had stopped to rest and drink strong hot tea supplied by Roger. But they had not come nearly as far as they had expected.

"I'll rest, but only for a few minutes." She found a wide rock beside the stream and sat. Behind her she sensed the men breathing a collective sigh of relief.

She was exhausted. At times she felt as if she were floating. She had stumbled and nearly fallen twice, and once she had been so overcome by dizziness she had believed the future was about to present itself again. But nothing had presented itself to her except doubt. If she could fly with the eagles, if she could soar above Glencoe and look down upon it again, she would be sure they were in the right place. But she was earthbound, and she couldn't be sure at all.

"Is there room for two?"

She moved over to let Duncan sit beside her. "What will you say to Lisa when we find her?" she asked.

"What a strange question."

"It will be the measure of what sort of man you really are."

"What should I say?"

"I can no' tell you that. It must come from your heart."

"It will depend on whether my daughter is alive and well."

She put her hand on his. "She is, Duncan. I'm sure of it."

"And Lisa?"

"Alive."

"I hope so. I don't wish Lisa any harm."

"Do you no'?"

"I told you, I've made mistakes."

"This is no' one of them." She withdrew her hand.

"Are *we* one of them?"

"This is no' the time to talk about that. There are too many things still to be settled."

He stood, rebuffed. "I'm going to go consult with Geordie and see if he has any idea how much farther we have to go."

They started out again a few minutes later. A half hour or so farther in they came to a pile of enormous rocks that blocked the burn and seemed to spell an end to it.

"We cross to that side now," Geordie said. "But the rocks are slippery. We'll have to go one at a time." He started across even before he'd finished speaking. Duncan should have gone next, but he waved Roger in front of him. "Come on, Mara, I'll go first, but I'll stay in easy reach if you need me."

She waited until he had made a good start, then she followed. The rocks were icy, even more so than they looked, and her knees were weak. She struggled to maintain her balance, but she slipped again and again. And each time she did, Duncan was there to steady her.

On the other side he held out his arms and sheltered her against him as she struggled for breath. "You did well, lady. I know how hard you're working to keep up."

"We have to move on."

"We can't forget that we have to go back the way we've come, Mara. And we have to leave time to rest and still be back to the bus by dark. It will be safe to go a little farther, but we can't keep going for miles and miles. There just isn't time."

"I will no' be turning back until April and her mother are with us."

He stepped away from her. The others had crossed and were waiting. "Let's go," he said tersely.

She tried to make her mind a blank, but no matter how hard she tried, there were no images, not even the most obscure. She was aware only of the cold, of the struggle to lift one foot and plant it in front of the other, of the murmur of the burn that suddenly reappeared on the other other side of the rocks and led them into the corrie.

Everyone stopped and stared. The corrie was a level stretch of meadow, snow-crested now, but probably green and sprinkled with wildflowers in warmer weather. On either side the sheer rocky face of mountains closed it in, and the burn flowed through the center.

There was little to block their view. For as far as they could see there was nothing except snow and mountains and a burn flowing far beyond them.

A new wave of dizziness swept over her. Mara closed her eyes against it. She could feel her body sway in protest, but she was powerless to stop it. Then she saw cattle, shaggy, black and stocky, and she heard the laughter of men as they herded them into place. The image flashed across her mind, then disappeared along with the dizziness, but in that instant she knew they had come to the right place.

"They're here," she said.

"I don't see a tent. There's no sign anyone's been here since the snow," Duncan said. "I don't see a single footprint, and I don't know if you're going to make it another mile."

"They're farther in." She started along the burn. The walking was easier here, flatter and at a lower elevation where less snow had fallen. She turned when she realized the others hadn't followed. "I will bring them out alone if you dinna follow me," she said. "And then what will your wives and children say tomorrow when they find that a woman did the rescuing alone?''

Roger broke into a grin, and Geordie laughed out loud. Only Duncan didn't smile. "Come, Duncan." She beckoned. "Your daughter's waiting."

The sun was high in the heavens when Mara saw the tent. It hadn't been visible from a distance because it was tiny and white like the surrounding snow, and there was no movement near it to attract their eyes. She pointed. "There! Where the burn curves."

Duncan stopped and shaded his eyes from the glare of sunlight on the snow. Then he started to run, and several of the men loped after him. She purposely slowed her pace and waved the others ahead.

By the time she reached the tent April was outside of it held tightly in Duncan's arms. She saw tears on his cheeks, tears he probably wasn't even aware of crying.

"Are you really all right, Springtime?"

She was crying, too. "Mommy's not."

"I know. But she's going to be all right. We're going to get her out of here."

"I couldn't wake her up this morning. I tried, and I couldn't."

"You did the right thing by staying in the tent with her."

"She made me. When she was still awake she told me not to go outside. I wanted to find you."

"Mommy was right. She knew what to do."

"She slipped on the rocks by the river and hurt herself and we couldn't leave. And then it got so cold and she made me wear all her clothes and sleep under her sleeping bag, too. Then she fell asleep and I couldn't wake her up."

Duncan looked up and saw Mara. "Mara's here, Springtime."

Still clinging to him, April turned her head. When she saw Mara she gave a small cry and stretched out her arms. Mara took her and held her tight.

Roger backed out of the tent and stood. "Duncan, it looks like she's got a broken leg and maybe a concussion.

She's got a knot on her head and her skin isn't much warmer than the snow." He looked at April, then he motioned Duncan to one side and finished his assessment out of earshot.

"Is she going to be all right?" April asked. "Is Mommy going to be all right?"

"Yes, dearest. I know she is. The men will carry her back to the road, and then we'll drive her to the nearest hospital." Even as she said the words she watched the men team up to efficiently slide Lisa from the tent in a sleeping bag. Mara looked at the face she had only seen in a photograph and felt a deep compassion.

Geordie covered Lisa with the remaining sleeping bag while the rest of the men took down the tent and used the frame and canvas to construct a stretcher.

Duncan crouched beside her, and Lisa's eyes opened. Mara couldn't look away.

"April?"

"She's right here. She's fine."

"I thought... I'd show you I could take care of her." Tears seeped down Lisa's cheeks.

"Hush now. We're going to get you to a hospital."

"You'll never let me see her again..."

"Don't worry about that now."

"She's my..."

Mara looked away. She couldn't bear the pain on the other woman's face. Lisa had lost her daughter forever. After this Duncan would never allow her to have contact with April again.

"Yes, she's your baby," Duncan said. "And we'll work something out so you can visit her. I promise. You shouldn't have taken her, Lisa, but you did everything you could to keep her safe. I'll always be grateful to you for that." He stood.

April squirmed in Mara's arms, and she set her on the ground. April ran to her mother's side. "Mommy!" She grabbed Lisa's hand.

Lisa threaded her fingers through April's and closed her eyes.

"Let's go," Duncan said.

Deftly the men placed Lisa on the makeshift stretcher and lifted her, two to a side with April still holding Lisa's hand. Then they started through the corrie.

Duncan watched them for a moment, then he turned to Mara. "You've given me back my daughter."

"And you've given her back to her mother. It's a good day's work."

"After today your place in Druidheachd will be secure forever."

"Aye. I'll be the seer who lives on the mountain. There'll be respect and even friendship from those courageous enough to risk it. It's more than I've dreamed of in years."

April called to them. Mara started after the men, but Duncan put his hand on her arm. "Mara..."

"Dinna confuse gratitude with anything else, Duncan."

"Is that what I'm doing?"

She couldn't answer, because she didn't know for certain. There was very little that she knew now that she had found Lisa and April. The strength that had carried her this far had disappeared, and love and fear warred inside her.

"We're not finished," he said. April called to him again, and he dropped his hand and started toward the others.

He turned after a few paces. She was still standing in the same place. "We're not finished, my lady. And if you think we are, it's one of the few times you really can't predict the future."

Chapter 18

The hotel pub was crowded, as it had been every night in the week since the weather had changed. There was no better place to commiserate with friends about a summer that had been too short, or to talk about the mysterious rescue of Duncan's ex-wife. In the far corner Geordie, drunk on attention and not a drop of liquor, was relating the story for the eighth night in a row.

"And so it becomes the best tale ever told in a Druidheachd pub," Iain said to Duncan. "Reduced to that."

"Don't underestimate it. There've been tales told in here for centuries. If Geordie's is the best, I'll go down in history."

"And that's how your name will be remembered." Iain lifted his glass in toast. "At least it *will* be remembered when you're back in America or wherever you're off to."

"What makes you think I'm off to anywhere?"

"Carlton-Jones tells me you've been negotiating with him on a price for the hotel. You're a good businessman, Dunc. Anyone else would have taken what he offered for this pile of rubble."

Duncan leaned back and signaled Brian for a dram. "I've been interested to see how high he would go when pushed."

"And?"

"It's safe to bet there's no one else anywhere in the world willing to pay what he is. It should give us all pause. He bears watching."

"Why? Just consider yourself a fortunate man. You found your buyer right off."

"No." Duncan downed his drink. "I didn't."

"You're not going to let something as insignificant as Martin's wee weasel eyes stop you from taking his offer?"

"I'm not taking anybody's offer. It's the Sinclair Hotel. I've spoken to Fiona. We'll be keeping it."

Iain lifted a brow. "Will you now?"

"Oh, come off it, Iain. You've known all along that I would. You've been enjoying this, haven't you? You like watching the mere mortals suffer and squirm and act like idiots while you rise above it all."

"You Americans have no respect for your betters."

"There *is* no one better."

Andrew joined them, and they made room for him at their table, which was easy since everyone else edged away.

As always, Duncan was annoyed. "What in the hell do they think is going to happen just because we're sitting together?"

Iain ignored him. "Duncan tells me he's not going to sell the hotel," he told Andrew.

"Is that so? And what is it you'll be doing with it, Dunc?"

"Living in it. Running it. Running a business out of it, I think. I'm appalled at the state of advertising in the Highlands. We've got more to offer than knobby masculine knees and grinning Loch Ness monsters. I've got some thoughts on how to tastefully present what we're about."

"We?"

Duncan leaned forward. "You don't have any idea how much this place irritates me sometimes. There's nothing to do, and the weather? My God, the weather's the worst in the world! And then there are the attitudes. I half expect to wake up one morning and find druids sacrificing victims in the middle of High Street and everybody else nodding and going about their business. And the two of you are no better than anyone else in the village. You're set in your ways and you're lazy and you keep coming back here no matter where else you go because you think, for some crazy reason, that this place, this Brigadoon rising from the mists every day of every year, is home.''

''And?'' Iain asked.

Duncan sat back. ''And, damn it, I guess it is.''

Andrew signaled Brian, and in a moment there were three drams of the hotel's best whiskey on the table.

''To the men of midnight,'' Andrew said. He held his glass high.

And the three of them drank in unison.

He had a Scot's tolerance for his native drink and a Sinclair's disdain for talking about his feelings. Now one warred with the other as Duncan drove the road up Bein Domhain to Mara's. He hadn't had enough whiskey to impair his driving, but two drinks had been all it had taken to convince him that tonight had to be the night to confront her.

He'd driven the road already this week. Twice, in fact. And both times he'd turned around just before he reached her croft because he hadn't been sure what to say.

What could he say to a woman he loved beyond reason but to whom he had never mentioned that fact? How did he tell her that he was a stubborn, overbearing and sometimes blind fool who had learned much too early not to take any emotional risks? How did he promise that he had learned from his mistakes and wouldn't make them again, when he wasn't sure, himself, that he *had* learned. Not totally.

Because he was only human and, sadly, perpetually fallible.

Something rolled against his foot and Duncan kicked it to the other side of the car. A glance affirmed that it was a ball that April had been trying to teach Primrose to fetch. She hadn't taken either the dog or the ball when she'd left town with her mother two days ago, but she would have lots of time to play with both when she returned.

April was staying with Lisa for the remainder of the week, at a hotel near Loch Ness where Lisa planned to recuperate before her long flight back to the States. She had plans to come back at Christmastime and take April to London for a few days. Lisa didn't want custody, only the right to visit her daughter. And she had proved that she could put April's needs above her own now.

After the rescue Lisa had been surprisingly honest about her difficulty accepting responsibility, and she expected to work on her problems for a long time to come. But she wanted to be part of her daughter's life, and for everyone's sake, Duncan was going to let her. Sometime in the last year she had stopped searching for easy answers.

Sometime in the last year he had *started* searching for answers. His search had led him back to the village of his birth and his boyhood friends, and to a compromise with Lisa that was going to help his daughter grow into a happy, healthy adult.

Now he had to face his last and possibly his most difficult challenge.

Duncan's thoughts had taken him a good distance up the mountain. He realized he was close to the passing place where he had seen the fountain of light that had probably saved him from a fatal collision. On a whim, and because he still wasn't sure what he was going to say to Mara, he pulled over and got out of his car.

It was a cold night and mist rose like icy fingers from the ground. If there was a moon tonight, it wasn't visible in the cloud-layered sky, and not a single star shone. An owl hooted from the lone tree at the edge of the cliff, and somewhere on the ground below, a small animal, a vole or a shrew, perhaps, rustled in fright.

The view—or lack of one—was desolate. Cold and mist and a starless sky, the faintest shadows of distant peaks, the stark silhouette of leafless trees. And the remnants, the faintest dusting, of last week's snowfall.

He took a deep breath of the frost-laden air and filled his lungs.

And he finally knew what he would say to Mara.

The rest of the trip went quickly. He parked at the bottom of her drive to give himself a few extra moments to prepare. Over the hill he could hear the tinkle of a bell and the hypnotic whisper of fleece against fleece as the sheep huddled together for the night. For the first time he truly understood Mara's enchantment with this place, why she had struggled to resurrect it from the earth, and why it had given her the courage to move beyond it. Now he could picture himself here, too. Winter nights beside a peat fire, spring days exploring daffodil-dappled meadows. There was little he couldn't imagine if Mara was at his side.

He crested the hill and looked toward her house, still a good ways in the distance. The chill that stole his breath had little to do with the autumn air. Just in front of her cottage was a familiar fountain of pale green light.

He stared, transfixed. The light glowed against the stone walls with an unearthly radiance and transformed everything in its path. For that moment he was rooted to the earth, unable to move. The light swayed and rippled against the stone, then slowly, so slowly, coalesced into the form of a woman.

"My Lady Greensleeves." He breathed the words. Fear clutched at him even as he admired her beauty. He had seen this sight, this ghost of Perthshire and now of Druidheachd, twice before, and each time it had been a warning of danger. "Mara!"

He began to sprint toward the light. He had no thought except to find Mara. His fear was for her safety, and not for his own. He would **fight ghosts** for her; he would slay dragons.

He was closer now, and the light blazed brighter and didn't fade away. He could see a clearer outline, the soft feminine curves, the long, pale hair. And then she was running toward him.

He held a flesh and blood woman in his arms, a woman dressed in a flowing green cape, her hair loose and wild on her shoulders. He covered Mara's face with kisses and tasted the salt of tears on her cheeks. The lantern she carried brushed his back as she clasped him against her. His lips found hers and he knew he would never let her go again.

"My lady," he whispered over and over. He held her close. She seemed to flow against him, her body as supple and yielding as light, her skin as soft and as warm.

"I knew you'd come."

"Did you? How? Did you see our future?"

"No. I've waited for you every night. I've come outside for every passing car. I believed in you."

"In us." He kissed her again and filled his hands with her hair. She swayed in his arms and the feel of her body as it brushed against him set him on fire. "I believe in us, too, but I haven't known what to say to you."

"You dinna have to say anything, Duncan." She slid her hands under his belt, under the waistband of his trousers and pulled his shirt free. "There's nowt you could say that would be better than this."

He felt her hands against his bare skin. He felt the rhythmic sway of her hips against his. He groaned, torn between trying to tell her what was in his heart and showing her.

"I love you," he said. It was too little, too late, and he was ashamed.

"Aye, I know." She rose on tiptoe and ended the conversation. He kissed her back and let desire consume him.

As if she knew, she led him inside and kicked the door closed behind her. He was surrounded by the fragrance of smoldering peat, of sage and chamomile and lavender. The air was warm against his skin as they undressed each other and the mattress was soft against his flesh.

In bed she moved against him, her legs entwined with his, her breasts indescribably perfect against his chest. He told himself to wait, to savor so that he could remember this always, but he was inside her before the words had ended, and they were moving together.

He could feel the velvet warmth of her surrounding him. He had asked for so little, and somehow, he had been given so much. She was part of him in a way he had never dreamed a woman could be, and he belonged completely to her.

He didn't know what stars they reached for, what answers they sought and found together. He wasn't aware of the passing of time or of beginnings or endings. The pleasure he felt was beyond words, and he knew it was her pleasure, too. When there was no way to prolong the ecstasy, when the agony of prolonging it was too excruciating, he gave himself up to one all-consuming moment.

And there was no time except infinity.

Mara was the first to speak. It might have been yesterday or tomorrow, a minute or a millennium. He didn't know and more important, didn't care.

"You took your time, Duncan."

Time might have stood still when they were wrapped in each other's arms, but he suspected she wasn't talking about their lovemaking. He laughed. "Did I? Someday I'll have to show you what it's like when I really take my time."

She playfully tapped his cheek with her fingertips. "You know that's no' what I meant. You took your time coming back to me."

"I needed to think."

"Did you?"

"I've been up Bein Domhain twice this week, Mara, and both times I left without seeing you."

She stroked the cheek she had slapped. "Is it so hard to tell me what's in your heart?"

"I haven't been able to think of a way to tell you. I'm only good with words when it's not myself I'm selling."

"Ah. And must you sell yourself to me?"

"I think so. Yes."

"Even though I knew already that you loved me?"

He turned to his side so that he could see her face. "Did you know?"

"Aye. And I know how much that frightens you."

"I haven't been very good at love, Mara. I couldn't love Lisa enough to help her surmount all the problems in her life. And I didn't love April enough to protect her when she needed to be protected or to help her have a relationship with Lisa when it was so clear she needed one."

"You loved them both, and you loved them both enough. And you did what you thought was best. Always. And sometimes, no matter how hard we try, it is no' enough to make things perfect."

"You're very wise."

Her eyes sparkled. "Well, I've come by it at great cost. I wish sometimes I were only half as wise."

He smiled and lifted to kiss her. "I would like to take you exactly as you are, wisdom and all, if you'll let me. But can you forgive me?"

"For what?"

"For never trusting you enough. For telling you I believed in your second sight, then refusing to believe that Lisa and April were at Glencoe?"

"What is there to forgive?"

"I didn't trust you. I called my attorney and asked him to meet the plane that I thought they'd be on. I didn't really believe that you could be right."

"And so?"

"Mara, are you saying you forgive me?"

"There was nowt to forgive, Duncan. Could I be angry that you took no chances with April's safety? Had I been you, I would have done the same. There was no shame in it. And you trusted me enough to come with me. I'll never ask for more than that."

He kissed her again, slowly and thoroughly. "Then there's one thing more."

"Aye?"

"There's something I've only just admitted to myself."

She smiled. "Only one thing?"

He laughed, but he sobered quickly. He touched her cheek, her hair. Then he tilted her face to his. "From the beginning I've used your second sight as an excuse to keep you at arm's length. But it's never been anything more than an excuse."

"No?"

He moved a little closer. "You've frightened me, but not because you can see the future."

"Why, then?"

He gathered her close, and rested his lips against her cheek. He feathered a trail of kisses to her ear, and then he whispered the truth he had only just come to know.

"Never because of the future. You've frightened me, my extraordinary lady, because you've turned the present into something magical."

Her smile trembled and her eyes misted. "Have I?"

"And it will always be so." He found her lips with his. She settled against him with a sigh, and he felt the peace and pleasure of a man who had everything. He reached down for the comforter to cover them, and then with a soft curse he sat up and swung his legs over the side of the bed.

"What's wrong, Duncan?" Mara asked sleepily. "Please dinna tell me you have to go back to the hotel tonight."

"No. But I just remembered that you dropped the lantern before we came inside. I'd better check to be sure it's out."

She took his arm to restrain him. "Come back to bed. There's nowt to worry about. I'd yet to light it before you came over the hill."

"What are you saying? You never lit it? It was never on?"

She reached up and dragged him back down beside her. "No. I was waiting to see if it was needed."

"I saw..." His voice trailed off.

"What is it you saw?" She kissed his cheek, his nose, and then, his lips. It was a lingering kiss, full of promise.

He sighed and wrapped his arms around her again. "I may ask you to prove from time to time that you're really flesh and blood."

"Would now be as good a time as any?"

He smiled, and his hands searched for evidence. "Now and forever, my lady. Now and forever."

* * * * *

Get Ready to be Swept Away by
Silhouette's Spring Collection

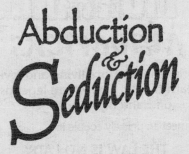

Abduction
Seduction

These passion-filled stories explore both the dangerous
desires of men and the seductive powers of women.
Written by three of our most celebrated authors, they are
sure to capture your hearts.

Diana Palmer
Brings us a spin-off of her Long, Tall Texans series

Joan Johnston
Crafts a beguiling Western romance

Rebecca Brandewyne
New York Times bestselling author
makes a smashing contemporary debut

Available in March at your favorite retail outlet.

™ *Silhouette*®

MONTANA
Mavericks

Stories that capture living and loving
beneath the Big Sky, where legends live
on...and mystery lingers.

This March, meet an unlikely couple in

THE LAW IS NO LADY
by Helen R. Myers

Why would an honorable court judge want to marry
a disreputable outlaw? Was it because she loved the
child he sought custody of, or had she simply fallen
for a rugged loner who could give her nothing but
his name?

Don't miss a minute of the loving as the passion
continues with:

FATHER FOUND
by Laurie Paige (April)

BABY WANTED
by Cathie Linz (May)

MAN WITH A PAST
by Celeste Hamilton (June)

COWBOY COP
by Rachel Lee (July)

Only from ▼ *Silhouette*® where passion lives.

Silhouette celebrates motherhood in May with...

**Debbie Macomber
Jill Marie Landis
Gina Ferris Wilkins**

in

*Three
Mothers
& a Cradle*

Join three award-winning authors in this
beautiful collection you'll treasure forever.
The same antique, hand-crafted cradle
connects these three heartwarming romances,
which celebrate the joys and excitement of
motherhood. Makes the perfect gift for yourself
or a loved one!

A special celebration of love,

Only from

Silhouette®

—where passion lives.

ROMANTIC TRADITIONS

Patricia Coughlin

Graces the ROMANTIC TRADITIONS lineup in April 1995 with *Love in the First Degree*, IM #632, her sexy spin on the "wrongly convicted" plot line.

Luke Cabrio needed a lawyer, but high-powered attorney Claire Mackenzie was the last person he wanted representing him. For Claire alone was able to raise his pulse while lowering his defenses...and discovering the truth behind a vicious murder.

ROMANTIC TRADITIONS: *Classic tales, freshly told. Let them touch your heart with the power of love, only in—*

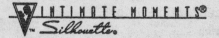

INTIMATE MOMENTS®
Silhouette

SIMRT7

Southern Knights

Join Marilyn Pappano in March 1995 as her
Southern Knights series draws to a dramatic
close with *A Man Like Smith*, IM #626.

Federal prosecutor Smith Kendricks was on a
manhunt. His prey: crime boss Jimmy Falcone.
But when his quest for justice led to ace reporter
Jolie Wade, he found himself desiring both
her privileged information—and the woman
herself....

Don't miss the explosive conclusion to the
Southern Knights miniseries, only in—

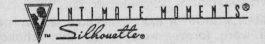

INTIMATE MOMENTS®
Silhouette®

KNIGHT3

Men and women hungering for passion to soothe their lonely souls. Watch for the new Intimate Moments miniseries by

Beverly Bird

It begins in March 1995 with

A MAN WITHOUT LOVE (Intimate Moments #630)
Catherine Landano was running scared—and straight into the arms of enigmatic Navaho Jericho Bedonie. Would he be her savior...or her destruction?

Continues in May...

A MAN WITHOUT A HAVEN (Intimate Moments #641)
The word *forever* was not in Mac Tshongely's vocabulary. Nevertheless, he found himself drawn to headstrong Shadow Bedonie and the promise of tomorrow that this sultry woman offered. Could home really be where the heart is?

And concludes in July 1995 with

A MAN WITHOUT A WIFE (Intimate Moments #652)
Seven years ago Ellen Lonetree had made a decision that haunted her days and nights. Now she had the chance to be reunited with the child she'd lost—if she could resist the attraction she felt for the little boy's adoptive father...and keep both of them from discovering her secret.

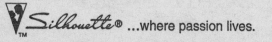

Silhouette® ...where passion lives.

BBWW-1

You won't want to miss...

by Merline Lovelace

Starting in May 1995, Merline Lovelace brings her
new miniseries, CODE NAME: DANGER, to Silhouette
Intimate Moments. And the first title, *Night of the Jaguar*
(IM #637), is also an INTIMATE MOMENTS EXTRA.

Alias: Jaguar. *Agency:* OMEGA. Secret Agent
Jake MacKenzie hadn't planned on rescuing
Sarah Chandler and three frightened children from
the jungles of Central America. Then a drug bust
gone awry made him an unwilling savior—
and all-too-willing lover.

Coming your way in August 1995 is
The Cowboy and the Cossack (IM #657).

Join the excitement of Merline Lovelace's
CODE NAME: DANGER, as the daring men and
women who comprise the Omega Agency find love
despite the most perilous odds, only in—